"I know how this goes."

Lacy paused before adding, "There are two kinds of men here. The first doesn't think a woman like me should be anywhere near a bull because we might do better than them and that would obviously be the end of the world. The second thinks I'm nothing but a one-night stand that hasn't happened yet." She pointed a finger at him. "Guess which one you are."

His lips...nice lips, rounded and full and—*no, stop it, Lacy.* She was not going to start thinking about his lips! All they were doing were twisting off to the side, as if he was thinking about laughing at her but trying not to.

Unfortunately, in trying so hard not to stare at his mouth, her gaze drifted back down to his chest. The wet T-shirt left nothing to the imagination. Pecs, nipples!

She snapped her gaze to the front windshield of the truck. She wouldn't look at him. That was the best solution.

"Have you considered," Ian Tall Chief said in an amused drawl, "that there might be another kind of man here?"

Dear Reader,

Welcome back to the rodeo, where dreams are made—and broken—in eight seconds in the arena on the back of a two-ton bull.

Ian Tall Chief has something to prove. He's got a secret, one he guards with his life: he's got a son he gave up for adoption. It's been six years and he wants to be someone his son can be proud of, which is why he's determined to make it to the rodeo finals as a bullfighter.

But his path is blocked by one very stubborn woman. Lacy Evans. She's the owner of the Straight Arrow Ranch and her bulls have been giving Ian nothing but trouble. Lacy is as tough as nails, yet there's something vulnerable about her that makes Ian want to protect her.

When Lacy's hidden past comes to light and collides head-on with Ian's, will these two make it out of the arena?

One Rodeo Season is a sensual story about accepting your past and fighting for your future— and falling in love. I hope you enjoy reading this book as much as I enjoyed writing it! Be sure to stop by sarahmanderson.com and sign up for my newsletter at eepurl.com/nv39b to join me as I say, Long Live Cowboys!

Sarah

SARAH M. ANDERSON

One Rodeo Season

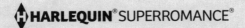
HARLEQUIN®SUPERROMANCE®

Recycling programs
for this product may
not exist in your area.

ISBN-13: 978-0-373-60957-4

One Rodeo Season

Copyright © 2016 by Sarah M. Anderson

Printed in U.S.A.

Sarah M. Anderson may live east of the Mississippi River, but her heart lies out West on the Great Plains. Sarah's book *A Man of Privilege* won an RT Reviewers' Choice Best Book Award in 2012.

Sarah spends her days having conversations with imaginary cowboys and American Indians. Find out more about Sarah's love of cowboys and Indians at sarahmanderson.com and sign up for the new-release newsletter at eepurl.com/nv39b.

Books by Sarah M. Anderson

HARLEQUIN SUPERROMANCE

Rodeo Dreams

HARLEQUIN DESIRE

The Nanny Plan
His Forever Family

The Bolton Brothers

Straddling the Line
Bringing Home the Bachelor
Expecting a Bolton Baby

Visit the Author Profile page at Harlequin.com, or sarahmanderson.com, for more titles!

To Hannah and Willa and to parents everywhere who love the children they gave up and the children they adopted.

CHAPTER ONE

"COME ON, COME ON." Ian Tall Chief bounced on the balls of his feet, adrenaline dumping into his system. The bull rider in the chute apparently couldn't get his grip and kept resetting. The bull kept trying to rear up and Ian couldn't blame the animal. This was taking forever. This was the last ride of the long goes, the opening round of the rodeo. "Come *on*, Randy."

Ian had met Randy on the Total Championship Bulls Ranger circuit—the minor leagues of the TCB Challenger circuit—last year. He was friends with most of the riders. They were little more than kids, but hell, he wasn't that much older. Bull riders were a good time on a Saturday night.

If they made it that far. Randy was in no hurry to get on with his eight-second rush. At this rate, they would be in this arena in Hays, Kansas, all night long.

From behind him, he heard his partner, Black Jack Johnson, snort. Later, Ian knew, Black Jack would give Ian crap about his impatience. A good bullfighter waited. A good bullfighter did not rush in early. Bad bullfighters rushed in and spooked a bull. That got a bullfighter or a bull rider or even a bull hurt.

Ian's job was to stand back and wait until a bull rider dismounted. Or was bucked off. Didn't matter. All riders had to get off a bull one way or another, and when they did, Ian and Jack were on the ground, ready to make sure no one got gored or crushed to death.

Hadn't happened yet. That wasn't to say no one had gotten trampled or tossed on Ian's watch—they had. Ian and Jack had kept things from getting worse. That was their job. But the fact that things could go bad kept Ian on high alert.

Finally, Randy nodded and the chute gate swung open. *About damn time*, Ian thought as the bull roared out, its hind legs flailing up and out with incredible speed. It was a monster of an animal—a mottled brown beast that was probably close to two-thousand pounds. Ian danced out of the path he thought the bull would take, barely clearing the back hooves. That bull had one *hell* of a kick.

A fact Randy was not prepared to deal with. The kid went sailing through the air after only a few seconds, landing in a heap behind Ian—which was a good enough place to fall.

But tell that to the bull. This was one mean—and fast—sucker that kept on coming. Jack jumped at the side of the bull, waving his hands to distract the bull from charging at where Randy was having a little trouble getting up, but all Jack got was knocked over for his troubles.

Oh, crap, Ian thought as he watched his partner literally bite the dust. Ian was on his own. He could get out of the way fast enough, but Randy couldn't and Ian got the feeling this bull wasn't going to quit anytime soon.

Ian had two choices. He could try to grab Randy and spin the two of them out of the way and hope like hell that Jack could get back on his feet or...

No time. Ian stood his ground in front of Randy and did the only thing he could.

When the bull got within feet of him—close enough that Ian could smell the rank bull snot coming out of his nose—he stepped to the side and grabbed the bull by the horns.

Bad idea, he thought as he dug in his heels and twisted to the right, trying to get his left arm under the bull's jaw. Normal steer wrestling meant falling on a five-hundred-pound castrated bull from the back of a horse. This bull was the moving definition of aggressive and weighed maybe three times that much. Plus, Ian didn't have momentum on his side. The bull was dragging him and bearing down on Randy and Jack was shouting and Ian was losing his grip. Hard. *Bad, bad, bad—*

Then the bull slowed, shaking his head as if Ian were nothing but a fly he could shoo away. Ian held on, fighting to drag the bull's head to the side. Out of the corner of his eye, Ian saw Jack grab Randy by the arm and haul him to the side. The bull slowed another half step, trying to decide if he wanted to change course to go after Randy or focus on Ian. That half step gave Ian the chance to get his grip.

He twisted the bull's head up. His muscles screamed at the awkward angle and for a second he thought the bull was going to throw him instead of the other way around. He put everything he had into getting the bull's jaw up and lifted. *Come on, come on.* If this didn't work...

He felt it the moment he gained control. Instead of being dragged along with the bull's momentum, Ian was suddenly able to get his heels into the dirt. Then it happened in less than a second. The bull's feet flipped out from underneath his body and the animal went down on its side with a muffled grunt of surprise.

Ian lay on the bull's neck and checked the arena. Randy was up and hobbling toward the fence. Jack was off to the side, staring at Ian with his mouth flopped open in shock. The handler on horseback had his lasso ready to rope the bull and drag him out.

The whole place—the arena, the cowboys waiting their ride, the spectators in the stands—

was eerily silent. The hair on the back of Ian's neck stood up. Bull riding was many things, but "quiet" wasn't one of them.

"O…kay…" Jack mumbled. "You need any help there, Chief?"

"Just gotta get up," Ian replied as the bull tried to lift its head. The animal made a deep bellowing sound, one of pure bovine anger. Getting up wasn't a problem. Getting up without getting kicked? That was another story entirely.

Jack came and stood within an arm's reach, crouched down on his heels and braced himself. "On three?"

Ian nodded. *One, two*— He let go and rolled to the side as fast as he could. Everyone always worried about getting a bull's horn up the ass, but any cowboy worth his salt knew that the hooves were what killed a man. And this bull had all four hooves pointed at Ian.

Jack latched onto Ian's arm and yanked him up so hard it made the world spin. Both men took off for the fencing as fast as they could.

The bull stumbled to his feet, but by the time he got all four on the floor, Ian and Jack were climbing up the fence to safety and the rider had the bull roped.

It was only when the bull had successfully made it down the chute and Ian was straddling the fence that he heard it—the roar that swelled with each passing second until it damn near deafened him.

"Damn, man," Jack shouted over the noise. "Where the hell did you learn to do that?"

"Back on the ranch," Ian yelled back. Which was partially true. He'd done plenty of bulldogging back on the ranch.

But never a bull that size. Never from the ground.

Adrenaline pumped into his system. Had he really done that? Taken down a charging bull in a test of strength and skill?

Hell yeah, he had. Damn, he felt *invincible*. The number of men who could do that and not get killed could probably be counted on one hand. He turned to the stands and took off his hat, waving it for the crowd. They yelled their approval. A pretty blonde caught his eye and blew him a kiss.

God, he loved this job. Best damned job he'd ever had.

The rodeo clown joined in with the crowd. "That's our very own Chief, everyone! Using those Indian superpowers to save Randy Sloap from certain death!"

Ian gritted his teeth. It wasn't that he hadn't been called Chief. When your last name was Tall Chief, it was unavoidable. But he hated it when people ascribed his hard-won physical skills to some mystical Indian gift.

Ian was a cowboy, a linebacker, a bullfighter. He was not some noble savage who communed with bulls, dammit all.

From somewhere behind the chutes, he heard what sounded distinctly like a war whoop. Ian rolled his eyes at Jack, who shrugged helplessly. Just another day on the job.

He looked back at the chutes, and a cowboy caught his eye. At least, it looked like a cowboy. A little shorter, a little rounder. With a jolt of awareness, Ian realized it was not a cowboy, but a cowgirl, which was unusual enough. Aside from his cousin, June Spotted Elk—who was one of the better bull riders in the world—there weren't usually a whole lot of women behind the chutes during the rides. Buckle bunnies had no place back there. Ian tried to think. Had there been a cowgirl out in the arena for the preride introductions and prayers—another rider? He didn't think so.

But what made her more unusual was that the cowgirl was glaring at him as if Ian had personally slapped her on the ass and told her she should be pregnant, barefoot and in a kitchen somewhere. What the hell?

He nodded his head at her, which only made her scowl harder. Everyone else in the arena tonight was his biggest admirer. To hell with what one woman thought.

Randy limped up to him. "Man, I owe you one for that."

Ian shrugged. "Just doing my job."

Randy grinned. "It's one hell of a job, ain't it?" He slapped Ian on the leg. "I'll catch you tonight at the bar—drinks on me!"

Ian nodded and grinned. After that save, the bar was going to be a lot of fun tonight. It'd been more months than he wanted to admit since he'd picked anyone up. Maybe he'd cut loose and find a beautiful woman to spend the evening with. He might not have the street cred of a bull rider, but bull riders tended to be on the scrawny side of things, like Randy. That kid probably didn't weigh 170 pounds wet. Ian brought a certain physicality to the table. It went with the whole football player thing.

Even as he was thinking about buckle bunnies, his gaze drifted back over to where he'd last seen the angry cowgirl. She wasn't there.

"Did you see that woman?" he asked Jack.

"The blonde? Damn straight I saw her," Jack replied with a low whistle. "She didn't see me, though. Only had eyes for you, curse your red hide."

Jack was about the only man on the planet who could say something like that to Ian and not get the pulp beat out of him, mostly because Black Jack Johnson was, in fact, black. Aside from a few Brazilians and Mexicans, there weren't a lot of men of color on the circuit. Jack and Ian stuck together.

"Never seen anyone pull a stunt like that in the arena," Jack went on, shaking his head. "Damn foolish, too. What if you'd hurt the bull?"

"I'm fine, but I appreciate your concern," Ian retorted as they hopped down off the fence and headed back toward the water. They had about twenty minutes before the short goes started. "This isn't the first time I've wrestled a steer. I know what I'm doing."

Mostly, anyway. And he had a feeling he wasn't entirely fine. The right side of his body was screaming from the strain now that the adrenaline was wearing off. He must have pulled something. Ian did a couple of preliminary twists and felt a twinge. Damn. The latissimus dorsi on his left side was definitely strained. Looked like he would have to take an ice bath tonight.

"Don't do it again," Jack said, and Ian had to nod in agreement. Jack had been a bullfighter for close to twelve years and this was Ian's first year at this level. Bullfighters made it to the bigs as a team. Jack was calling the shots like a quarterback. Ian was, once again, the linebacker doing the blocking. Funny how the more things changed, the more they stayed the same.

Ian dumped half a bucket of water over his head to knock the dust and sweat down a layer. Bullfighting might be a lot of fun, but it was a dirty job on the best of days. As the water dripped down the back of his neck, he said, "Don't get knocked on your ass again, old man." Jack had been a much higher ranked bullfighter before he'd gotten stepped on in a bad wreck two years ago. This season was about him getting back on top of his game. "Then I won't have to save—"

"Hey! *You!*" An angry voice cut through the din.

Ian whipped his head around to see the cowgirl he most definitely had *not* imagined stalking toward him. The look on her face might turn a lesser man to stone, but Ian held firm. Besides, he had the advantage of height. This woman was a little thing, probably a solid foot shorter than he was—but she clearly made up for that in sheer ferocity. She might even be pretty, if she wiped that scowl off her face.

But *pretty* was not the word for her. *Violent* would be better. Ian opened his mouth to say something—"hi" was always a good place to start—but she cut him off. "What was *that*?"

"A damn good save," Ian replied confidently. He stood up straight and puffed out his chest.

Her eyes widened and a spark of electricity flowed between them as her features softened. She *was* pretty, he noticed. Delicate features, wide eyes with fringed lashes. Her skin was tanned, but she had a smattering of freckles over her nose. Her lips were lush and lightly parted. Her face was diametrically opposed to the un-sexed cowboy outfit, almost as if she were try-ing to hide herself under a cowboy hat.

The electricity between them felt good. He admired a lot of beautiful women in the bars, but that spark—he hadn't felt that in a long time. "Hey," he said in a more seductive voice, hoping to fan the flames a little. "Tonight at the bar—"

Anything pretty or sparky or electric about her disappeared as she sneered up at him. "You do *not* touch the bull, you understand?"

"What?" Ian said, bristling. "I've got a job to do. I'm there to protect the riders. I protected the rider. I don't give a damn about the bull."

A look of hatred twisted her features. "That animal is worth a hundred grand. You so much as rub his fur the wrong way and I'll sue you for everything you're worth." She gave his dirt-and-muck-stained pants and the red-and-black shirt that matched Jack's a dismissive glance. "Which obviously isn't much."

"What is your problem, lady?" Even as he said it, he realized what she'd said. She'd sue him.

"He's *my* bull," she snapped. "Touch him again and you will live to regret it."

"*You're* the stock contractor?" But he said it to her back as she turned and stomped off in the direction of the pens. "She's the stock contractor?" he asked the only other person who was listening.

Jack didn't answer. He was too busy laughing.

Ian twisted back around and tried to see where she'd gone. Who was she?

Someone tiny and fierce and unafraid of him. Someone who had a hell of a lot of spark.

It wasn't as if Ian hadn't been yelled at before—he had. Especially the time he'd dated two girls years ago. Yeah, that hadn't been his smartest idea. But Ian was a big guy—especially compared to a slip of a girl. Most women—hell, most men—wouldn't confront him like that. She'd gotten the drop on him, and that, he didn't like. Next time—if there was a next time—he didn't want to be caught off guard.

He hoped there was a next time.

He located her as an older man in a ten-gallon hat stepped in front of her. The huge hat topped off a face pinched into a permanent sneer. The long mustache did nothing to improve the man's appearance. Neither did the potbelly that hung over his belt buckle. Aside from the belly, everything else about the man was scrawny—scrawny mustache, scrawny legs, scrawny neck. He was ugly and mean looking, but the cocky grin on his face said loud and clear that he enjoyed the meanness.

The man said something to her. Even at the distance of twenty or so feet, Ian saw her reaction. Her shoulders tightened and she took a nervous step backward. The older man said something else, and the woman backed up again.

The hackles went up on the back of Ian's neck and he started moving. Okay, so that woman might have dressed him down in public, but Ian didn't like the way the man was leering at her and he especially didn't like the way the woman was reacting. Where was the no-fear, take-no-prisoners woman who had threatened him within an inch of his life? She was gone, replaced by a small woman who was afraid of the older man.

Not on Ian's watch, that was for damn sure.

Well, he amended as he heard her snap something out at the older man, maybe *afraid* wasn't the right word.

As Ian got within earshot, he heard the older man say, "...to see something bad happen to a pretty little thing like you, Evans," in tones of mock concern.

Evans what? Surely that wasn't her first name.

The man's tone was dismissive and threatening. Ian had heard plenty of men talk to his cousin June that way because she wanted to ride bulls. Ian had backed June up when she wanted to ride. Just because Evans didn't necessarily like him didn't mean she didn't deserve the same.

"You wouldn't," she shot back. Her voice wasn't quite as sharp as it had been with him. "You'd only hate it if someone else got first crack at the Straight Arrow." She held her ground and, as Ian came up behind her, stood as tall as she could. "Stay the hell away from me and my bulls, Slim."

Okay, so these two had history—that much was clear. A small gathering of cowboys had formed around Evans and Slim. Ian noticed that most of the cowboys were standing behind Slim. Evans looked small and very alone.

Nope, not happening on his watch.

Slim smiled the oily smile of a man who would get what he wanted, one way or the other. "Or what?" he asked, the mock concern replaced by sheer menace.

Ian cleared his throat and crossed his arms. She started, but didn't make a noise. Instead, she glanced over her shoulder and made eye contact with Ian. He gave her a curt nod that he hoped said, *I'm on your side.* At least in this matter.

The corner of her mouth twitched, as if she wanted to smile but wasn't going to. Then she turned back to Slim, who was now glaring at Ian with undisguised hatred. "Do you really want to find out, Slim? Because I guarantee you won't like it. I'm not afraid of you." This statement was only slightly contradicted by the way her voice wavered. "My father wasn't afraid of you, either."

Slim spat. "He can't protect you anymore, you little—"

"Watch your mouth around a lady," Ian growled

as he flexed his muscles. That was a threat, plain and clear. And sometimes, a threat had to be met with a threat.

Slim snorted. "What are you going to do about it, *Geronimo*? Scalp me?"

Ian charged. His vision narrowed until all he could see was Slim. Just like when he'd been on the football field, when all he could see was the quarterback, the ball. His body primed for the hit, the satisfying crunch of pad against pad, bone against bone.

He didn't make it. Suddenly, he was jerked to the side. At the same time, Evans turned around and put both hands on his chest, pushing him back.

"Dammit, Chief," Jack hissed in his ear. "You'll get kicked off the circuit."

"Don't," Evans said, her wide eyes all the wider with a mix of horror and fear. Then she pitched her voice up louder. "He's not worth it."

Ian's vision widened enough to see that Slim was now standing behind two riders Ian didn't know real well. Ian could have easily taken them both. "What's the matter?" he asked, shaking off Jack. "You'll threaten a woman but you're too much a coward to man up?"

"Boy," Slim said, spitting the word out as if it was an insult. "You don't know who you're dealing with." Then he turned on his heel and walked off.

Ian watched him go and then turned his attention to Evans. "There," he said. "That should—"

"What the hell is your problem?" Evans demanded, cutting him off. "Are you trying to ruin my life or what? Because you're doing a damn fine job."

"I was *trying* to help," Ian said through gritted teeth.

"Well, don't. I don't need any help, certainly not from you. I don't know how I can make it any clearer, buddy— Leave. Me. Alone."

And with that, she turned and stormed off for the second time in less than fifteen minutes.

Ian blinked, but this time she really was gone.

"What the hell happened?" he asked Jack.

"I think," Jack replied, his Texas drawl stronger than normal, "you made her mad."

"Yeah, thanks for that insight," Ian shot back. He looked again, but he didn't see Miss Evans from the Straight Arrow Ranch anywhere.

Ian started after where he'd last seen her, but the promoter began shouting that the short goes was starting and everyone needed to stop standing around and gawking like schoolboys.

Ian had to get back to work.

But he wasn't done with Miss Evans.

CHAPTER TWO

HER HANDS SHAKING, Lacy Evans walked back to where Rattler was penned after his go. *Please let the animal be okay*, she prayed. Without Rattler…

The thought brought on a wave of nausea so strong it almost stopped her in her tracks. She didn't stop, though. She couldn't afford a single sign of weakness. No throwing up. No hysterics. And absolutely no crying allowed.

What would Slim Smalls do if he caught Lacy in a true moment of weakness? Bad enough he'd obviously seen the bullfighter take Rattler down—worse that he was hoping Rattler would never get up. Lacy had no doubt about that.

Rattler was the only thing keeping the Straight Arrow going. If she lost that bull, Slim would say something misogynistic about how a "pretty little thing" like Lacy had no business in stock contracting, no business running a ranch—no business existing. And when she broke—or he pushed her too far…

She tried to swallow down the rock in her

throat that was pushing against her tongue, but it didn't budge. So she kept walking.

She saw Rattler in the pen and for a moment, she thought he was holding a leg funny.

She tried to push the panic away as she hurried to the pen. Without getting in there with him, she looked over the bull as carefully as she could—especially his legs.

He shifted his weight onto the leg. Thank God.

In place of the panic, a new emotion took root—anger. The anger felt good. She was furious with that bullfighter. What the hell had he been thinking, twisting her best bull to the ground like that? For God's sake, he could have killed Rattler! Snapped a leg—or several legs, given the force with which he'd dropped Rattler, as if the eighteen-hundred-pound bull was little more than a stuffed animal someone had thrown at him. Who the hell did that bullfighter think he was?

Chief. That's what the other bullfighter had called him. The thorn in her side had a ridiculous name like Chief. Of course he did. Lacy didn't know if that was his real name or another dig at him being an Indian. Because she was pretty sure he was an American Indian. There'd been his faint accent, a different way of clipping his vowels. But beyond that, it was Chief's dark hair and dark eyes and bronzed skin and eagle nose and strong jaw and muscles moving beneath his shirt.

Not that she'd noticed all those muscles when she'd put her hands on his chest and held him back.

A very small part of her brain replayed the scene again. The whole thing hadn't taken more than twenty seconds. The bull rider hadn't made it past five, which was good for Rattler's statistics. Then there'd been the few agonizingly long seconds where the bullfighter had thought about running. Lacy had seen it in his face. Anyone else would have dodged out of the way. Rattler was no pussy cat—he was a mean son of a bitch who'd broken her father's arm once and launched Murph, one of her hired hands, fifteen feet into a fence.

But the bullfighter hadn't run. He hadn't abandoned the downed rider. He'd stood his ground, absorbed the impact and redirected the bull's energy into the twist.

If it hadn't been her bull, her livelihood—she would have been cheering with the rest of them.

But it *was* her bull, her livelihood. If something happened to Rattler...

She refused to think about that worst-case scenario as she shooed Rattler from one end of his narrow pen to the other, watching his gait the whole time. Rattler seemed okay. No pulling up lame, no favoring one foot.

She needed him to be okay. If that Chief so

much as touched her bull again, he wouldn't have to be worried about getting gored. Lacy would see to *that* herself.

Reluctantly, she left Rattler. Her other bull, Peachy Keen, was due up soon. Peachy wasn't half the bull Rattler was, but that didn't mean Peachy wasn't a good bull. He was perfectly suited to the Total Championship Bulls Ranger circuit. The riders here were all trying to break into the big league, the Challenger circuit. If they couldn't get past Peachy, then they didn't have a hope of making it to the finals in Las Vegas this October, a mere six months away.

Rattler, however, was a different story. He was amassing points every time he was loaded into the chutes. If he had a good summer, he could be bumped up to the bigs. And the bigs paid better.

She needed that. The Straight Arrow was hanging on by what felt like the thinnest of threads. She'd cut every expense she could. If Rattler didn't have a good year with a strong finish in Vegas, she'd have to start selling off the beef cattle that paid at least half of the ranch's bills.

And if that happened...

She would do anything to keep the ranch. If she lost the Straight Arrow, she didn't know what she'd do.

She didn't know *who* she'd be, without that ranch.

It wouldn't come to that. Rattler was going to have a strong summer. Peachy and Chicken Run would earn their keep. Then there was Wreckerator. Some rides, he was every bit as good as Rattler. But other rides were a total disaster. She couldn't bet the ranch on Wreckerator. Not yet, anyway.

Everything was riding on Rattler.

She made her way to the chutes as Peachy went in. She didn't recognize the rider's name, but he tipped his hat and said, "Ma'am," when she slung her leg over the railing to grab Peachy's flank strap.

She nodded at him. Well, that was a nice change of pace. At least half of these cowboys treated her like a pariah at a family picnic, as if the mere fact that she had boobs meant she shouldn't be contaminating the air they breathed. Never mind that she'd been a working rancher since she was old enough to sit in a saddle. Never mind that she did a man's work all day, every day. It didn't matter. She was not welcome here.

But every so often, one of the cowboys was a decent human being, as her father had been. Dale Evans never let anyone talk down to her or any other woman. It wasn't the Straight Arrow Ranch for nothing.

She'd never understood what had started the feud with Slim Smalls. At this point, it didn't matter. Not even Dale's and Linda's deaths were enough for Slim. He wanted more. He wanted Lacy's ranch.

She pulled the flank strap as another rider pulled the bull rope. Peachy shifted nervously in the chute as the rider got his grip. Lacy realized he was praying under his breath. "Have a good one, Preacher," the other rider said.

The Preacher? Fitting, she thought as the man nodded his head. The chute swung open.

Normally, Lacy watched the rides, making notes on how her bulls did, where they were stronger, where they were weaker. She and her father had always done that, breaking down each ride together until Lacy understood bulls better than her dad did.

But not this time. This time, she was watching a bullfighter named Chief.

Now that she knew Rattler was okay, she almost felt bad for tearing into the man. Of course he was doing his job. Of course he didn't know about Rattler or Lacy Evans or the Straight Arrow or even Slim Smalls. He'd only known how to take down a charging bull with his bare hands. It had nothing to do with her.

And he had been trying to help her, hadn't he? He'd cut Slim off before he could start cursing, and Lacy would be willing to bet that he'd have taken Slim down in much the same way he'd taken Rattler down. For her.

Even if it was all macho posturing—still, he'd

been willing to throw down on her behalf. And that was after she'd yelled at him. The first time, anyway. She didn't know if he'd be so eager to defend her again after she'd told him off a second time.

Okay, she did feel bad. She'd been upset and angry and she hadn't been able to take all of her anger out on Slim. Somehow, Chief had seemed safer. Maybe it was because she didn't know him. Or maybe it was something else.

She'd pushed him. She'd put her hands on his chest and shoved to keep him from beating the hell out of a man who richly deserved it. She'd felt Chief's body tense at her touch, which was bad enough. But what was worse was the way he'd looked down at her, as if he hadn't expected to find her there but he was glad she was.

Then she had to open her big mouth. Again.

She'd apologize, she decided as the Preacher made the time on Peachy. If she got the chance, she'd thank him for not killing her bull and for putting Slim in his place and for letting her hold him back. Then her conscience would be clear and that would be that.

Peachy obligingly trotted out of the arena. Lacy heard the announcer say the Preacher had gotten a seventy-four—not a great score for either the rider or the bull, but it was enough. She was done here. There were only a few riders left, and then the rodeo would be over except for the belt buckles. She could load up her bulls and begin the long trip home to the Straight Arrow in Wyoming.

She couldn't say the prospect excited her. If she went home to the empty house, there'd be no distractions, good or bad. She'd be utterly alone, except for when the hired hands did their work and even then, there wasn't a whole lot of interaction. It'd be just her and the truth she kept trying to avoid.

A little distraction could be good. Hell, it might even be great. As she thought it, she looked back at Chief. She might see him again, she might not. Bullfighters didn't always follow the same schedule as the bulls and the riders. This could be a one-off, for all she knew.

At that moment, Chief looked up and caught her eye. She tensed. She couldn't exactly apologize or thank him across an arena but what if she didn't get another chance?

He was staring at her. She only knew this because she was staring back. His head dipped forward in a polite nod. Wow, she thought. Polite and tough and hot? He was the kind of guy who could be very distracting.

Then he winked at her, his mouth curving up into a suggestive smile.

She scowled. Great. It hadn't been no-strings-attached, that little show he'd put on earlier with Slim. Chief wanted something in return. Did it matter that she'd been thinking about nearly the same thing? No.

She did not hook up and she did not hang out, not with bull riders or fighters or stock contractors. That was *that*.

She pushed away from the chute and went to get her animals. She could not afford to be distracted by a bullfighter with a testosterone imbalance. She had a ranch to save and contracted bulls to deliver. Anything outside of that was…

Well, it was unlike her. Dale and Linda Evans's daughter did not allow distractions.

But even as she thought it, sadness gripped her. Sure, Dale and Linda's daughter didn't hook up.

But Lacy wasn't their daughter, not really.

The lump was back and breathing was difficult. The only thing that kept her from falling apart was the sheer number of people milling around. She would not cry or weep or, God help her, sob. Cowgirls didn't cry. Certainly not in public, anyway. She was not weak.

She got to her truck and sat there for a few minutes, taking deep breaths until the lump passed and she had things back under control. She drove over to the pens. It was really a two-person job but she wasn't about to ask for help. Besides, she'd been loading bulls since she was a kid. She could do this. She had to.

"Come on," she grunted at Rattler. He lowered

his head and bellowed. Lacy glared at him. "I'm not the one who grounded you. Don't take it out on me. Now get up!"

Rattler gave her a look and blew snot in her face and walked into the trailer. Peachy followed his traveling buddy, thank God.

Slim and his "pretty little thing" could go to hell. She could do this—deliver her bulls and get them back home. She could do the job—which meant she could keep her ranch.

She climbed into the cab of her dad's F-350 and fired up the engine. No, this wasn't his truck anymore. He'd been gone for seven months now. The truck, the bulls, the Straight Arrow and every single bill were hers now. Distantly, she thought she might be hungry. When was the last time she'd eaten? No lunch today. Had she had breakfast? Well, she'd eat when she got home.

Hays, Kansas, was only about six hours from the Straight Arrow, which sat between Cheyenne and Laramie, Wyoming, although it was closer to Laramie. Laramie was where her mom had taught second grade and, therefore, where Lacy had gone to school.

The Straight Arrow was set on the high plains near the base of the Laramie range. The winter held lots of snow for forts and snowball fights. In the summer, the Laramie River was only a short horse ride from the house. It didn't matter that the river never got much above sixty degrees, even in the warmest part of the year. Lacy would ride out and jump in again and again until her lips were practically blue, and then she'd lie out in the sun until she warmed up. Or until her mom rang the dinner bell. Then they'd all sit around the table and talk about the day before they watched the movies her dad had loved so much.

She'd never have that back, that sense of perfect belonging. It was gone now. The only part of her life still recognizably hers was this—bulls in the trailer, sitting in the truck, driving home from a rodeo.

God, she missed her parents. She missed being their daughter.

She was so lost in thought that she didn't see the tall figure in a white T-shirt flagging her down until she almost ran into him. But the man stepped to the side, neatly avoiding having his toes squashed, just as he'd avoided Rattler's horns.

Lacy slammed on the brakes—at least she'd only been going about ten miles per hour. Otherwise, she wouldn't have been able to stop. "Dammit!"

Because it was Chief again. The pain in her neck, come back for more.

He leaned against her driver's-side mirror and waited for her to roll the window down, looking cool and graceful and hot all at once, dang it.

She lowered her window. "What now?"

"I'm sorry about the bull," he said. "I'll pay for any treatment he needs."

She blinked at him. "What?"

"The bull." He shifted and she realized the white T-shirt he was wearing was soaked through. It clung to his body, highlighting muscles and more muscles and then, down a little lower...

Chief cleared his throat, making Lacy startle. "Is he okay?" he asked again.

She needed to come up with something that wouldn't have her breaking down in grateful tears that Rattler was, in fact, okay. It would be best if that something she came up with didn't let Chief off the hook or give away the fact that she was having a hard time not looking at his chest. "I won't know for sure until the vet checks him out." There.

"Let me know."

She nodded in agreement and waited for him to move back, but he didn't. "Yes?"

The corner of his mouth curved up into the kind of smile women like her didn't often get from men like him—confident and sensual and interested. If Lacy had been a normal single woman, it was the kind of smile that would make her want to melt into his arms and kiss him.

But she wasn't a normal single woman. She had responsibilities.

"We got off on the wrong foot. I'm Ian Tall Chief." He stuck out his hand.

And waited while Lacy looked at it. "Are you serious?"

He dropped his hand, looking offended. "Did I look like I was joking?"

Oh, hell—had that come out wrong? She wasn't trying to make fun of his name. Actually, given that everyone called him Chief, she was relieved to hear that was not some sort of derogatory nickname.

So she clarified, "I'm not interested. I don't hook up."

That got both eyebrows up and moving as his face relaxed.

"Are *you* serious?"

"Look," she said in exasperation, "I know how this goes. There are two kinds of men here. The first doesn't think a woman like me should be anywhere near a bull because we might do better than them and that would obviously be the end of the world. The second thinks I'm nothing but a one-night stand that hasn't happened yet." She pointed a finger at him. "Guess which one you are."

His lips—nice lips, rounded and full and—*No, stop it, Lacy*. She was not going to start thinking about his lips, which were twisting as if he was thinking about laughing at her but trying not to.

Unfortunately, in trying so hard not to stare at his mouth, her gaze drifted back down to his chest. The wet T-shirt left nothing to the imagination. Pecs, nipples—

She snapped her gaze to the front windshield. She wouldn't look at him. That was the best solution.

"Have you considered," Ian Tall Chief said in an amused drawl, "that there might be another kind of man here?"

"No."

"What'd that old man say to you?"

"What?"

Ian leaned forward. "Before I got there to back you up. What'd he say?"

"Look," Lacy said in frustration, "it's really not a big deal."

Ian dropped his head to one side. "That's not what it looked like to me. It looked like he was threatening you. Sounded like it, too. Does he always go after you like that or was today a special occasion?"

She tried to shrug, as if another verbal battle with Slim Smalls was no big deal. "I appreciate you trying to help, but I can handle it."

Ian snorted. "You shouldn't have to 'handle' it."

She glared at him. "I was doing fine without your help, Mr. Tall Chief. I can handle Slim. I can handle my bulls. I'm not some silly girl who's in over her head. I've been bringing bulls to rodeos for over fifteen years now." But she'd had her father with her then.

Didn't matter. She could still handle this—all of this. Slim, the bulls, the fighters and the riders—she could even handle Ian Tall Chief.

"Any woman who can load two bulls by herself is not silly." Ian met her gaze and held it with his own. At least, she thought she could handle him. It'd be easier if he were wearing a dry shirt, though. Or if he stopped looking at her like that, with some mix of protectiveness and—dare she say it—respect in his eyes.

He crossed his arms over his chest. Unfortunately, that put a whole lot of biceps right at eye level. Good lord, was any part of this man not muscled and ripped? He had some interesting tattoos on his right side—not the standard stuff, but something that looked like a circle in red and black and yellow.

"There's no shame in asking for help," he said. His voice was surprisingly soft—gentle, even. "Or accepting it."

Warning bells went off in her head—loud, clanging bells that beat a fast rhythm. For some ridiculous reason, she felt exposed, even though he was the one standing around in a practically see-through T-shirt. She wanted to look away—she desperately needed to—but she couldn't break his gaze.

"I don't need any help." It came out as a whisper. It was a lie and she knew it. And, given the way he looked at her, he knew it, too. But she couldn't accept what he was offering, whatever it was. She couldn't be in anyone's debt. Not his, not Slim's—no one's.

So she tried again. "I don't need any help."

There. That was better. She just had to keep saying it.

After what felt like a long time of staring into his eyes—deep, dark pools with things hidden in their depths she could only wonder at—Ian nodded and took a step back. "All right, then. Have a safe trip home."

She blinked. *What?* Was that it? After that long, lingering look? She hadn't even told him her name yet. Was that the end of the conversation?

Was he going to take her at her word?

He was. How freaking weird.

"You, too," she said, because it was the most polite thing she could come up with.

She drove off. In her side mirror, she saw Ian Tall Chief stand there and watch her go.

She might not ever see him again. Bullfighters operated under a different schedule than the riders or the bulls. Her next contracted rodeo was next weekend, in Colorado Springs. Ian Tall Chief might be in Amarillo or even Baton Rouge, for all she knew. She certainly didn't want to see him again—not to risk having him hurt one of her animals or piss off Slim Smalls even more.

Before I got there to back you up, he'd said. That and, *You shouldn't have to handle it*. She could almost hear the word *alone* after that second statement.

Because she *was* alone.

Or at least, she had been. Until Ian Tall Chief had backed her up.

Maybe he'd be in Colorado Springs next week, after all.

CHAPTER THREE

LACY ROLLED INTO Colorado Springs Thursday afternoon. She was feeling good. Okay, *good* might be a bit strong, but she was feeling better. She'd been able to sleep the past few nights without too many nightmares about car wrecks, so that counted for something.

The night before a rodeo was her favorite time. The arena grounds were quiet, with only a few stock contractors and the promoter around to unload the bulls. The riders wouldn't show up until tomorrow, and then tomorrow night, the crowds would come pouring in.

This time was about the bulls. Had it been less than a year since she'd done this with her dad? They'd get in around dark on Thursday nights and unload. Dale would shoot the breeze with the other stock contractors and check in with the promoter.

She didn't want to run into Slim again. If she could get through this weekend without feeling as if she was losing her grip on—well, *everything*, that'd be great.

Lacy checked in with Mort and got the details on where she was to unload her bulls. She had three with her today—Rattler, Chicken Run and Wreckerator.

You can do this, she thought as she backed the truck up to the pens. Sure, unloading and loading two bulls by herself had been a challenge. Three would be downright hard, especially because Wreckerator was in one of his moods. She'd had Murph to help her at the Straight Arrow, and Wreckerator had almost charged the trailer. Which meant he'd have a good bunch of rides this weekend, but it didn't help Lacy right now.

She got out of the cab and looked around. The good news was, she didn't see Slim. But the bad news was, she didn't see anyone else, either. For some ridiculous reason, she was disappointed not to see Ian Tall Chief. Not that she wanted to. She didn't. She didn't need his help or his excessively large muscles, and that was that. Besides, he would have no reason to be here tonight. He'd probably roll in tomorrow afternoon with everyone. She was being ridiculous to even look for him.

Except Rattler was refusing to back out of the trailer and Lacy didn't want to push her luck going in to lead him out, not with Wreckerator behind him, pawing at the metal floor and bellowing with nervous energy. She needed to get the bulls out so they could stretch and get water.

She could go get Mort, but she didn't want to tell the promoter of the rodeo that she couldn't handle her animals on her own. That was the sort of thing that could be used against her in future contract negotiations, and the last thing she could afford was to weaken her bargaining position.

Nope, she was on her own here. She knew it; the bulls knew it. "Come on, Rattler—get up," she hissed, poking at his haunch through the slats. She didn't want to use the cattle prod, but if Rattler didn't get a move on, she would have to. Which would upset Wreckerator, which meant he would be practically unmanageable.

"You look like you need help," a man said from behind her—too close.

Lacy startled, banging her elbow against the trailer. She pulled her arm out and spun to see a cowboy standing less than three feet from her. Not Ian.

Oh, this was a good-looking cowboy, all right. He was maybe six inches taller than she was, on the lean side of things, wearing jeans and a black Western shirt with silver piping on the sleeves and white mother-of-pearl buttons. He had stubble that looked intentional on his chin and a leather cord with a silver cross on it around his neck. He was pretty and polished and he did nothing for her.

And he was talking to her chest. "Let me get that for you."

"I'm fine." The moment the words left her mouth, she knew she'd said the wrong thing.

The cowboy's mouth curved up into a predatory smile as he looked her up and down. After what felt like an hour of inspection, he finally looked in the vicinity of her face and said, "You sure are, sugar. What's a stunner like you doing unloading bulls?" He took a step toward her, effectively pinning her against the trailer.

Her heart began to pound as panic dumped adrenaline into her system. She didn't want to do this. This never would have happened if her dad were still here. And even that realization was depressing because he wasn't here and she was completely on her own.

She had two choices. Start swinging now or… She went with option two. She forced a smile to her face and said, "What was your name, *sugar*?"

"Jerome." The pretty cowboy smirked, bracing an arm against the trailer right next to her head. "I'm one of the riders. I'm sure you've heard of me."

She hadn't. If his ego got any bigger, it'd suffocate her. Dimly, she thought he might have been one of the cowboys standing around Slim last week, but she wasn't sure.

She made an effort to bat her eyelashes. She wasn't any good at it—hell, she couldn't pull off flirting even when she wanted to—but option two was to start swinging later. And if Pretty

Boy Jerome would shift his legs a bit, she'd have a clear shot to kneeing him in the groin. A girl had to do what a girl had to do to defend herself, because she hadn't lied to Chief the other week. There were two kinds of men at these rodeos—the Slims and the Jeromes.

Lacy was about to make her move when something in the air shifted. The hairs on the back of her neck stood up as they had last week when Slim had been threatening her—right before Ian had made himself known.

Ian.

Jerome leaned down, unaware of how the air had changed. His gaze dropped to her lips as he cupped her chin. *No, no, no.* She couldn't fight the shiver of fear that went through her body, but Jerome either thought it was a shiver of desire or he wanted her afraid. She shifted her legs, hoping she had a clear shot of his crotch. He ran his thumb over her lip and said, "Why don't we— *Oof!*"

Then Jerome was gone, being plowed sideways by something the size of a small bulldozer. No, not something—someone.

Two conflicting emotions hit her at the same time as Jerome hit a fence. One was sheer relief. She hadn't had to defend herself and she hadn't had to find out what a man like Jerome would do if he got his nuts crushed. For a second, she didn't feel so alone in the world because Ian Tall

Chief had her back—even when she was backed up against the trailer.

But the other was pure irritation. She *could* defend herself. She didn't need help—or him. But it was too late—he was already helping her, and that put her in his debt. She didn't want to owe him. She didn't want to owe anyone.

"Touch her again and I'll break every bone in your hand," Ian growled, lifting Jerome by his shirt clean off the ground. A tearing sound filled the air.

"Jesus—" Jerome's voice came out in a strangled squeak "—we were just talking!"

"Talk to someone else." Still holding Jerome off the ground, Ian spun and threw him to the ground. Jerome crumpled like an empty feedbag. "Clear?"

"Jesus, Chief," Jerome repeated, scrambling to his feet and spitting into the dirt. "What the hell is your deal?"

"She isn't here for you." Ian had the nerve to ball his hands into fists and take a step toward Jerome, who was now considerably less pretty. His face was an angry red, his shirt trashed and he was covered in dirt and worse. "Now move."

Jerome did as he was told—but not until he'd straightened his shirt and dusted off his butt. He gave Ian a long look. "Another time?" he said, sounding less squeaky and more threatening.

Ian smiled, as if this was what he'd wanted to hear. "Anytime, man."

Jerome nodded and turned. It wasn't until he'd disappeared around some trailers that Lacy felt herself breathe again. Her knees felt wobbly and she wanted to lean against the trailer and allow herself a moment to process.

She did no such thing. She couldn't, not with Ian standing there and watching her with an unsettling mixture of concern and anger in his eyes.

"Are you okay?" he asked, and damn him, he sounded genuinely concerned. "He didn't hurt you, did he?"

No. Yes. No.

How was it possible to be this irritated and this grateful at the same time? "I'm not here for you, either," she told him, completely ignoring the fact that at least part of her was more than a little glad to see him.

He gave her a fierce look before his face settled back into something that looked almost disappointed. "Yeah, you're welcome."

She should at least thank him. Why couldn't she? She didn't know. "Ian, I don't need your help. I wish you'd listen to me."

"No? So what was that all about? You can't tell me you wanted that slime bag to be touching you. He was going to kiss you, Evans. More, knowing him."

Evans? It felt weird to be called that. "Yes,

and when he did, I was going to knee him in the groin and then punch him." She turned back to her trailer. She had to get her bulls out and she'd be damned if she accepted any more help from one Ian Tall Chief. She couldn't be beholden to him. "The situation was under control. I didn't ask for a guardian angel." Never mind that she might need one. "I can handle myself."

"Yeah? What if Salzberg hadn't taken kindly to getting his nuts crushed? Or what if Slim had showed up? You collect an awful lot of enemies, Evans."

She gave him a pointed look. "It must be my sunny nature."

That got her a smile—a full-on smile that took the remaining adrenaline still pumping through her body and drove it down deeper, where an unfamiliar warmth started to spread up her back.

Jerome Salzberg might have been pretty, but Ian Tall Chief was something else entirely— broad and muscled and completely unafraid of anyone or anything. And for some reason, he'd decided to keep an eye on her.

She couldn't be his type. Hell, she wasn't anyone's type.

Something in Ian's eyes deepened. Good lord, was she blushing? No. Not allowed. She would not let her body betray her like that. She turned back to the trailer and the stubborn bulls that wouldn't get the hell out of it.

"Tell me you at least have a gun." His voice was so serious that she was forced to turn around and look at him again.

"In the glove box."

He scoffed. "Fat lot of good it's going to do you there. Can you use it?"

She jammed her hands on her hips and tried to glare him to death. "What do you think? I've competed in mounted shooting events, thank you very much. Won a few, too."

If Ian was insulted by her attitude, he didn't show it. If anything, he looked relieved. "Good. You should be wearing it. The next time someone gives you crap, shoot them in the knee."

She looked at him. It appeared, whether she wanted one or not, she had a guardian angel. This realization made that warm sensation that had spread up her back burn hotter, until she was afraid she was going to start sweating. "Why are you helping me?"

He tilted his head from side to side, as if he was debating how to respond. "I have my reasons. And they have nothing to do with getting you into bed," he added before she could snap off another insult. "Now, do you want help with your bulls or not?"

She knew she should say yes and let it drop. But she couldn't. She kept pushing what little luck she had and the only reason she could even remotely come up with was that it felt safe to push Ian. "Is that why you're here a day early? Because of the bulls?"

Ian gave her a little smile, one that somehow made him look innocent and yet not innocent at the same time. "I wanted to make sure I didn't owe you money for that one bull. What was his name?"

"Rattler." She stared at him a moment longer. She didn't buy that he was here to check on Rattler but she didn't *not* buy it when he said he wasn't trying to get her into bed.

And honestly? She could use a hand, at least for right now.

Up to this point, Ian hadn't done the best job following the simple directions to leave her alone. But he'd stood up for her—twice now. It was more than anyone else had done for her in the long months since her parents had died. What's more than that, he looked her in the eyes when he talked to her.

But you touched him, a small voice piped up from the back of her mind. She'd put her hands on his massive chest and felt his muscles and he'd halted in his charge on Slim. And at no point had he suggested that contact between them "meant" that Lacy wanted him or anything other than what it was—she'd asked him to stop and he had.

That had to count for something.

"This doesn't mean I owe you a thing."

He smirked. "Are you always this stubborn, Evans?"

"I'm not stubborn." Another lie. She ignored the incredulous look on his face and turned back to the trailer. "And my name's Lacy."

LACY. OF COURSE she was Lacy. Underneath that pricklier-than-hell exterior, she was probably soft and gentle.

There might be a part of her that was quiet and sweet—as there was a part of her that wanted his help—but it wasn't a part she was all that excited to share with him, and it'd be best if he didn't allow his thoughts to wander off in that direction. Even if she didn't have a pistol on her, she had a gun and she knew how to use it—and he'd basically told her to shoot him if he did anything underhanded.

Lacy Evans might not realize it, but he'd given her his word and he intended to keep it. This wasn't about getting her into the sack.

Of course, that didn't exactly explain what it *was* about.

That wasn't entirely true, either. It was about that *spark* she had. When she tore into him, her body language was completely different than what it had been when she'd been confronted by Slim or when Ian had come around the corner and seen her pinned against the trailer by Jerome.

She'd been physically shaking, pale and panicked—and then Jerome had touched her. And
that had been all Ian had seen before the world
narrowed to Jerome. That asshole would *not*
touch Lacy like that. Not while Ian was breathing.

"Why are you alone?" he asked as the first
bull emerged from the trailer. "This isn't a one-
man job."

"You really don't think I can do this, do you?"
she snapped before adding, "Get up, Wreck."

"I'm not questioning your skills. I'm saying
you have three bulls and you're by yourself. You
were by yourself last week, too. You should have
a traveling partner."

"I—" Oh, hell—he heard her voice catch. She
dropped her head and put her hands on her hips.
"I had a partner. He died."

"I'm sorry." Ian had the urge to put his arm
around her shoulder and hold her. He didn't do
it, of course—he wasn't particularly in the mood
to have his nuts crushed up into his stomach. But
the urge alone was troubling. It was obvious that
she'd loved the guy. Ian could only hope he'd
treated her well.

"All I'm saying," he went on, pointedly not
looking at her, "is that I'm only ever in the arena
with one bull at a time and I've got a partner.
And here you're traveling with three bulls. Don't
you have any hired hands or something?"

"I don't have to defend myself to you."

There, that was better. Her moment of weakness had been just that—a moment. Already she was back to her fighting self. "Lacy."

He had things he wanted to say after her name, but then she looked up at him and whatever speech he'd been about to make about safety died on his tongue. Her eyes were wide-open, a pale brown color with a darker brown ring around the outside.

He wanted to see what she looked like without that hat crammed down on her head. He wanted to tangle his fingers in her hair and tilt her head up and—

She looked away first, her cheeks turning a sweet pink. "Maybe if Rattler and Wreckerator have a good season," she said, her voice pinched, "I can afford to hire someone. But right now, I can't. There. Are you happy now?"

"I don't know why you'd think I'd be happy about that," he said, taking a step away from her. "Sounds like it's been a rough road for a while."

This observation was met with the kind of silence that made stone walls look cushy. They got the third bull out.

"That one's Rattler, right?" he said into the silence, pointing at the brown bull.

"You should remember him," she said. It ought to have come out snippy, but her voice was quiet—thoughtful, even. "He checked out, by the way."

"How much was the vet call?"

"Don't worry about it."

Now it was his turn to gape at her. "Seriously, Evans?" She flinched when he used her last name. "You're busy convincing yourself that me helping you unload the bulls doesn't mean you 'owe' me anything, but you won't let me cover the cost of the vet visit—which, I might add, I already promised to pay for? This isn't charity and I'm not taking pity on you. I might have injured your animal. Let me pay for the damn vet."

She turned toward him, her brow furrowed in what looked like confusion. Well, she could just be confused. He was completely turned around by a hard woman with a soft name and several chips on both shoulders.

"You helped unload the bulls. We're even," she said, her hand slicing through the air as if that was that.

It wasn't. "If this is you being not stubborn, I'd hate to see what you'd do if you really dug your heels in. I'm paying for the vet visit one way or the other. Either you tell me how much it cost or…"

She leaned toward him. It wasn't a big movement—she might not even have been aware she'd done it. But he noticed. Her big brown eyes were locked on his and her body was angled toward his and her lips were parted. When she tilted her head to one side, as if she wanted to be kissed, his self-control almost snapped.

The only thing that saved him from making a first-class fool of himself was Jack's voice echoing in his mind—a good bullfighter waited. A bad one rushed in.

Ian would not rush this. Not her.

So, despite the signals her body was sending, he did not pull her into his arms and he did not take the kiss she appeared to be offering.

"Or what?"

But by God, it would be easier to not kiss her if she didn't sound so soft and sweet. "Or I'll work it off. I'll help you load and unload the bulls when we're at the same rodeos, make sure the assholes don't treat you like crap." He couldn't help it, not when her eyes widened even more. He leaned forward, his voice dropping down a notch. "Either way, you'll get it out of me."

Then he waited. Either she'd punch him or kiss him or she'd walk off.

She didn't do any of those. "Why are you doing this?" she asked, that voice of hers so soft without all the hard edges she usually used. "I'm nothing to you. You don't even know me."

"You're not nothing. Not to me." She sucked in a quick gasp of air. "And rodeo is a family. I was raised to look after my own."

But even as he said the words, he could feel the ink over his heart start to burn, like he was having it carved into his skin all over again.

So it was a lie that he always looked out for his own. No one knew about Eliot, not even Ian's cousin June. All she knew was that he'd been seeing two girls at the same time before he went off to college. Leasha had left the rez to have the baby and hadn't told anyone she'd given the boy up.

Not even Ian. Not until the papers had arrived.

And Ian had— Well, he'd signed them.

He hadn't taken care of his own son.

Ian rubbed the tattoo on his chest until the pain edged back again.

"A...family," she said, turning back to the bulls. She sounded very faraway.

"We're not all like Salzberg or Slim," Ian felt obligated to point out. "Some of us are decent human beings. My partner, Jack, is a good guy. There's the Preacher, Randy—heck, even Garth is okay, if you get him before he's had more than three beers."

"You spend a lot of time with the riders?"

He shrugged. "I have connections." She shot him a sideways look. "There's always going to be the jerks who think you shouldn't be here. Let's just say I enjoy putting jerks in their proper places."

As he'd done at that first rodeo he'd gone to

with his cousin June. She'd been climbing the ranks of professional riders, but she'd had a problem with some of the riders. Ian had been more than happy to stand up for his cousin.

Before that rodeo, Ian had been an ex-football player without a team.

But after that rodeo? He was a bullfighter.

"No strings?" Lacy asked, a hint of worry at the edge of her eyes. She didn't trust him. *Not yet*, a quiet voice whispered in his ear.

"No strings," he agreed. Then he stuck out his hand. "Friends?"

She regarded him for a long second. Then she slipped her small hand into his, gave him a brief squeeze, and yanked her hand back. "Don't get carried away," she told him.

He grinned at her. Oh, she was a piece of work, but really, he didn't expect anything less from her. "I wouldn't dream of it."

CHAPTER FOUR

"HEARD YOU GOT into it with Salzberg," Jack said, giving Ian a look. "Can't take you anywhere, can I?"

Ian bristled. "He had Lacy pinned against her trailer. He's lucky I didn't kill him."

That got Jack's eyebrows up and moving. "Lacy, is it?"

There were days that talking with Jack was like talking with Ian's father, Dave Tall Chief. Dave had a way of making Ian feel as if he was still fourteen, big and wild and more than a little stupid.

This, apparently, was one of those days. "I reckon that girl can take care of herself," Jack said, lazily scratching his throat.

They were sitting behind the chutes. The rodeo didn't start for another hour, but the crowd had started to filter into the outdoor arena as people jockeyed for the best seats. The stock contractors were loading the bulls in order.

He looked around, but he didn't see Lacy. All

he saw were bull riders strapping on their spurs and chaps or rosining up their bull ropes.

Every athlete needed a pregame ritual to get their head into the game, he thought. When Ian had played football, he'd needed to smash helmets or bump chests with his teammates.

Ian and Jack had some collapsible chairs that they set up next to their watercooler. Jack liked to watch the bulls and try to guess which ones would give him the most trouble. Ian always had a hard time sitting still for this part—he'd always been a little hyper. But today was worse than normal. He wanted to find Lacy and make sure she was all right. At the same time, he was sure that doing anything remotely like that would get him in trouble.

More trouble than he was in, anyway. "I don't see what the big deal is. I watch your back. Why shouldn't I watch hers, too?" Jack snorted, so Ian went on. "I thought you were the one who told me that rodeo is a family and we look out for each other."

Jack sat forward, his massive biceps straining at his white T-shirt. Ian was big—but Jack was bigger. "I've fought too damn hard to prove that I'm not some gangbanger playing at cowboys and Indians for you to toss that aside for some chick. You dig?"

Ian glared at his friend. "All I'm saying is that we stick together because we don't fit in with *them*," he said, nodding toward where the all-white rodeo riders were gearing up. "And Lacy doesn't fit with them, either. You know some of them don't want her here because she's a woman. How's that any different from someone calling us names?"

"This ain't the Land of the Misfit Toys, man," Jack drawled in his strongest Texas accent. He only busted it out when he was being condescending—or when he was trying to pick up buckle bunnies. Either way, it grated on Ian's nerves.

"Like hell it isn't." Ian spotted her. She'd walked up alongside the chutes, her eyes on the bulls. "I'm keeping an eye on her," he stated. "If you decide to grow a pair and man up, you can do the same. I won't tell—it'll be our little secret that big, mean Black Jack Johnson's got a soft spot for misfits."

"Boy," Jack growled, "that mouth is going to get you into a lot of trouble one of these days." But he slumped back into his chair, the fight gone from his body.

"Too late," Ian said cheerfully. He'd won this round. Winning wasn't everything, but sometimes, it came close. "What do you know about that Slim fellow?"

"Slim Smalls?" Black Jack chuckled. "He's an ass. Always has been. There are some that don't think a black man should be in the arena and Slim is always leading that charge."

"The more things change?" Ian asked.

"The more they stay the same," Jack agreed. "But his bulls are rank and he knows how to grease the wheels. Got friends in high places and all that crap."

"And the Straight Arrow?"

Jack shrugged. "Man…"

"Come on, Jack. You know everything and everyone. I don't know a thing."

"Wait!" Jack dug his phone out of his pocket and held it up. "Say that again, Chief. I want it on the record."

"Ha-ha. But you know what I mean. She said she'd lost her traveling partner."

"Honest to God, I don't remember a lady stock contractor," Jack replied, pocketing his phone again. "I want to say that the Straight Arrow was owned by a guy named Dale? If I'm remembering right, nice guy. Never made a big deal about me one way or the other. Quiet, kept to himself." He gave Ian a blank look. "I suppose you're gonna want me to ask around."

Ian shrugged. "Don't put yourself out, man. I do have my own connections." He could always call Travis Younkin, June's husband and a former world-class bull rider in his own right. Travis would make a few phone calls and get back to Ian with all kinds of information.

But then, Ian could have already done that. And he hadn't.

He wanted to know. But for some ridiculous reason, he wanted her to tell him.

Like yesterday, when she'd finally told him her first name. He could have found out, but it was sweeter hearing the name come out of her mouth because he'd earned it. The fact that she trusted him with her real name was powerful stuff.

He wanted to show her that men weren't all Slims and Jeromes. He wanted...

Well, hell. He didn't want to be the man he'd been seven years ago.

Ian realized he was rubbing the ink over his heart again. "We gonna get to Vegas this year?" he asked Jack.

Jack notched an eyebrow at Ian. "Might," he drawled. "Assuming you stop pulling dumb-ass stunts like you did last week. Why?"

"No reason."

Except for Eliot. Ian knew the boy and his family lived in Las Vegas. If Ian could get to Vegas, maybe he could see if Eliot's folks would bring the boy to the rodeo. Maybe, after all this time, Ian could meet his son.

He found himself looking at Lacy again. What would a woman like her think of a man like him, if she knew about Eliot? Would she think he was a deadbeat dad? A serial womanizer who didn't care what happened to the women he loved and left?

Would she still trust him with her name?

Jack stood up and began to stretch. Ian did the same. They'd get loosened up, don their matching work shirts and suffer through the opening rounds of the same tired jokes that the rodeo clowns used at every stop along the way. Then it was time to dance with the devils in the late-summer light.

"She brought that bull I took down last week," Ian told Jack as he stretched. His back was still tight where he'd pulled it last week. "Rattler."

"Yeah? The bull wasn't hurt, was he?"

"Nope. She wouldn't even let me pay for the vet visit."

Jack cracked a wide smile. "You be careful. A woman like that doesn't take crap from anyone— not even the likes of you."

"Tell me something I don't already know."

They went out for the introductions and the opening prayer. The Land of the Misfits, Ian thought. It wasn't far off. He didn't fit anywhere else. He had a job back on the Real Pride Ranch and the rez would always be home, but he'd wanted more. He'd thought football was his ticket to the rest of the world, but it hadn't worked out like that.

He found Lacy. She was behind the arena fence, apart from everyone else. Instead of having her head down in prayer, her hands were clasped as she stared up at the dusk sky. For a woman who was not to be taken lightly, there was something fragile about her that pulled at him.

The fireworks shocked him back to himself. They were all noise and smoke, but they got the crowd energized after Preacher's solemn prayers for safe rides. Heavy metal music blared through the speakers as the riders got back behind the chutes and began to mount up on their bulls.

He couldn't think about Lacy right now. Distractions could be deadly. He had to focus on the bulls and the riders. He let the music push him until his adrenaline was flowing and his head was in the game.

Lacy would have to wait.

It was time to go to work.

CHAPTER FIVE

WRECKERATOR WAS NOT in the mood to be ridden. He came flying out of the gate awkwardly, slamming into the chute hard enough that Lacy had to grab onto the top of the gate to keep her balance. The rider had no such luxury—he lost his grip and went down.

The crowd gasped as the rider bounced off the ground. Then Ian and his partner were there. They threw themselves in front of Wreck, arms waving as they shouted at him.

Wreck's flank strap didn't fall off, which meant it was still irritating him. He was not the sharpest knife in the drawer and, in his pissed state, he got confused by the noise. Still bucking, he lowered his head and charged at Ian. Lacy held her breath. He wouldn't try to wrestle Wreck, would he? She wanted to shout at him, but her voice got stuck in the back of her throat and all she could do was watch in horror as Wreck bore down on Ian.

Ian made a stutter step to the right, and then spun left as Wreck blew past him. Lacy leaned forward, trying to see around her bull to where Ian was—had he gotten clipped?

But no. Ian was standing in the middle of the arena, hands on his hips, shaking his head as if Wreckerator—a fourteen-hundred-pound bull—was a naughty child. Lacy felt herself breathe again in relief as the crowd cheered.

Wreck's flank strap loosened and fell to the ground. Ian's partner, Jack, danced in front of Wreck, moving toward the open chute that would funnel the bull back to the pens. Wreck charged, but it didn't have the same murderous intent. When Black Jack dodged, Wreck saw the opening and kept right on going, still kicking up his back heels as he was shunted down the chutes.

"That'll earn Garth Whitley a reride, folks," the announcer proclaimed. "And let's hear it for our dedicated bullfighters Ian Tall Chief and Jack Johnson, ladies and gents! They're working hard for our riders tonight!"

Both men tipped their hats to the crowd. Lacy couldn't help but note that the sounds of female voices seemed to drown out male cheers. She realized she was scowling at the crowd and forced herself to stop.

Gah, she was being ridiculous. Ian was a good-looking man—well, they both were. Of course the ladies were going to cheer for them. Bull riders tended to be lightweights and the bullfighters were anything but. Ian and Jack were both well over six feet and even their dorky matching shirts couldn't disguise their muscles.

Muscles she'd touched. Muscles she'd seen in detail when Ian's wet T-shirt had clung to his chest.

She shook the image out of her head and wondered how many of the people here had heard about Ian wrestling Rattler to the ground. She'd meant to see if anyone had posted a video, but she hadn't been able to bring herself to walk into her father's office and turn on the computer, not when the box was still sitting on the desk, exactly where she'd left it. The Straight Arrow was far enough out in the middle of nowhere that Wi-Fi and broadband were still pipe dreams. Dad had sprung for a satellite connection when Lacy had gone to college so she and Mom could email, but Lacy couldn't get her laptop hooked into the system. Well, she probably could, if she could bring herself to go into the damn office. But she couldn't. Not yet, anyway. She would. Soon.

Besides, she hadn't had time to do any online digging into Ian Tall Chief in the first place. Murph, her hired hand, had come down with the flu and Lacy had been doing most of the ranch work herself. The vet had come to preg-check the cows and had looked at Rattler while he was there. After loading a couple of hundred cows into a holding chute, she'd barely been able to do anything other than stumble into the shower and collapse into bed. At least she'd slept. She had that going for her.

Lacy climbed down off the chutes and threaded her way back to the pens to check on Wreck. No one messed with her, not during the rodeo. Bull riders were a superstitious lot. No one wanted to risk her jinxing them before a ride.

She took a deep breath and let the smell of dirt and manure and bulls fill her nose. For a moment, she could *be*. It was as close to free as Lacy felt these days.

Wreck was safely in his pen, blowing snot on everything and bellowing his dissatisfaction with not getting to crush anyone to death.

"It was a good effort," she told the bull. "You have to get out of the chute, though. A no-ride doesn't do either of us any good."

If only Wreck could get it together—he could be such a good bull. But he was still too green to be reliable.

She headed back up to the front. Chicken was due up soon, and she liked to be near him. Where Wreck was all impatient, Chicken Run had gotten to the point where he'd seen this, done that. After this year, she'd retire him out to the ranch and he'd live out the rest of his bull days among the fawning herds of cows, hopefully making mean little bulls that would grow up to be as rank as their daddy.

That was the plan, anyway. The six months of the season felt like a long time to go.

She watched a few of the other rides from the side of one of the chutes, well away from the rest of the riders. She located Jerome Salzberg on the other side of the chutes. He was in the middle of a crowd and didn't seem to notice her. That was how she liked it.

But even looking at him caused her to tense up as she remembered the feeling of his breath on her cheek and the trailer biting into her back. She had to be smarter. She knew that. She couldn't let someone like Jerome or Slim surprise her again and she absolutely couldn't let anyone get close enough to touch her.

She didn't have a belt holster for her pistol and she wasn't sure how she'd feel open-carrying it around. Her father had never needed to pack heat when he traveled. The gun was there in case an animal got injured and had to be put out of its misery. She'd seen it happen a couple of times and it was a hard thing to watch.

Cowgirls didn't cry. Not in public, anyway.

Ian was in the middle of the arena, bouncing on the balls of his feet. All of his attention was focused on the chutes. She thought it was the same guy who'd nearly gotten crushed by Rattler— until Ian had saved his hide.

Ian really was good—there was a fearlessness about him that she admired. She wished she could be that certain, that confident. Instead, she was going through the motions, hoping everyone else didn't see how close to the edge of total collapse she really was.

Chicken had a good ride, bucking his rider off at the 6.8 second mark. A better rider would have made the time, but this one committed to the right when he should have gone left.

The moment he'd dumped his rider, Chicken trotted toward the gate. Ian hadn't even moved during the ride. She hadn't realized she was staring at him until he looked up and caught her gaze. She could feel heat build on her cheeks, especially when his mouth quirked into a smile. For her.

She didn't smile back. Yes, Ian had said they were friends. But because he'd said so didn't make it true. She would not do anything he might take the wrong way. She was smarter than that.

Still…

She touched the brim of her hat in acknowledgment. It was more than a nod, less than a smile. It was the best she could do.

He did the same back.

Not that it mattered. She wasn't here for Ian. She was here for the bulls. She followed Chicken back to make sure he made it into the pens without a problem, but she didn't have to worry. The old bull wanted some water and hay.

Part of her thought she should watch the rest of

the rides, but part of her wanted to stay back here with the bulls. When she was with the bulls, she didn't have to worry about sending the "wrong" signals or defending herself or any of that crap. She had to make sure they didn't step on her. It was easy in its simplicity. *Don't make a mistake. Don't get crushed.*

Rattler was going tomorrow. She hoped like hell he had a good ride. They needed another three-hundred-and-some-odd points before she could start negotiating with the promoters for appearances at the Challenger level.

She climbed into her truck. She had a good view of her trailer and the pen where her bulls were held. She should probably eat dinner. She knew she'd eaten breakfast—the hotel had served doughnuts and coffee, that sort of thing. But she wasn't sure she'd eaten lunch.

She had the feeling that, if her mom were still alive, she'd give Lacy that look and say, "Honey, I *know* you can do better than this." It was Mom's favorite phrase, one she deployed equally for underwhelming grades or a messy room. And then Dad would say, "Linda, go easy on the girl. She'll get it next time—won't you, honey?" And Lacy would nod and promise that next time, she'd do better.

As an only child, Lacy had often thought it was unfair that her mom expected her to be so perfect all the time. But now that Lacy knew the truth…

How much of that prodding had been Mom hedging against Lacy's true nature?

What *was* Lacy's true nature?

The answers were in the box. The box that Lacy couldn't bring herself to look into again.

She couldn't ignore that box for the rest of her life. At the very least, she needed to get back into Dad's office, sort through the bills that were way past due, pull the stock contracts out—that sort of thing. She couldn't let the box loom over her.

She wouldn't. Tomorrow, the bulls would buck and she'd load them up and drive home. And this week, she promised herself, she'd go into the office and face the box again.

She would do better. She knew she could.

TAP, TAP, TAP.

"Lacy?"

She started awake—wait—when had she fallen asleep? She blinked groggily as she tried to remember where she was.

Knocking, again. "Lacy?" the voice repeated, more concerned this time.

She swung her head to the left and saw him. He stood there like some sort of dream—although this time, he wasn't in a T-shirt, wet or otherwise. He was in a bright blue button-up shirt with white buttons. The sleeves were cuffed, revealing his massive forearms. He had a brown leather strap around one wrist and a brown felt cowboy hat on his head. He looked good, she thought dimly. He'd look better naked, though.

Wait—had that been real?

She rolled down the window and, to her horror, heard herself say, "I liked the wet T-shirt better." Which was shortly followed by, "Oh, hell—did I say that out loud?"

Ian blinked. "If you did," he said, giving her an easy out, "I didn't hear it. You're not sleeping in this truck alone, are you?"

"I wasn't sleeping," she lied. "And I have a gun."

He gave her a look that was probably supposed to be stern, but didn't quite make it. "Is it still in the glove box?"

"Maybe." The cobwebs started to clear out of her head.

"Where are you sleeping tonight?" he asked. She didn't much care for his tone. It was too much like the way she'd always imagined big brothers talking to their irritating little sisters.

At least he hadn't made it sound as if she should be sleeping with him. Even if she might have been dreaming about doing just that. Even though it hadn't been real, none of it, an image of his mouth closing around her nipple flashed back through her mind. She shuddered. "I have a hotel room."

He nodded. "Have you eaten today?"

"Yes." She wasn't quite sure when. "I know I had breakfast. Doughnuts."

That got her another irritated big-brother look. "I'll buy you dinner."

"No," she said quickly. "You don't have to." Dinner after the rodeo was something she'd always done with her dad. They'd make sure the bulls were secure for the night, and then hit a local diner or something. Lacy had always spent so much time with her mom, going to and from school, that those times with her dad had been special.

As nice as it was of Ian to offer, she didn't want to replace Dad in that ritual.

Not that Ian knew that. "I know I don't. But I want to."

She didn't like the sound of that. "Another time?" she said, because that seemed like something her dad would say.

Ian gave her a long look then, one she couldn't hide from. Most people looked past her. She wasn't a pretty woman—never had been, never would be. And she didn't fit into anyone's neat little box about how a woman should think or act. As a result, most people ignored her, which suited her fine.

But Ian? He did not ignore her. He didn't look through her.

He saw *her*. God, it was unnerving.

Finally, he said, "I'll see you tomorrow?"

"That'd be good." She realized she meant it. She wanted to see him tomorrow. To see what he'd do in the arena, to see if he'd tip his hat in respect to her.

It had nothing to do with the dream.

"I'll help you load the bulls up after the rodeo. That's our deal," he added before she could protest. "I keep my word."

"You know that's not normal?" The words were out before she could think better of them. She must not be as awake as she'd thought she was. "Most people don't."

Up until that moment, he'd kept a reasonable distance between him and the truck. He was fond of leaning against the driver's-side mirror, she noted.

But when she said that, he leaned forward, his hands on her door, his face where the window would have been if it'd been rolled up.

For the first time, he entered her space. Not because he wanted to shake her hand and seal the deal, and not because she was in between him and a man who had it coming.

This wasn't incidental. This was intentional. They were close enough to touch.

Close enough to kiss.

Her body tightened with awareness, taking the vague frustration leftover from the dream and making it painful. She heard herself gasp, but she felt as if she was holding her breath. His eyes were a deep, dark brown—maybe black. She couldn't tell in this light. But they were intense—and focused on her.

Kiss me. Don't. The two thoughts hit at exactly the same moment, swamping her in confusion. She couldn't lean in and she couldn't lean away. She couldn't do anything but stare into those eyes and wonder what he saw when he looked at her.

When he spoke, his words were a quiet whisper that she somehow felt deep down in the very center of her body. "I'm not most people, Lacy."

Then he was gone, leaning back and tapping his hand against the hood of the truck. "Get some dinner and some sleep. I'll see you tomorrow."

He started to walk away, and Lacy blurted out, "Ian?"

He paused and turned back. "Yeah?"

"It was a good rodeo tonight." No, no—that's not what she'd wanted to say. Of course, she didn't know what she wanted to say. Something that wasn't bitchy or dazed, something that said that they were friends.

"I mean, you were good tonight. In the rodeo." Ugh, that was not any better. "I mean…"

He saved her from death by embarrassment. "Thanks." Then he was gone, walking off into the night.

Lacy fired up the truck. Dinner. She'd go get some dinner.

For the first time in a long time, she was hungry.

CHAPTER SIX

THE RODEO DIDN'T start until seven that night. Ian rolled into the arena grounds at four thirty.

He wouldn't be surprised if Lacy had actually slept in that truck. And then, when he'd asked about dinner, she'd gotten a fuzzy look on her face and had admitted that she couldn't remember if she'd eaten lunch. He'd put the odds on her actually eating something after he left her last night at maybe fifty-fifty.

He had almost two hours before he needed to start his prerodeo warm-up. If she wouldn't let him take her to dinner, then he'd go get some food and bring it back to her. She was too thin, the circles under her eyes too dark.

She was entirely too stubborn. He got the feeling that if he tried to tell her to breathe, she might hold her breath to show him that he wasn't the boss of her.

The way she'd held her breath last night, when he'd leaned into the cab of her truck. He hadn't intended it to be an erotic thing. He hadn't even touched her.

But she'd sucked in that little gasp and hadn't let it back out. Instead, her eyes had gone wide and her pupils had dilated as a sweet blush heated her cheeks—and his blood. The spark that he felt when he was around her had threatened to catch and ignite a hell of a fire.

He'd almost kissed her. It would have been easy. He'd only had to lean forward another few inches and take her mouth.

And he hadn't. He hadn't kissed her, hadn't touched her. Instead—and he still didn't quite believe this—he'd gone back to the cheap hotel room he shared with Black Jack and ordered a pizza and watched some cheesy movie from the '80s.

It didn't make a damn bit of sense to him. Lacy wasn't his type. She was as tough as nails and twice as sharp. But underneath that—there was a vulnerability that had him at the arena hours early to make sure she ate dinner.

He parked and headed toward her truck. Something told him that, even if she had gone back to her hotel, she'd be here early.

He was not disappointed. She was sitting exactly where he'd left her. The only difference was she had on a different shirt, a pale green shot through with pink.

She still had her hat on. He was more disappointed than he cared to admit.

"Hey," she said when she saw him.

"Hiya," he replied. Her brows furrowed. Now what had he done wrong? "What?"

She tilted her head to the side as she looked at him. There was something about her face today that was softer. He took back everything he'd ever thought about her being not traditionally beautiful. She was *gorgeous*.

"Your accent."

"What about it?"

"Now it's gone. It was stronger." She shrugged.

He allowed himself a small smile. "Yeah, it comes and it goes, depending on who I'm talking to." It was always strongest when he went home and everyone spoke the same way. But sometimes, when he was hanging out with someone he was sure wouldn't hold his accent against him, it slipped out.

"It was pretty," she said without looking at him. Then her face scrunched up as it had last night when she'd sleepily told him she liked the wet T-shirt. It was a look that said pretty loud and clear *I can't believe I said that*.

"You eaten today? Something more than doughnuts?"

"I remembered to have lunch."

There was something about the way she said it that struck him as weird. "You *remembered*? Is that something you usually forget?"

"I eat when I'm hungry." But she didn't meet his eyes when she said it.

He tapped the hood again. "Come on. Let's go grab something before the show."

She shook her head. "I'll stay here, thanks. I want to keep an eye on my bulls."

"Did you sleep in the truck last night?"

The color on her cheeks deepened. "No."

That admission made him want to smile. She'd done as he'd asked. He got the feeling that didn't happen too often. "And yet, the bulls were fine?"

That got him a sharp look. Her whole face was transformed from one of surprisingly feminine beauty to a tough, tomboy scowl. "Yes."

"Then they'll be fine for another hour." Again, he wondered who Dale was to her. He couldn't tell how old she was—he'd guess Lacy was in her twenties, although whether that was twenty-two or twenty-nine was up for debate.

She could have been married. Or not, he thought, checking out her ring finger. No tan lines. But she was certainly old enough that she could have been in a long-term relationship. Of course, it was also possible that Dale had been someone else entirely—not a lover, but a friend, a brother...family.

She opened her mouth, to argue no doubt. Ian shot her a hard look. "I'm betting you're going to load up those bulls and head straight for home, wherever home is. I'm betting you won't stop until you get there. I'm betting that you'll 'forget' to eat then. So dinner now."

Her eyes narrowed, but then, unexpectedly, she gave in. "Fine," she said, cranking on the engine. "But I'm driving."

He snorted. "Yeah, I'm not surprised." He crossed around the front of the truck and climbed in. "You know where you want to go?"

THEY WOUND UP at Denny's. If Ian had any reservations about her choice, he didn't voice them.

For some reason, her dad had loved Denny's. And every single time they ate at one—which was frequently—he cracked the same "Moons Over My Hammy" joke. And Lacy laughed. Always.

Part of her felt as though bringing Ian to Denny's was wrong, somehow. She hadn't been able to face eating here alone. Somehow, with Ian, it felt as if…

As if she could do this.

"What are you going to get?" he asked when they slid into a booth that looked out onto the street.

"I'm not that hungry," she said. When he looked up at her sharply, she said, "I ate today. Really."

For a moment, she thought he was going to scold her like a child—much as he'd all but scolded her bull last night. But then his mouth twisted off to one side and he said, "Easy, Evans. We're just friends here."

"Yeah?"

"You don't sound like you believe me," he said from behind his menu.

"I'm not very good at having friends," she admitted. It'd always felt like such a failure, that she wasn't any good at maintaining friendships. Her mother had once said that Lacy was an out-of-sight, out-of-mind kind of person, and it was true.

He tried not to laugh but didn't quite make it. "You don't say."

She rolled her eyes. "I suppose you're friends with everyone?"

"Most everyone. I'm either friends with them or they deserve to be flattened by a bull."

"Or by you?"

"If need be," he told her. "Did you have a history with Jerome before this rodeo?"

She physically flinched at the mention of that jerk. "No. Didn't even know his name. I don't normally pal around with the riders."

He let that set for a moment. The waitress came over, poured the coffee and took their orders. Lacy ordered a salad but Ian ordered three appetizers and a steak dinner with sides. The waitress gave his physique a once-over before she left the table.

Lacy looked with her. Today, Ian had on a gray shirt. It was still cuffed at the elbows and he still had that leather strap around his wrist. He'd taken his hat off and set it on the windowsill. The hat was brown felt, but the band wasn't horsehair or leather. Quills? That would make sense, she guessed. He was an Indian.

Ian cleared his throat. "Or the fighters?"

She didn't want to answer that question because admitting that she'd never hung out with a bullfighter before felt as if she was admitting something. That Ian might be an exception.

So she changed the subject. "Is this your first year as a fighter? I think I would have remembered you from last season." If she could get him to talk about himself, then maybe he wouldn't ask any questions about her.

He went along with her tangent. "Yeah. I used to play football—"

"Shocking," she said, a smile on her face. A real smile. Then she made the mistake of letting her eyes drift over his shoulders and down to that chest.

Ian leaned forward, a playful smile on his lips. "You know, you're actually quite funny when you want to be."

Was that a challenge? It sounded like one. "Don't tell anyone. It'd ruin my reputation as that bitch with the bulls, and then where would I be?" She ignored the way her face warmed at his compliment, and she really ignored the way he noticed it. Something in his eyes shifted— deepened.

"Wouldn't dream of it," he said, his voice

lower. She felt it in her chest. But then, he leaned back, breaking the spell. "Anyway, I got lucky getting to tag along with Black Jack. Otherwise, I'd probably be down at the level below this one. Black Jack was up in the bigs for a long time before he got into a bad wreck. He thinks we can get back there if…"

She arched an eyebrow at him and actually smiled. "If you stop throwing bulls to the ground?" She was teasing him, she realized. When was the last time she'd teased someone?

"Yeah, that."

The waitress set down a huge mound of onion rings and mozzarella sticks. "Be right back with those chips," she said, and Lacy swore she winked at Ian.

If he noticed, he didn't show it. Instead, after offering Lacy some cheese sticks, he said, "How about you? How long have you been rodeoing?"

It was a perfectly innocent question, the kind someone asked when they were making polite small talk. But suddenly it was harder to breathe. A weight was on her chest and she wished she'd ordered the Moons Over My Hammy, just for Dad.

"I've been coming for as long as I can remember. My dad was the stock contractor. The Straight Arrow was his business."

"Ah," Ian said, as if that had answered all his

questions. "This your first year without him?" His voice was kind.

She nodded, a small movement of her head.

"I'm sorry," he said.

She tried to shrug, but it wasn't a smooth thing. She was not a smooth woman.

She couldn't hold up under his intense gaze, so she grabbed a cheese stick and began to eat it to hide her anxiety.

"Is your mom doing okay?"

She blinked a few times. She would not cry. Hell, she would not even tear up. Absolutely no moisture would leak from any orifice in her body. "I... I really don't want to talk about this." She set her half-eaten cheese on her plate. "If you don't mind."

He tilted his head from side to side. "If you decide you want to talk, you let me know."

"Why?" It came out so quietly it barely made it to the level of a whisper. She tried again. "Why would you want to listen to me?"

"Because," he said simply, as if that were the only answer that mattered.

It wasn't. Honestly, what was he doing here with her, besides trying to feed her fried food? "This isn't a date," she reminded him. "I'm paying for my half of the food."

He pointedly looked at her cheese stick. "Seriously, Evans? I'm buying your salad. Consider it part of my payback for the vet bill."

"You can't keep using that excuse."

"Sure I can," he said as he ate another cheese stick. "You act like if I buy your dinner, I'll expect you to put out or something."

"Most guys would. Most guys would have expected something in return for saving me from Jerome. Not that I needed saving," she hurried to add, because she realized she was making herself sound weak and she was not weak. She *wasn't.*

"And you're right. This isn't a date."

"Yeah?" She should have been pleased with his agreement. She wasn't. What the hell was her problem?

Ian leaned forward again. The air between them seemed to thin away to nothingness. She forgot how to breathe. She forgot how to think.

"I'm only going to say this once more, Lacy. I'm not most guys. I'm not sitting here with you because I think it's the best way to get you naked. I'm sitting here—with you—because we're friends."

Flashes of that dream came back to her. Naked. With Ian.

His gaze dropped down to her lips. He took a deep breath, his eyelids drifting to half-mast, as if he were smelling her and not the overpowering scent of fried onions. "Besides," he added in the exact same voice she'd heard in her dream, pure sex in the air, "you want me, you know where to find me."

"Wait—*what*?"

"You know what I mean," he said, leaning back. The waitress brought her salad and the chips, but Lacy couldn't even acknowledge food right now.

Had this man promised that they were friends, and then immediately offered—well, something? Something that he probably didn't offer his other friends?

Yes. Yes, he had. The look he was giving her was exactly the stuff that dreams were made of, and for a moment, she considered the possibility that, once again, she'd fallen asleep in the cab of the truck and that at any second, all of her clothes were going to fly off and Ian would be reclined on a bed, promising her that she wouldn't be able to think straight by the time he was done with her.

"I'm not the kind of man who boxes a woman into a corner—or pins her against a trailer— without her permission. That's not how I operate. Me trying to be a decent human doesn't mean you owe me a damn thing. Yeah, I'm attracted to you. There's something about you…"

His voice trailed off as his gaze drifted over her face, her chest. He took another deep breath and exhaled. Lacy knew her jaw was on the ground, but she couldn't believe what she was hearing. Had he just— Did he *want* her?

"If you're not looking for a good time, then

no harm, no foul," he went on. "You've got a lot to deal with right now and I respect that. But if you want to have a little fun, you know where to find me. No strings."

"I can't—I can't be hurt. I can't take any more pain." The admission was out before she could do anything about it.

He leaned forward and cupped her face in his palm. His touch was a kind of electric that she wasn't sure she'd ever felt before. Not from another man. Not even from her handshake with Ian a few days ago.

His thumb stroked over her cheek and she knew she should lean away. She should break the contact and put an end to this madness that he'd started. That she'd started.

"I won't hurt you, Lacy Evans. And I'll do what it takes to make sure no one else hurts you, either."

Good lord, he *was* serious. He barely knew her and he was touching her and promising to—to what? To protect her? To be her friend? With benefits? But only if she wanted to? Did any of that even make sense?

Nothing made sense. It made even less sense when the look in his eyes changed—she felt it where his skin touched hers.

Once, she'd been caught out in a summer storm while she'd been swimming in the creek. The skies had opened up and she'd barely gotten out of the water before lightning started striking. She'd grabbed her horse, Jacks, and dragged him out of the cover of the trees into the open grass. Moments after they'd made it to safety, lightning had struck one of the trees. The air around them had taken on a charged feel, making her hair stand on end. It was as close to being struck by lightning as she'd ever been.

But here? With Ian touching her, looking at her with the kind of intensity that made talking, *thinking*, nearly impossible? All she could do was feel the way he cupped her face, his massive hand tenderly holding her, his thumb stroking over her skin as if she was a jewel of the highest value.

And then his hand dropped away from her, breaking the spell. He sat back and said, "No strings, either way. It'd be fun. Nothing more."

She wasn't so naive that she didn't get his meaning. He'd sleep with her if she wanted him to—but any relationship they might have would be limited to friendship.

So she might have had an erotic dream about Ian Tall Chief. So he could reduce her to a quivering, wordless mass with a look and a simple touch. So he might be the most gorgeous man to ever look at her. It didn't matter.

"Honey, I know you can do better than this."

Mom's voice floated up through Lacy's memories. Her parents had raised her better than to

tumble into a relationship that was no strings—
and no promises.

She could do better than a not-relationship
with Ian Tall Chief. And she would. She would
not give in to these—these *urges*, for lack of a
better word, to rip his shirt off and pin him to a
bed and let him do things to her and...

She wouldn't let go. She couldn't.

She could do better.

So she forced her lungs to breathe and dug
deep for a voice she hoped like hell wasn't desperate. "How is this supposed to work? Because I don't understand how we're supposed
to be friends after you say something like *that*.
You don't make that kind of offer for your other
friends."

That got a laugh out of him—deep and rich
and genuine. "No, can't say that I offered that
to Black Jack. I feel pretty sure he'd turn me
down." Then he looked up at her, his face open
and, well, joyful. "We can be friends because I
can control myself."

"It's not enough," she pressed on. His eyebrows jumped as he chewed his meat. Suddenly,
she had to know *why*. "Yes, hurrah, you have
self-control. That doesn't explain why you insist on helping me, if you're not trying to sleep
with me. You said you had your reasons, and I
don't want to hear about how you're making up
for Rattler. Spill it."

He let that demand sit for a moment before he said, "Eat." She glared at him, which only made him smile. Which only made her glare more. "Eat," he said again, this time in a more pleading voice.

She picked up her fork and stabbed a leaf of lettuce. "There, happy?"

He waited until she'd actually started chewing. "I can't believe you haven't heard about this already," he finally said when she was into her third bite. "It's fairly common knowledge, at least among some of the riders."

"I don't hang out with the riders," she mumbled around a mouthful of tomato. Ranch dressing made everything better, she decided.

"No, I reckon you don't. You ever hear of June Spotted Elk?"

She paused midbite. "Of course I've heard of her. She's the woman who rode No Man's Land—the bull no man could ride. That was *huge*."

Ian nodded his head in acknowledgment but didn't immediately fill in the blanks for her. Instead, he dropped his gaze to his plate and fiddled with the leather strap on his wrist.

Wait—why did he look so sheepish? Oh, lord—had June been his girlfriend? Or his friend with benefits? And if so, why would that matter? She'd married, hadn't she? Yeah, Lacy thought she remembered reading that. She'd been dealing with the fallout of Mom's and Dad's death, but even the world's most famous female bull rider marrying one of the more famous male bull riders had penetrated through Lacy's grief.

Ian still hadn't said anything. Dread filled Lacy's stomach and it did not mix well with ranch dressing. She felt sour. Ian was a bullfighter because he was trying to win June back. It made sense. They were both American Indians. Gah.

"Whoa, whoa—simmer down over there." She looked up to find Ian grinning at her. "You look like you're going to stab someone with your fork. Hopefully not me."

"What? No. Just—a bad cucumber."

Ian nodded in a way that made it clear he knew she was lying, but he would let it go. "June is my cousin, Lacy."

"Your—*cousin*?" The word was a squeak. Oh, why couldn't she sound cool, calm or collected? She knew she'd never be all three but even one would be great.

He grinned and started eating chips. "Yup. We were always trying to one-up each other back on the rez. I'm bigger and stronger, but she's faster. Anything I could do, she could do better." He actually looked depressed. "It's not so bad—she's a world-class rider. She's not just better at bull riding than I am, she's better than nearly every single man out there."

"Still don't see what this has to do with me,"

Lacy murmured. But at least she wasn't some rebound in the making.

Ian pushed his empty plates away and leaned back, his hands behind his head. Lacy didn't think this was the best time to be caught staring at his massive biceps, so she focused on the salad. Yay for ranch dressing.

"When she was on this circuit," Ian explained, "she got a lot of crap from some of the riders. There were only a few who treated her with any respect—the Preacher, Mitch and the Brazilian, Travis, in his own way, I guess."

"Travis Younkin?" Ian nodded. "She married him, right?"

"Eventually," he said in that big-brother tone of voice she'd heard a couple of times. "But not everyone was willing to give her a shot." He leaned forward. "Not everyone wanted her there. And a few people weren't above threats or intimidation."

This was beginning to sound suspiciously as if it might have something to do with her, after all. "So?"

"So—and I'm going to be completely honest here—it drives me nuts that I can't beat her at this. I hate losing in general. My high school football team was undefeated when I was playing. My college record before I broke my leg was fourteen and three. I hate losing to a girl even more. But being bested by my own cousin?" He shook his head.

"All right, so that might explain why you're a bullfighter and not a rider," she told him. A storied football career cut short would also explain those muscles. Not that she was looking, because she wasn't. "But again, so?"

"If I'm going to be beaten by my cousin, by God, it's going to be fair and square. It's not going to be because some jerk decided girls shouldn't ride, that sexual intimidation was the best way to get rid of her."

"But she's family," Lacy protested. "I'm not. I'm nobody."

He cut her off with a look so intense, so heated, that she had no choice but to be quiet. "I don't want to hear you say that again. I'll admit it—the first time you tore into me, I wondered what the hell your problem was. But then I heard the way Slim talked to you. I saw how you reacted. And you know what? It was like watching some of those men try to put June in the place where they thought she belonged." He clenched his hands into fists. "It's like listening to people try to put *me* where they think I belong because I've got a name like Tall Chief."

She didn't know how to respond to that. If there had been a time when she'd thought him nothing but a bunch of muscles he'd completely blown that image away.

"I know it's not the same," he went on, sounding tired. "I know it's not a competition for you. And I'll never be the best bullfighter in the world. But I need to be good again. I need to be able to say I'm *one* of the best at something. I've got—" He paused and rubbed his hand over his heart. "I've got to prove myself."

He'd stopped being honest. If his body language hadn't given him away, his voice would have sealed it. He had another reason he did what he did. It couldn't be bills. There were easier ways to make a buck than this mad obsession they all had with the rodeo.

"It's not like you can win or lose at being a stock contractor," he went on, his voice unnaturally level. "But I don't want people to tear you down, and then say you failed because you were a woman in a man's world. If you're going to fail, you should fail on your own. Not because they set you up that way." He gave her a sheepish look. "If that even makes sense."

"It does." It was a lot to take in. "I won't let anyone tell me I can't do this."

"That's why."

She thought about what he'd said. "You ever help June out like you help me?"

Oh, my—that smile on his face? Wow. "I only had to once. Had a brief run-in with Red Willis."

Lacy choked on her coffee. "Red Willis?" He was another rider up in the bigs now. She hadn't realized how deep Ian's connections went. "You beat up *Red*?"

"As I understand it," he said, his voice something that would have been lazy if it hadn't been so menacing, "he keeps well clear of her now. A perfect gentleman at all times." He shrugged, as if assault were no big deal. "If Jerome's got half a brain, he'll do the same." He waved at the waitress, who brought the check. Lacy opened her mouth to protest, but he fished out two twenties and handed them to the waitress. "Keep the change. Ready?"

She nodded. She was tired, she realized. This was more talking—more feeling—than she'd allowed herself to do for a very long time. "So now what?" she asked as they walked back to the truck.

"It's up to you," he said in all sincerity. "I promised to help you with your bulls and I aim to keep that promise. We can keep hanging out. Or…" Even though he was a good three feet from her, she felt that lightning's-about-to-strike sensation again.

Or.

Or they could get naked in the vicinity of a bed.

"We could hang out some," she said, trying to sound as though she was 100 percent certain about it. Then, before he could react, she added,

"And I don't want to seem ungrateful about the bulls. I... I appreciate the help."

"There, that wasn't so hard, was it?" They'd stopped at the tailgate of the truck, she realized, as if each going to their separate side of the truck would somehow end the conversation. "Where are you going to be next week?"

"Nothing on the schedule until Clinton, Oklahoma, in two weeks."

"Where's home?"

It was a perfectly innocent question. So why was her pulse beating an extra hard rhythm right now? "Not too far from Laramie, at the foot of the Laramie Mountains."

"Beautiful country."

"It is. It's home." And she couldn't lose it.

If that meant she had to accept Ian's help and ignore this attraction, then that's what she had to do. She couldn't lose the ranch to Slim and have life as she knew it come to an end. Without home to anchor her, she'd be...

Lost.

She cleared her throat. "What about you? Where's your next stop?"

"West Virginia, if you can believe it." He sighed heavily. "It's different out East, when you've got a name like mine." He scowled. "Plus, it's a hell of a long way. I'm going to have to fly. I hate flying. I don't fit in the seats."

She tried to picture him folded up into an airline seat. Laughing, she leaned against the truck. "Will you be in Oklahoma after that?"

"Yeah." He looked down at her then, his gaze a caress. "Here." He looked away and dug his phone out of his pocket. "This is my number. Call or text me for any reason."

She got out her phone and entered the number on his screen into her contacts list. "I'll let you know when I get into Clinton?"

He smiled encouragingly. "And I'll help with the bulls."

"Because we're friends."

"Sure are." That's what he said, at least. But the look in his eyes?

Not friendly.

Not even close.

Two weeks felt a *long* way off.

CHAPTER SEVEN

LACY HADN'T GIVEN him her number. And Ian hadn't asked for it.

Instead, he'd chosen to put himself in the uncomfortable position of hoping a woman would call and being pretty sure she wouldn't. And all he could do was hope she was doing all right and focus on his job.

West Virginia was a different world. He'd grown up on a sea of grass, the Badlands half an hour away. It was flat and dry and every so often, there'd be a low line of hills covered in pines. South Dakota was a beautiful place, all the more beautiful because it was the kind of land that could kill you if you let your guard down. A summer storm, a blizzard—hell, even a grass fire could do you in. If the weather didn't get you, a coyote or a snake or a buffalo might. A man had to be aware of his surroundings.

West Virginia, however, was all lush green hills and deep valleys filled with rivers. And people. Houses were hanging on the edge of hills and the roads were wedged in underneath. The whole thing was claustrophobic.

Morgantown wasn't like any cow town Ian had ever been to, either. The arena was indoors in a coliseum on a college campus, for crying out loud. The place had a concrete roof and the echo was terrible. He'd done indoor arenas before, but they'd never been this freaking loud.

"You okay?" Jack said as they set up their chairs on Friday night. "You don't look so good."

"Rough flight," he admitted.

"Hey, at least you can afford a plane ticket," Jack snapped. "Where's your girlfriend?"

"First off, she's not my girlfriend. Second, she's not here." He got out his phone and checked to make sure he hadn't missed a text from her.

Jack chuckled. "You're gonna get your head in the game, right?"

"You have to ask?" No messages of any kind. Damn. "I don't like the echoes in this place."

"Yeah, neither do some of the bulls. Stay on your toes, man. I don't need you screwing up my comeback because you're making puppy-dog eyes at a girl."

"What are you, six? What's your problem?"

Jack gave him a mean look, but then looked away. "Long trip," he said. "My bad."

"No problem," Ian said. But now he was worried. Jack wasn't normally this tense before a rodeo. "Anything I can help with?"

Jack sat back in his chair and stared up at the horrible roof. He seemed older today than he had last week. More beat down. "We gotta get to Vegas this year, Chief."

"Working on it."

Vegas. He'd almost told Lacy about Eliot. About how he needed to be someone his son could be proud of. Yeah, Jack needed to get to Vegas and everyone could use more money but...

Ian hadn't been able to tell Lacy about that part of him. Hell, he should probably be more surprised that he'd told her what he had. Sure, people knew June was his cousin, but he didn't randomly reveal that it drove him nuts, her being better than him.

So why had he told Lacy?

She needed to have faith that he wasn't just putting himself in the friend zone until the perfect opportunity struck. He'd needed to give her a reason to trust him.

But that wasn't it and he knew it.

And, despite what Jack might claim, Ian was *not* making puppy-dog eyes at her. She wanted him. She had to be the one to pull the trigger—so to speak. He wasn't playing games with her because he didn't play games anymore. The last time he'd thought he could play a woman—two women—he'd wound up fathering a child.

He checked his phone again and began to

stretch. The loudspeakers started blasting heavy metal. God, his ears were going to start bleeding.

He had to focus. Too much was riding on this season. No matter what was going on with Lacy—friends or something else—he had to keep his eyes on the prize. If he made it to the bigs this year, he'd ask Eliot's parents if he could meet his son.

So he focused. He had a job to do.

IAN SAT AT the end of the bar, nursing a beer and watching the crowd and subtly trying to stretch out his shoulder. He'd caught a glancing blow trying to keep Jerome Salzberg from being turned into a mud puddle and the impact had strained a muscle. Not that Jerome was appreciative of Ian's effort. The asshole was on the other side of the bar, surrounded by fawning women who wanted to hear about his brush with death. Jerome hadn't bought Ian a beer or even nodded his thanks.

Well, Ian supposed he had that coming. After all, he'd hit the man long before the bull had taken a shot at him.

Ian didn't care. Not much, anyway. But he kept taking his phone out and glancing at the screen.

Waiting on a girl, he thought with disgust. He'd never waited on a girl before. He'd never had to. He'd been a big man in high school, a bigger man on campus. He'd never wanted for feminine company.

He thought of Leasha, Eliot's mother. Ian hadn't loved her. He wasn't sure he'd ever loved any of them. They'd had a lot of fun together, but that hadn't stopped Ian from seeing Pammy on the side. When Leasha had found out—because June had ratted on Ian—it'd been over and done. The fight had been epic, but the break had been clean.

Or so he'd thought. And then Eliot had happened.

All these girls here, they were about the same age Leasha had been when she'd had the boy. He didn't even know why she'd given up the baby. Because she had plans? A job waiting for her? Or because she couldn't raise him herself—because she knew she wouldn't get any help from Ian? He hadn't exactly proved himself to her, after all. He'd been a lousy boyfriend. A lousy man.

He had to make up for what he'd done.

Ian's phone buzzed. He glanced at his phone.

A text message. No name, no picture. Just a number. Wrestle any bulls today?

Lacy.

He chugged the last of his beer and headed out to the rental car. By the time he'd climbed into the driver's seat, he had three more messages. It's me, which was followed by, Lacy, and then

Lacy Evans, as if he had so many Lacys in his life that he couldn't remember which one was which.

He could almost see her, sitting there, frowning at the phone the way she frowned at him and wondering if maybe she shouldn't have texted him in the first place. I figured it out after the bulls question, he texted back. No, I didn't wrestle anyone or anything today. Almost got stepped on once, though. How are you?

The little bubble thought for a moment. Fine, she finally said. You? How was the rodeo?

Okay. The arena had a concrete roof. Louder than hell, he texted back. Now that he was in the relative quiet of the car, he could hear how much his ears were still ringing. Where are you?

The pause was long. It felt longer because not even the little thought bubble was there to tell him she was typing something up.

But it was worth it when she texted, In bed. You?

He let his mind spin out a fantasy of Lacy in, well, lace, curled up under the blankets, looking soft and sweet and…

In my car, in a bar parking lot, he texted back.

The response was quick. Oh. Sorry to bother you. Have fun.

Whoa, girl—I'm done here. Heading back to the hotel, he texted back as fast as he could. Rather be texting with you than watching the riders get drunk.

Oh. Okay. He swore he could hear the hesitation in her voice, as if she didn't believe him.

There was only one problem with his mental picture of her in bed. Question, he texted before he could think better of it.

Yes?

Do you sleep in the hat?

Of course not.

He grinned at his phone. Pictures or it didn't happen.

It wasn't as if he was asking for a picture of her bare breasts or anything. This wasn't sexting. Or if it was, it was the least sexual sexting ever.

He wanted to see her hair. He wanted to know what she looked like when she wasn't working so hard at being a tough-as-nails cowgirl.

This time, the pause was much longer and Ian wondered if he'd pushed her too far. Her hair was like her name—she'd reveal it in her own sweet time.

Then she was there, looking up at him from his phone. It was not, technically, a good photo. The colors were a washed-out gray, and she'd only managed to get a little over half her face in the shot.

But it didn't matter. Because Lacy Evans was looking at him. Her eyes were wide and maybe a little nervous. She was curled up in bed. He could see the edge of a smooth shoulder that was bare except for the strap of a tank top.

And her hair. Oh, Lord, her hair—deep, dark waves that fell in thick curls around her face and down her neck, ending at her shoulders. Something in his gut tightened, and Ian knew that if she'd revealed her hair to him in person, he wouldn't have been able to fight the overwhelming urge to bury his fingers in it and let the softness of those waves tangle around him until he was hopelessly caught up in her.

Wow, he texted back. Beautiful. His finger hovered over the send button. She wouldn't like to be told how pretty she was, he knew. She'd probably turn an interesting shade of pink and scowl at her phone and remind him this didn't mean anything because they were just friends.

He hit Send.

Then, without waiting for her response, he took a selfie—without his hat on—and sent it. Not his best work. He looked like he'd spent several hours being deafened in an arena and getting pushed around by bulls. Even? he asked.

I already knew what you looked like without your hat, she replied.

But did you know what the inside of this crappy rental car looked like?

I'm not going to tell you you're handsome, if you were fishing for a compliment.

That made him grin. She could be damnably prickly when she wanted to. I only fish for trout, he texted back. Did you eat today?

Yes.

He wasn't entirely sure he took that at face value. Are you going to be able to sleep tonight?

There was a pause. I think so. Thanks for talking with me.

Hey, that's what friends are for. He sent the text and then sat there for a moment. Will you let me know how you're doing tomorrow? It was still her move to make. She could text him if she wanted, but he wouldn't intrude on her time if she didn't want him to.

Yes. Then, a moment later, You won't show that picture to anyone, will you? Never sent a text picture before.

Never? Maybe that explained what took so long? Obviously, she was a different kind of woman, but then something she said seemed to click into place. She wasn't very good at having friends. It was possible she'd never had anyone to send a picture to before.

And she'd sent one to him. Won't, I promise. Just between you and me.

I'll hold you to it.

He grinned at his phone again. I expect nothing less. Night, Lacy.

Night, Ian.

He sat in the dark for a bit, thinking. They were friends. She was probably the most unusual friend he'd ever had, though. Aside from June, he didn't make friends with women—and June didn't count because they were cousins. When he'd been younger, he'd been too busy getting busy to be friends with girls. And his world now didn't lead to a lot of chances to hang out.

He tapped until he had cropped half of the blue-gray background out of Lacy's photo, so that it was her face, her shoulder, her hair. Then he saved it as her contact photo.

He could see her curled up beside him in bed, looking at him with those big brown eyes. He could feel her lying in his arms, her face propped on his chest. It wasn't a sexual image, but there was a closeness to it that he wanted.

He shook the vision out of his head. Ian had the feeling that if Lacy ever found anyone in her bed, she'd probably shoot them. And most likely not in the kneecap.

He would not show her picture to anyone; that much he knew for sure. Not even to Jack, and Ian trusted Jack with his life. That photo of her, soft and innocent and vulnerable, that was just for him.

"Good night, Lacy," he murmured to her picture. Then he fired up the car and headed for the hotel.

LACY LAY IN BED, scrolling back to the beginning of the whole text conversation and rereading it. She almost hadn't sent him that text. She'd assumed he'd probably be in some bar, pretty women fighting to be the one who went home with him.

And she hadn't been all wrong about that. He had been in a bar. And, if he'd looked the way she'd seen him look—the close-cut Western shirt with the sleeves cuffed to the elbows, that leather strap around his wrist, those intense eyes—yeah, there'd been women. There had to have been.

But he'd been in his car. If the photo could be believed, he'd been alone. She couldn't imagine any self-respecting woman sitting patiently next to him for twenty minutes while he'd texted Lacy.

She looked at his picture. He was wearing a dark shirt and there was the leather strap on his wrist. He looked tired—like a man headed back to his bed to sleep.

Night, Lacy.

She touched her fingertip to the screen. She was terrible at being friends with people, especially with people who were technically not there.

But she'd texted him. He'd texted back.

And she was beautiful. He wouldn't say something like that if he didn't mean it, would he? Or was it that he was still softening her up, making her like him more than she wanted to? She wasn't beautiful; she knew that. Striking, maybe. But not beautiful and nowhere near pretty.

He must have been saying "thank you" when he'd said "beautiful," she decided. *Thanks for sending the picture—you look nice.* She could accept that, right?

"Good night, Ian," she whispered to his picture. Then she turned off her phone.

It took a long time to fall asleep.

CHAPTER EIGHT

IAN'S PHONE BUZZED. Lacy. I'm here. You?

Twenty min away. Will be there ASAP, he texted back. "Can you drive any faster?" he asked Jack.

K, was the only reply he got from Lacy.

"Keep your pants on," Jack grumbled. "I'm not speeding for you or anyone else. I've had trouble in these here parts."

"Fine," Ian said, trying to sound as if putting along at seventy miles per hour was no big deal. If he were driving, he'd be pushing a hundred, easy.

But Jack was driving, so Ian kept his damn mouth shut. It'd either been ride with Jack or get back on a plane to South Dakota, and then drive down to Oklahoma. Jack had invited Ian down to his family's ranch in Texas after the West Virginia rodeo.

Which was great. The Johnson family ranch had been about two hours north of Dallas—pretty land. Jack's parents still worked the ranch and his brother lived nearby. It'd been a boisterous family reunion with so much barbecue that Ian had gained almost five pounds.

And every night, about 9:00 p.m. Wyoming time, he'd gotten a text from Lacy. The conversations were often short—mostly *hey, how are you, doing good here, good night.* He'd told her about hanging out with Jack's family, but that had been the extent of it. No more pictures of her in bed. This morning she'd texted that she was on the road with three bulls—Rattler, Wreck and Peachy.

Now she was in Clinton and he was still half an hour outside city limits with the world's most cautious cowboy driver.

"And how is your friend who is a girl?" Black Jack asked.

Ian snorted. "She's okay."

"Already at the arena, I gather? I hope your sorry hide appreciates that I left home a day early for this."

"I do, man. She needs help with the bulls. She's got three this time. It's a lot to handle."

"Why's she doing it alone? Seems kind of reckless."

"Her dad—that's the guy you remembered, Dale—he died. She's still working through it. They traveled together."

"I see." Jack was quiet for a moment longer. "I don't remember her. But if she always dressed like a boy, I guess I wouldn't."

"Yeah." Ian could see it, too. A stock contractor's kid, not a stock contractor's daughter. No doubt that between the Slims and the Jeromes of the world her father had assumed she'd be safer that way.

"You'll help with the bulls, won't you?"

Now it was Jack's turn to snort. "You're not going to lecture me on that whole 'misfits have to stick together' thing again, are you?"

"Depends. You going to help or not?"

Jack shot him a side-eye look. "You're gonna owe me one for this."

There was something in his tone that made it clear that this was going to go above and beyond Jack taking Ian to Texas and having his family put Ian up for a few nights and eating his food. This favor Jack was banking on didn't have to do with Vegas, either.

"Yeah, okay."

"I'm serious, now."

"I am, too. I'll owe you one and you'll help keep an eye on Evans."

Jack stuck out his hand and Ian shook it. "Done."

They pulled into the arena grounds twenty-three minutes later. Jack had goosed it up to a whopping three miles over the posted speed limit and they hadn't gotten pulled over, so he was in a good mood.

Ian spotted her silver truck. Jack parked and

they walked over to discover Lacy standing next to three bulls, all snorting around a holding pen. She had all that glorious hair hidden up under her cowboy hat. When she saw Ian, a cautious smile crossed her face. But then she saw Jack and that smile fell away.

"I thought you were going to wait for us," Ian said with no other introduction.

This time, her smile was huge—and almost feral. "I managed," she said, sounding as if she wanted a fight.

"Lacy, it's not a good idea for you to do this on your own." Even as he said it, though, he knew it was wrong.

A scowl wiped that smile off her face. "I appreciate the offer, but I know how to handle my animals. I don't need your permission to unload them."

Jack unhelpfully snorted. Ian heard his partner mutter, "Misfits," under his breath.

"I thought we had an agreement," Ian said, stepping toward her and lowering his voice. "I was going to help you out and you were going to accept my help as payment for the vet bill you won't let me pay."

"First off, I did accept your help at the last rodeo. Second off, I didn't need it today so I don't see what the big deal is. And third off— you don't get to tell me what to do. I'll eat when

I'm hungry, sleep when I'm tired and handle my bulls as I see fit."

He took another step toward her. She stood her ground. "I didn't show anyone your picture," he said in a voice so quiet he was sure no one else could hear him.

Her eyes went wide. Something was wrong. Up close now, he could see that the dark circles were back under her eyes. Without that big smile on her face, she looked drawn. "Lacy," he said, a weird mix of fear and anger gripping him, "what happened?"

"Nothing," she snapped. But she took a step back and dropped her gaze.

He hoped like hell she didn't play poker. *"Lacy."*

"*Nothing*, okay? Look, I've got to do what I've got to do and you've got to do the same. Okay?" Behind her, one of the bulls bellowed and started pacing. "See?" she hissed. "You're upsetting the bulls. I was doing fine without you."

He stared down at her and she glared up at him and he didn't want to let this go but what the hell choice did he have? He wasn't white-knighting her. She wasn't so helpless that she couldn't function without him. He knew that.

By God, if Slim or anyone else had so much as laid a finger on her, they'd spend the rest of their very short lives regretting it. "Fine. When you're ready to talk, you let me know."

"I don't need your help," she said in a cutting whisper.

He wasn't going to win this argument. He didn't even know why they were arguing. He was positive that half an hour ago, she'd texted him and nothing had seemed off. She hadn't said, "I've got this," or anything that might have clued him in that she didn't need his help. In fact, nothing in the past week had said that she was sick of him.

Something had definitely happened. By God, he was going to find whoever was responsible.

"We aren't done yet," he growled, turning away from her. "Come on," he muttered at Jack.

"What's going on?" Jack asked.

"Don't know, man."

Jack fell into step next to Ian, occasionally glancing over his shoulder. "She always like that?"

"No." Which wasn't strictly true. She was *usually* like that—prickly and borderline belligerent. But he'd thought that, since the restaurant, maybe she wasn't like that with him.

Was it because Jack was with him? She could be almost human around Ian, but anyone else was a threat?

"She's a hell of a tough nut to crack," Jack said. "I wonder…"

But whatever he wondered was lost underneath a sudden crash and shout. Both Jack and Ian spun to see Lacy stumbling back from the pen. A fence panel had come loose and one of the bulls was out.

"Wreck!" he thought he heard Lacy shout, as if she could reason with the bull. "No!"

But all that did was draw the bull's attention to Lacy.

Ian was running without being conscious of telling his feet to move. "Lacy!" he hollered. "Get out of there!"

She didn't. Maybe she couldn't. She backed up a step or two but it wasn't enough to get her to her truck or behind anything that could protect her. The animal lowered his head, pawed at the dirt and charged.

Jesus. She was defenseless, stuck in the middle of no-man's-land. "Jack!" Ian bellowed.

"Hiyaaa!" Jack shouted, hands waving wildly as he tried to draw the animal's attention away from Lacy. He wasn't as fast as Ian, though.

Ian got in front of her seconds before the bull hit her. He tackled her with everything he had, but instead of flattening her as he might a quarterback, he wrapped his arms around her body and rolled into it. Ian felt the heat of the bull's body pass behind his back, and then the two of them hit the ground with an audible *whump*. Pain jolted his shoulder, but he didn't care. He kept rolling, trying to keep her out of the bull's way. Lacy let out a pained shriek as Ian's back hit something hard and metallic.

There was a horrific crash from off to the side, and then the air was filled with the screams of an animal in pain. Seconds later, everything shook as something large hit the ground.

"No!" Lacy cried out, trying to break free of Ian's arms. "No! No, no, *no*!"

Still rolling, Ian got his feet under his legs and hauled himself up, carrying Lacy with him. "Don't look," he said. He hadn't let go. He couldn't.

"No!" Lacy screamed, hitting at his arms. "Wreck—oh, God—Wreck!"

Jack came skidding to a halt in front of them. "Okay?" he shouted.

Ian gave a curt nod of his head. He wasn't dead and neither was she. Lacy hadn't been trampled or gored.

"No," she yelled again, her voice cracking on the high note. "Wreck!"

Ian looked at Jack. His partner shook his head *no*.

"The other bulls," Ian said.

"Got them," Jack said. "Couple of contractors are here. They're penned."

"Who's got a gun?" someone demanded.

"Wreck..." Her voice cracked over the word again and Ian recognized it for what it was. She was about to start crying. She leaned her head back and looked up at him. Her eyes were glazed with pain and her hat was gone. "Don't let them kill my bull."

Ian tucked her head against his chest and half turned to see a cowboy with a pistol stand over what was left of Wreck. Wreck was a wreck—that much was clear. Ian didn't need to be a vet to see the animal wasn't going to make it. He was on his side but instead of his legs all pointing out away from his body in the same direction, one of his front legs was angled up toward the sky—until the hoof, which dangled awkwardly. The bull was trying to stand, screaming in pain the whole time. His other three legs were thrashing madly.

The bull had hit the trailer, Ian realized. His leg must have hit the wheel well or something. He thought he could see blood dripping off the rim of the well—which was six feet off the ground. The animal had hit the trailer hard enough to flip the whole damn thing on its side.

Jesus. If Ian hadn't gotten to Lacy in time, she'd have been pinned between the bull and the trailer. She would have been crushed to death.

"Don't let them," Lacy begged.

"Medical tent?" Ian yelled over the noise. A cowboy he didn't recognize looked up and pointed in the opposite direction.

A shot rang out. What was left of Lacy's bull went silent and slumped against the ground.

"No!" Lacy howled against his chest. She began to beat her fists against him. *"No!"*

"Lacy, hon—come on," Ian tried to say gently. She was coming apart at the seams, and he knew that if he let her fall apart in front of all these men, she'd hate him for it.

He swept her legs out from underneath her and cradled her to his chest. Then he took off in the direction of the medical tent.

Her breathing had left ragged behind and moved on to deep, painful gasps that didn't come at any regular interval. He couldn't tell if that was because she was so deep into the panic or if it was because he'd hit her at full speed.

But he'd had no choice, he reminded himself as he ducked into the tent. It was either she get hit by him or get hit by the bull.

The tent was empty. A cot was off to one side and a table that held a small fridge full of ice was on the other. No EMTs, no doctors. "Dammit."

"I—can't," she gasped in his arms, and then she tried to twist out of his grip. He almost dropped her, the movement caught him so off guard. "I have to—"

He staggered to the cot and managed to set her down without flat-out dropping her. Lacy looked up at him with dazed eyes. "I want to wake up now," she said in a whisper that was nothing but pain. "God, please let me wake up now."

It hurt him so bad. "Lacy, babe—just sit. I'll find the EMTs and—"

"No!" she screeched. "Don't leave me. Not until I wake up."

Well, hell. He was not a medical professional, but he had a degree in sports kinesiology. "I won't leave," he promised as he crouched in front of her. "But I need to check you for injuries. Will you let me do that?"

"Am I...hurt?" She looked down at her body.

"I need to find out. I'm going to take your boots off and check your ankles, okay?" He grabbed the left one and tugged. It came off so suddenly that he wound up sitting on his ass in the grass.

He saw Lacy physically shake herself, as if she really was trying to wake up. Then her eyes focused on him again. "Oh, God—this is really happening, isn't it?" She stood and started to walk out of the tent, with only one boot on.

"Lacy—wait!" He hopped to his feet and caught her by the arm. "I need to check you for concussions."

"Ian..." Her chest hitched up and fat tears streaked out of her eyes.

He sat down on the cot next to her and pulled her onto his lap. "It's okay. I'm here." He held her. That was all.

She collapsed in heaving sobs.

He started rubbing her back. As he did, he let his hands feel along her ribs. "It's okay," he murmured into her hair.

"It's not, is it? Don't lie." She leaned back, shifted and buried her face into the crook of his neck. Her arms went around him and, for the first time, she was holding him back. "It's not okay." She took a shuddering breath. "I'm so tired of death, Ian."

"I know, babe." So far, she hadn't reacted to his gentle pressure on her back. That was a good sign. The biggest risks of the hit had been a concussion if her head hit the ground or cracked ribs.

"Wreckerator..." She sucked in air.

"I'm sorry," he said, and he was. "He didn't suffer long."

"Oh, God," she repeated.

That was all she said for a while. The crying evened out. There was no stopping those tears, though.

So he held her. At some point, he realized he was stroking the top of her head. He didn't know where her hat was and he knew she would want it. But for right now, he would let her dark waves slip under his fingers. He'd wanted to see her hair, to feel it—but not like this.

Eventually she cried herself out. When she was down to a few sniffles, she whispered, "This wasn't a nightmare, was it?"

"No. I'm sorry."

"Rattler? Peachy?"

"Black Jack made sure they were secure. He's watching them now."

She nodded against his neck. "Wreck…"

"I'll deal with it," he told her, hoping like hell she wasn't about to start crying again. "But I need to do something else first."

That got her to lean back. Not enough to look him in the eyes, though. "What?"

"I need to check you for injuries. I need to make sure you don't have a concussion or any broken ribs."

"Oh." Her voice was small. "Okay."

He slid her off his lap and set her on the cot next to him. "I'm going to feel your ribs," he told her. "I'm not trying anything funny, okay?"

"Okay," she nodded. She looked as awful as was to be expected, but at least her eyes were focused on him now and she was breathing regularly.

Ian pressed along her ribs. "Let me know if you feel any pain," he said as he moved his hands forward, underneath her arms. He kept his pressure slow and steady and his hands as far away from her breasts as he could.

When he touched under her right breast, she sucked in air. "That…hurts," she said in surprise.

Ian nodded, mentally noting the spot. He finished checking the left side and then said, "I'm going to check your sternum, okay?"

She nodded. He put his hand between her breasts and forced himself to think about the muscles and bones—not her skin or her bra. She was almost painfully thin around the waist. He wanted to remind her to eat, but now wasn't the time. "Does that hurt?"

She shook her head.

"Are you breathing?"

She managed a look that was almost normal. "I'm trying. But this is…"

"Awkward, yeah." He tried to grin at her. He didn't make it. "I'm going to touch where it hurt again. Tell me how it feels."

He put his hands back underneath her breast and felt along the rib cage. She tensed at the same spot. "That's sharp."

"Take a deep breath." She did as she was told and winced. Ian closed his eyes and pictured the human skeleton. "You have a fracture here," he said as he felt the sore spot. "That's my fault. I'm going to take you to the hospital."

"No—I mean, I can't," she quickly corrected. "I can't afford it. And what are they going to do, anyway? Take an X-ray, maybe wrap it?"

"Probably not even wrap it," he admitted. "But I'm the one who broke your rib. I'll pay for it."

She shook her head. He supposed he should be glad she was getting back to normal—prickly and ready to throw down. That was a good sign that the shock had passed. "No hospital."

He sighed. "I need to check for a concussion, though. Does your head hurt?"

"No. Well, I mean, yes—but that's because I was crying."

He cupped her face in his hands and lifted her chin so he could study her eyes. They focused on him clearly. "Where are you?"

"In a medical tent in Clinton, Oklahoma."

"What's your name?"

"Lacy Evans."

"How old are you?" Not that he'd know if she answered correctly or not, but these were the questions he'd been asked a few times after a few hard hits.

"Twenty-three."

"How much is seven times eight?"

"Fifty-six."

"Good." She hadn't hesitated. He let go of her face and looked around. He didn't see a flashlight anywhere, but the light in the tent was muted. "Here." He pulled her to her feet and walked her over to the tent flap. Then, watching her pupils, he opened the flap and let the light hit her in the face.

"Hey!" she yelped in surprise.

He leaned forward and stared at her pupils. They'd both contracted at the same time and were even. "Does the light hurt?"

"No, you idiot—it's bright!" She socked him in the shoulder. "I'm okay now."

He let the flap fall behind them. "Are you sure? I'd feel better if you got checked out."

This got him a half-worried look. "And you're not a medical professional?"

"I have a degree in kinesiology," he told her. "If I'd stayed in school, I could have been a physical therapist. I know enough to patch myself up when I do something stupid like wrestle bulls to the ground." He smiled, hoping she would smile back.

She made a face that might have started out as a grin but was quickly buried under a cloud of gloom. "I need to check on my other bulls." She took a deep breath and reached up to cram the hat that wasn't there back onto her head. "I'm sorry I fell apart."

"What?"

She tried to step around him, but he wasn't letting her go. So she stopped. "I need to make sure Rattler's okay. I can't let anything happen to him. If I lose him…" She shuddered.

"Lacy, you don't even have your boots on."

She looked down at her feet in surprise. "Oh?"

Damn. Maybe she hadn't managed to avoid a knock to the head, after all. He led her back over to the cot and sat her down. "What's my name?" he asked, watching her reaction.

"Ian. But I'm fine."

"My full name?" he insisted. He reached up to brush her hair away from her ears so he could check for bruising along the side of her face.

As his fingertips stroked over her skin, she tensed. Her pupils dilated again. "Ian Tall Chief. Everyone else calls you Chief. You're a bullfighter. You used to play football, but now you don't." Something in her voice changed. It wasn't a huge difference, but suddenly there was a husky quality to it that hadn't been there a minute ago. "You promised to help me out and I didn't let you. I should have." Her eyes began to water. "I *should* have. It's my fault."

"It wasn't your fault, Lacy," he told her. Lacy wasn't in charge of setting up the pens. But that didn't mean that other mistakes couldn't have been made. He didn't see any bruising or knots that would indicate she'd hit the ground hard. "Does this hurt?" Slowly, he pressed his fingers along her scalp.

"No." The huskiness was stronger now. He honestly couldn't tell if she was about to cry again or not. "My hat..."

"It came off when I tackled you. If you want, you can wear mine until you get yours back."

She reached up and took his hands in hers, and then lowered them until they were resting on her lap. "Why are you doing this?" she whispered.

"Because we're friends," he told her truthfully. "I've done this whole workup on Jack—he'll tell you."

He disentangled his hand from hers, then lifted his hat off his head and put it on hers. It sank down until it was covering her eyebrows. "There," he said, brushing a stray curl back up under the hat. His fingertips skimmed over her jawline. He was having trouble breathing, he realized—and he couldn't blame it on the bull. "All hidden."

She moved again. This time, instead of pulling his hand away from her face, she pressed it against her cheek. "Why are you doing this for *me*?" she demanded, her voice soft and hard all at once.

"Because we're friends," he repeated. He was vaguely aware that he was leaning closer to her, but he couldn't help himself. "Because I like you."

He wanted to kiss her and he didn't want to kiss her. She was having one hell of a bad afternoon and she'd already been disorientated and anything he did that crossed the line would be jerky.

But she was holding his hand to her cheek and she was soft and warm and looking at him with huge eyes—eyes that focused and moved at the same speed—and damned if she didn't look like a woman who wanted to be kissed.

He couldn't. She had to make the move.

"Will the owner of the Straight Arrow please come to the stage?" The announcement boomed over the loudspeaker, the voice distorted by static and echo.

Lacy started. "Oh," she said, looking embarrassed. "I should go."

Yeah, she should. Ian stood back and watched as she jammed her feet into her boots. "Promise me that, when the EMTs get here later, you'll get checked out. And if you feel a sneeze or a cough coming on, try to hold a pillow or a stuffed animal to your chest. It'll take the pressure off your ribs."

She opened her mouth to argue, but then appeared to think better of it. "I will," she promised. Then she was up and moving—thankfully, her steps were quick and sure.

When she reached the tent flap, though, she paused and turned back. "You won't—you know—tell anyone I had a breakdown, will you?"

Ian walked over to her. "You should know me better than that by now," he said. He picked up one of her hands and pressed a kiss to her palm. She gasped as he then pressed her hand over his heart—right over the ink of Eliot's heart. "I swear that all your secrets are safe with me, Lacy."

She exhaled the breath and gave him a curt nod. Then she was walking away from him with her head down and her arms wrapped around her waist.

All he could do was watch her go.

CHAPTER NINE

MORT, THE RODEO PROMOTER, was sitting in a folding chair behind a folding table up on the stage behind the arena. He was already sweating, but it was only late April. Lacy fought the urge to step away from him and his sweat-stained shirt.

Mort was pinching the bridge of his nose. "What happened?"

"One of my bulls got loose. It charged me. The bullfighters were right there and pulled me out of the way. The bull…" Her voice stopped working. She tried to swallow down the lump that had taken control of her throat, but nothing happened.

Ian stepped up next to her. She startled. Unlike Mort's repulsive sweating, Ian smelled of leather and sawdust. She fought the urge to lean into him. "The bull hit a trailer, broke its leg and had to be put down."

Lacy tensed at the bare recitation of facts. But she would not cry—not again, that was. She supposed she should be thankful that she'd been alone in a tent, safely hidden behind canvas walls when she'd lost it.

Well, she hadn't been alone. Ian had been there. Just as he was now.

Mort gave her a cautious look. "You okay?"

"Fine." She didn't even cop to the busted rib, which was throbbing more every minute.

She could still feel Ian's hands moving over her body with a kind of gentleness that she wouldn't have given him credit for. She'd seen him throw a bull, tackle men—hell, she'd been tackled by him. And yet, when he'd touched her chest, oh-so-carefully avoiding her breasts the whole time—when he'd threaded his fingers into her crazy hair—

When he'd stroked her face and looked at her with something that hadn't been just concern?

She swallowed. She didn't know what to think about right now. She didn't want to think at all, because if she thought about Wreck, she might lose control again. She didn't know how she was going to fall asleep tonight without seeing Wreck charging or hearing his screams of pain—or the gunshot that ended him.

And that was bad enough. Worse were the long-term problems she was looking at now. Without Wreck, her ranch would be teetering on the brink of bankruptcy and no doubt Slim Smalls was waiting in the wings to take the Straight Arrow away from her.

But if she thought about Ian, she might do something totally irresponsible like ask him to spend the night having sex with her so she wouldn't have to think about it. Any of it.

No strings, Ian had said. And given the way he'd kissed her palm and held it against his heart? They were friends. Because he liked her.

If she wanted to spend the night getting lost in his body, he'd say yes. He'd make sure she didn't think anymore; that much she was sure about. It'd be a relief, frankly. Instead of nightmares, Ian would make it good for her. She knew he would.

But it wouldn't last. If she lost herself in him tonight, what new problems would she have to deal with in the morning?

Would they still be friends if they slept together?

A bead of sweat on Mort's forehead slid down his face. She focused all of her attention on it. It would keep her from making a fool of herself with Ian.

Mort sighed wearily. "Which bull was it?"

"Wreckerator." She got the name out without her throat catching, so that was pretty good.

"Hell," Mort muttered. "This puts us down one bull for the show." He scrolled through his phone. "Hopefully someone local has a bull they can get out here..."

The last voice she wanted to hear right now

spoke from below the stage. "Mort, now you know I like to come prepared. I have an extra bull."

Lacy stood stock-still. She would not react to Slim Smalls. She would not wonder out loud about the coincidence of Slim having an extra bull available mere minutes after one of hers mysteriously got loose and died. And no matter what, she would not show weakness in front of that man, because she knew he'd twist it around.

She would not give in to him and that was final.

Next to her, Ian growled. She felt the noise deep in her chest and winced. She didn't remember any pain when he'd tackled her, but she sure as hell felt it now. Which was good. The physical pain was something she could feel without having to think about it. She took a deep breath to feel that sharp jab again. It kept her in the here and now.

Mort looked up in surprise. "Well, Slim, that's good news. Who'd you bring?"

"Brother-in-law," Slim said, climbing onto the stage. He didn't look at Lacy, but she felt his sneer, anyway.

Mort wrote it down. "Okay, we'll go with our standard terms. Evans, I'm sorry but we won't be able to pay for that bull since it didn't die during the show." He wrote something down on a scrap of paper and handed it to her. "Call them about the carcass."

No, of course they wouldn't pay for the bull. She'd have to cover the cost of the removal. Where was she going to get the money?

She'd have to start selling off some of her heifers ahead of schedule. That'd get her through now, but this fall, she'd come up short again.

She nodded. She wasn't ready to think of Wreck as a carcass. He'd been her bull and he could have been a damned good one.

No—no crying. She would not cry. She'd think about…

Slim turned to her, a slimy grin on his face. "I know it's been a lot for you to handle since your folks died, sweetie," he said in a voice that was probably supposed to sound caring but was only patronizing condescension. "I wish you'd let me take some of that burden off your shoulders. That ranch and those bulls are too much for a darlin' like you to handle on your own."

She felt Ian bristling with anger next to her, but Mort was the one who spoke first. "Which trailer got tipped?"

Lacy blinked at him for a moment. A trailer had tipped over?

"The Straight Arrow's," Ian answered when Lacy didn't.

"We'll see about getting it righted," Mort said

in a way that made it pretty clear the conversation was over.

"Much obliged," Lacy managed to get out. She turned and headed for the stairs, Ian right behind her.

Neither of them said anything as they walked back to the scene of the accident. Her rib poked at her and she wondered dimly if maybe she should have let Ian take her to the hospital. But God only knew what Slim would have done with that. She had no choice. She had to prove to that man—to all of them—that it wasn't "too much for a darlin'" to handle this.

Ian had been telling the truth—Jack, his partner, stood next to the pen that still held Peachy and Rattler. At least it hadn't been Rattler, she tried to tell herself. She really would have been screwed if it'd been Rattler.

This attempt at optimism did not work.

Several other cowboys were standing around what was left of her bull. The hum of male conversation washed over her. She caught a few words here and there, words like, "a damn shame," and "check on my bulls."

And, yes, there was her trailer, flipped on its side with a massive dent where Wreck had slammed into it.

"Hey," Jack said, tilting his head to indicate that Ian and Lacy should join him. "The panel right there?" Jack pointed with his chin.

"Someone's jacked it up. The connector pole's been cut." Ian started toward the panel, but Jack grabbed him by the arm and said, "Whoa. No one else has seen it yet. Wait to see who shows their hand." Ian nodded, his face unreadable.

The pole had been *cut*? That meant the pen panel had swung open like an unlocked gate without that pole to hold the panels up.

Swirling rage and pain and those stupid tears all ran headlong into each other, seemingly colliding in the back of her throat until she had trouble breathing again. This wasn't an accident. Someone had done this on purpose.

She glanced over at the upended trailer, careful not to let her eyes fall on Wreck's body. She could have been trapped between her animal and her trailer. She would have been—if Ian hadn't been there.

She might be sick.

"I tried to tell Mort she couldn't handle her animals, but you know what a soft touch he is for anything sweet." Slim's voice was pitched so that everyone in attendance could hear him loud and clear. "That girl has no place at this rodeo."

Lacy cringed. She didn't know what part of that statement was worse—that she was nothing more than "anything sweet" or that now everyone would think the accident was her fault.

She turned and started for him. Whatever his problem was, it stopped *now*.

Except she didn't make it to Slim. Someone grabbed her arm and said, "No," in her ear. Then Ian put himself between her and Slim. "Smalls," he said in a booming voice, "you best move on down the line right now."

The hum of male voices died away as Slim turned to face Ian. "You don't scare me, *Geronimo*."

"Slim," one of the other cowboys said, trying to lead him away. "Maybe…"

"Maybe nothing. She's busy hiding behind her boy toy. What's the matter, Evans? Can't fight your own battles anymore?" He turned his attention back to the other cowboys. "I want to know what the hell she's been doing instead of taking care of her animals. Well?" he sneered at Lacy. "Been too busy with your Indian Chief here to pay attention to your job?"

Ian went very still. "I'd be a might more careful if I were you, Smalls."

Slim snorted. "Or what? You don't scare me one bit."

Lacy had to do something because if all hell broke loose, she knew she wouldn't be able to handle it. But Slim was right about one thing— she couldn't let Ian fight her battles for her. Not every situation was best solved by a flying tackle.

So she did the only thing she could do.

"Why'd you bring an extra bull?" she announced into the tense silence.

Slim's gaze snapped to her. His eyes bugged out with what looked like fear. "What?"

She liked knowing she could make him feel the same way he made her feel—nervous and off center. She stepped around Ian. "Why'd you bring an extra bull? I was standing right next to you when you told Mort you'd brought an extra bull. It's a hell of a long way from Wyoming, you know. You don't haul an extra bull for shits and giggles unless you *need* it."

She looked to the other cowboys. Most of them looked as confused as she'd felt on that stage. They knew the same things she did—things her father had been teaching her for the past decade and a half. Travel wore on a bull. It wasn't like loading a puppy into the front seat. Every trip in a trailer was a risk. "Anyone else here bring an extra bull?"

Several of the contractors shook their heads no.

"But you did," she said, turning back to Slim. "Why is that? Banking on a bull getting injured so you could get a bigger paycheck?"

The contractors and cowboys were all looking at Slim now. His face was turning an interesting shade of red that deepened closer to purple with each passing second.

She almost smiled, because by God, for once in her life, she had the drop on Slim Smalls, and it was his own fault. He could have waited another five minutes to tell Mort he had that bull, but no—he'd wanted to rub her nose in it. He'd been so busy trying to smear her that he'd overlooked the one thing she could use to smear him.

She didn't smile, though. Not with Wreck's carcass right there on the ground. Not with the way her chest felt. Not when things had become life-and-death so suddenly.

"Could have been anyone's bull," she went on, speaking to the group. "Someone could have gotten hurt."

"I didn't sabotage your pen, if that's what you're implying," Slim spat out.

But the cowboy who had tried to lead Slim away let go of his arm and took a step back. "That true, Slim? You brought an extra bull?"

Oh, she shouldn't be enjoying this. But she was. She stood a little straighter, her shoulders a little farther back. So she'd lost it in the tent earlier. She could still be the tough-as-nails contractor she had to be in public.

"I didn't let her bull loose, Jerry, for God's sake," Slim snapped. "I didn't even get here until maybe half an hour ago!"

"You didn't have to," she said in a quiet voice. "You just had to know it was going to happen." She made certain to phrase it neutrally like that. Cutting a pipe would have taken time and made a hell of a lot of noise. Someone would have heard it.

Slim might have had his back against the wall, but he wasn't done yet. "Anyone could have tampered with that pen," he snapped. "You know those animal-rights activists are always sniffing around, trying to make the rodeos look bad. Why don't you look into them, huh? I had nothing to do with it!"

She didn't say anything. She held her ground and met his gaze with one of what she hoped was steely determination.

Slim would not be cowed, however. He sneered at her so hard she could almost hear him say, *You've won this round, but I'll be back!*

The cowboy who'd tried to lead Slim away cleared his throat. "We've got to get this bull out of here."

"I'll make the call," she said. Her voice was strong, thank God. She sounded as if she knew what she was doing. She was in control. She was not some little girl that had nearly gotten trampled and broke down in hysterics and was unable to manage her bulls. She was a stock contractor, dammit.

Slim walked off. She knew this wasn't over, not by a long shot. But she'd stood up for herself. She'd stood up for the Straight Arrow. And she'd done it all without throwing a punch or calling names.

Her daddy would have been proud of her.

This unbidden thought pushed that lump back

into her throat and she had to turn away from the crowd. The moment had passed, anyway.

She found Ian watching her, a half grin on his face, his thumbs tucked into his belt loops. His shirt was still a mess, both from where they'd hit the dirt earlier and from where she'd sobbed into his shoulder, and he looked off without his hat.

Oh—she was still wearing it. She needed her own hat back.

But she couldn't look for it, not while Ian held her gaze and gave her that smile. "That was impressive," he said.

"It was?"

"It was," his partner said, coming up beside him. "Didn't get him to cop to anything, but you put him in his place. A man like Slim needs to be taken down a couple of pegs." He held out his hand. "We haven't been formally introduced. I'm Black Jack Johnson."

She knew his name, of course, but they were being polite, so she gave his hand a quick shake. "Lacy Evans. Why do they call you Black Jack—are you good at blackjack?"

Ian made a choking noise and started to laugh. Jack blinked, and then broke out in a huge grin. "Ma'am," Jack said in all seriousness, "it's because I'm black."

Heat flamed over her cheeks. "Oh. Right. I mean—oh," she finished lamely.

"It's all right," Ian said. "We're all friends here. He's black, I'm Indian and you're a woman."

"Misfits," Jack added with a kindly smile. "I understand you might need a little help now and then?"

She ducked her head. "I might. I should have—"

Ian cut her off. "Don't apologize. Everything you said to Slim was true. Someone cut that pole and even if he didn't do it, he sure as hell seems to have known about it in advance. It could have been anyone's bull." He stepped toward her. "And someone could have gotten hurt."

She felt him studying her eyes as he'd done in the tent. "Although, after watching you put Slim in his place, I'm not so worried about a concussion right now."

This time, she allowed herself to smile back. But not for long.

She forced herself to turn around and look at what was left of Wreck.

"How much was he worth?" Ian asked, his voice somber.

"Probably only fifteen thousand. But in another year or two..." No, she couldn't allow herself to think of what would never be. Wreck would never become a better bull and be a shining star for the Straight Arrow.

She turned away and dug out the scrap of paper Mort had given her and called the number. While she talked to the cleanup guys, Ian and Black Jack took pictures of the pen and the cut pipe, as well as the trailer and the bull.

"How much is this going to cost?" she asked the cleanup guy.

"The animal was thirteen hundred pounds? That's going to be close to a grand." He cleared his throat. "We'd need half up front. We could bill you for the other half..."

"Yeah, okay." She couldn't come up with a thousand, but she could scrape five hundred out of the bank account without overdrawing it.

Not for the first time, she wished her parents hadn't died. It wasn't only that they'd left her alone or that they hadn't told her about the box—that they'd never trusted her with the truth.

But it was also that paying for the funerals had taken the financial cushion her dad had been socking away and destroyed it. And now she had to pay to bury the bull in addition to losing the fees from his rides.

It wasn't fair.

"Here." Startled, she looked up to see Ian with her hat in his hands. He lifted his hat off her head and settled her own back down over her hair. It felt tight after his loose one. He tucked one of her curls under the brim. "Better?"

"I guess."

"How's the rib?"

"Sore," she admitted. Then she looked around,

afraid someone might have heard her. "Where'd Jack go?"

Ian grinned at her. "He went to find some chains and a new pole connector. We're going to lock the pens down."

"Oh. That's probably a good idea."

He notched an eyebrow at the *probably*. "You need to carry chains with you, Lacy. Double-check the pens before you get the bulls out."

He was scolding her, she realized. Well, maybe she had that coming. After all, if she'd waited for him—okay, so it wouldn't have changed the fact that someone had cut the pole. But together they might have realized the pen had been sabotaged. They might have helped keep Wreck calm.

But no. She'd convinced herself she didn't need help.

"Hey, now." She didn't so much see Ian step closer as she felt his presence. Then her cheek was in his hand again and he was lifting her face. "I'm not blaming you."

"You should," she whispered.

"Did you cut that pole?"

"Of course not."

"Then it wasn't your fault. Jack and I will take turns watching the bulls."

"You don't have to—"

He cut her off when his fingers tightened against her skin, drawing her closer. "Lacy," he said, his voice deep and low and for her ears only,

"I know I don't have to. Neither does Jack. But we're going to, anyway." His thumb stroked over the apple of her cheek, leaving a trail of tingles in its wake. "So let me do this for you."

He'd be so good. So good. He'd touch her like this and whisper those words in her ear, and then he'd pop the buttons on her shirt and...

And she had to stop thinking about it. Right now. First off, she had a fractured rib and wild sex was probably not the best treatment plan for that. Second off, she could not leave her animals.

If anything happened to Rattler, she'd be in a world of hurt—the kind of hurt that made a busted rib and a thousand dollars look like child's play.

She might have bested Slim in a battle of words, but she was still losing the war.

Ian's thumb moved over her cheek again. "Do you have a hotel room yet?"

Oh, God—this was going to happen. She'd sent out signals that she was open to sex, and Ian—being Ian—had picked up on them. A shudder went through her body.

Ian felt it. His eyes darkened and his jaw clenched.

Then he dropped his hand and stepped back. "I think you should lie down for a while," he said in a different voice. He almost sounded as if he was being strangled. "You need to rest."

"Why? I won't sleep. I rarely do."

He scowled at her. "You're being prickly again. Look, you need to rest. You need some aspirin and some ice. Knowing you, you probably need to eat. You can either do those things now, or you can do them tonight." He cast a judgey look over her. "Either way, you're going to rest. If you find a bed now, Black Jack will watch the bulls until we get back tonight. Or you can fight me about it now until you pass out from exhaustion and pain tonight and I put you to bed myself."

"You wouldn't." She didn't know why she said that. Apparently, she was being prickly.

"I would and I could."

"I can't leave my bulls."

"Then I'll stay up tonight with them." When she opened her mouth to protest, he cut her off with a wave of his hand. "You will sleep, Lacy. I promise."

She frowned at him. What were her options? She could go get a hotel room and try to nap now, or she could wait until tonight to try and sleep.

Damn Ian for always being right—she was tired. And sore. "Will you guys keep an eye on the bulls now? I'll take the night shift. I'd feel bad making you both stay up all night."

"Fine."

"But I can't go anywhere until the pens are secured, the trailer's been righted and the…carcass has been picked up," she added.

This was not what Ian wanted to hear. "If I get

some medicine, will you at least take it? You've got to be hurting."

She almost told him she wasn't—but the way he was looking at her made it pretty damn clear he wasn't buying that. "A little," she admitted. She put her hand on her ribs, right below her underwire. "Here."

"There, that wasn't so hard, was it? I've got ibuprofen in my pack."

Black Jack came back with some chains and a guy in a truck pulled up and a different guy with a massive tractor arrived and everything happened at once.

She wrote a check for four hundred and fifty-three dollars and twenty-seven cents, because that was what was in her account. The cleanup guy didn't give her any crap, not after he got a good look at the trailer. The tractor guy didn't ask for anything, so Lacy had to assume that Mort had taken some small measure of pity on her.

Then it was all done. She was one credit card bill away from flat broke. Wreck was gone to that great pasture in the sky. Her trailer was upright, and Ian hosed the blood off the wheel well. The water mixed with what was left of Wreck's blood on the ground, turning the red dirt a deep rust color.

And she was tired. The pills Ian had given her were taking the edge off her pain, but as she watched the trailer with Wreck's remains drive off, she felt as if she could fall asleep standing up.

She was so tired of death. More than that, she was so tired of being the one who had to clean up after the death.

Then Ian's arm was around her shoulder. "Come on," he murmured, and she had no choice but to follow as he guided her toward her truck.

He turned her around, and then his hands were on her waist. He lifted her up into the cab of her truck as if she weighed nothing at all. "Keys?"

She managed to fish them out of her pocket and buckle her seat belt as he slid behind the wheel.

The next thing she knew, Ian was saying, "We're here, babe," as he undid the seat belt and helped her to her feet. He slid an arm around her waist, and she let him take some of her weight as they headed into a hotel lobby.

"Did I fall asleep?"

"Yeah," he said. "Did you sleep last night?"

"I don't... No?" She didn't recognize the hotel, but at this point, she didn't much care so long as she could lie down for a little while.

"I didn't think so."

She leaned on Ian as he got her a room. When he went to pay, she tried to protest. "I can get it."

"No, I've got it," he said, sounding amused. "If you're going to stay up tonight, there's no need for separate rooms. Black Jack will sleep here tonight after we get to the arena."

There was something about that statement that didn't make sense, but then Ian was walking her toward the elevator and they were going up and she was swaying, dammit all, when the thing came to a stop.

Ian held her up, and then they were at the door to the room. He let go of her long enough to get the door open. Then he pulled her inside and set her down on a bed and pulled her boots off.

He lifted the hat from her head, then leaned her back on the pillows and pulled the covers up over her. "Sleep now."

Her eyes started to drift shut, but she forced them open. She didn't like being this tired. "I'm okay, right?"

"You're okay," he said in a reassuring voice. "But if you feel off when you wake up, will you let me take you to the doctor?"

She nodded. He was standing there, looking down at her and it could have felt wrong. It *should* have felt wrong.

It didn't. She felt safe.

"Will you be here when I wake up?"

He crouched down next to her. His fingertips touched her forehead, brushing her hair away from her eyes. Then they stroked down the side of her face. She sighed at his touch. "I'll be right here. Get some sleep."

Amazingly, her eyes closed.

And there was nothing but darkness.

CHAPTER TEN

LACY'S EYES CLOSED. She turned her head to the side, and within seconds, she was breathing regularly.

Ian exhaled heavily. He hoped like hell he hadn't gotten his no-concussion diagnosis wrong. She'd been entirely lucid for a good two hours or so, starting when she'd finished crying it out in the medical tent right up until the carcass guy had pulled away with what was left of her bull.

But then she'd curled into herself like a leaf falling off a tree, and he'd seen that she was almost to the point of collapse. Of course, if she hadn't slept last night—well, it'd been a long-ass day.

He watched her sleep, trying to dismiss the worry that crowded his thoughts. She didn't do anything symptomatic of a greater problem, though. She just slept. So Ian quietly left the room and went back down to the truck.

Behind the driver's seat, he found a gym bag. He peeked inside to make sure there were clothes, but he didn't want to look too closely.

Yes, she probably had a pair of panties, but there wasn't a shot in hell he would look at them without her permission. If she wanted to show him her underwear, then he'd wait for that as he'd waited for her name and her hair.

He was a strong man. Or so he liked to think. But there was something about her—that had to be why he'd offered to take care of her. And she'd taken it to mean a very specific kind of care.

She'd wanted him. And he could have taken her. He could have brought her back to this hotel and stripped her down and climbed into that bed with her.

He hadn't. He wouldn't.

He hefted the duffel out and stopped to get some coffee in the lobby. He wasn't particularly looking forward to sitting up all night, but he'd be damned if he left her in that arena all alone with some joker cutting pipes and God only knew what else under the cover of darkness.

She hadn't moved when he got back into the room. He wanted to take a shower, but his clothes were still in Jack's truck. He couldn't leave her because there was always a chance he'd missed something.

Whoever had cut that pipe—and he was going to find out who had—was still out there. But his first responsibility was to the woman who wanted him to be there when she woke up.

He kicked off his boots and stripped off his

work shirt. His T-shirt wasn't as trashed. He let the cold water run in the sink before he scrubbed his face and neck.

Then he sat down on the edge of the other double bed and watched her. Her chest rose and fell regularly, and she wasn't wincing, so that was good. Hopefully, it was just the one rib.

He stretched out on top of the covers and tried to sleep. He didn't, though. Normally, he could sleep at the drop of a hat. Anywhere he could catch fifteen minutes, he'd close his eyes and zone out.

Not today. He heard her gentle breathing from the other bed. He couldn't stop replaying the way he'd hit her, the way she'd fallen apart in the tent—and the way she refused to go to the hospital.

He sat up and scrubbed his hand through his hair. She still hadn't moved. He'd feel better, he decided, if he could reassure himself that she was okay.

He got up and walked around the far side of her bed. When he lay down—on top of the covers—she stirred. "Hmm?"

"It's okay," he whispered. "I'm here."

"Hmm," she repeated, turning her head toward him. She managed to work one hand free of the blankets.

He wrapped his hand around hers and gave it a little squeeze. Her hand was warm and small in his. She had these moments of vulnerability that killed him. "I'm here," he whispered again.

She sighed and was still again, except for her steady breathing.

He'd be right here when she woke up.

He'd promised.

SHE WASN'T ALONE.

This realization was startling—so startling, in fact, that her eyes popped open.

She was *always* alone. She'd never even had a puppy who'd climbed into bed with her. Mom hadn't wanted any animals in the house. Lacy had struggled sharing a dorm room in college because it meant listening to another person breathe.

And yet, there was someone doing just that in the bed—holding her hand.

For a second, she panicked. Who was touching her? Where was she?

She tensed and a dull pain stabbed her chest. The ache brought a measure of consciousness with it—her rib. She'd broken it.

Wreck. The trailer. The pipe.

Ian.

She turned her head. Ian was next to her. Holding her hand. His other hand was tucked under his head—even at this angle, she could see his massive muscles. His eyes were closed.

She was in bed. Sleeping with Ian Tall Chief.

Okay, so yeah, they were both still dressed and—
she tried to assess the situation without moving—
it appeared she'd been tucked in and he was on
top of the covers.

Still, her heart pounded. What was a girl supposed to do when she woke up in bed with a man
she didn't exactly remember going to sleep with?

Then Ian's eyes opened.

She couldn't get her eyes closed so she could
pretend she was still asleep. All she could do was
watch in a mix of horror and fascination as Ian
blinked a couple of times and turned his head
in her direction.

"Hey," he mumbled sleepily.

Then he stretched out like a cat. Without letting go of her hand, his body lengthened, every
muscle taut and tight. She wanted to lick him.
Just run her tongue over his body and taste him.

Wait—no—no, she did not. No licking. No
touching. No *nothing*.

Then Ian's other hand swung out over his
head. It was like watching a symphony of muscles work together in perfect time.

Something she dimly recognized as *want*
tightened her muscles in response to his body's
movements. She had a vague memory of Ian saying, "Let me do this for you."

This could still be a dream, she decided as
Ian rolled onto his side without letting go of her
hand. This could be a dream like the one she'd

had where she stripped him out of his wet T-shirt. And if it was, she was going to do a hell of a lot of licking.

"How do you feel?" he asked when he had himself settled—only inches away.

Not a dream. Oh, hell—now what?

"Okay."

He smiled at her, a small movement that felt intimate nonetheless. She was in bed with Ian and that might not be a bad thing.

He was so close she could feel his breath on her skin. "How's the rib?" he asked. Then—oh, Lord—he moved. His hand hovered over her sore rib—over her right breast. He was going to touch her.

Please. Don't.

The two thoughts collided in her head like a high-speed wreck.

He didn't touch her. Instead, he pulled his hand back and laid it along his thigh.

"A little sore. Nothing I can't handle," she added. She was pretty sure she was back to "prickly" again.

He took it that way, too. "Yeah, you're all right." Then, God help her, he stretched again.

Her rib began to throb with the physical effort of not licking him. But the pain was good. It pulled her out of the crazy fantasy in her head where she ran her hands over his body, where she grabbed his shirt and pulled, where—

He propped himself up on his hand and looked at her as if he expected her to do something. If only she knew what.

"If you want," he said in that voice that was way more than friendly but wasn't quite romantic, "you can take a shower."

Her face got real hot, real fast. "A…shower?"

The corners of his eyes crinkled with humor. "Yes. A shower. You'll feel better after," he added. "The heat will relax your muscles."

Did she look that bad or—worse—smell that bad? And was this a solo shower or a group thing? "Um…"

"I'll get us some dinner while you're in the bathroom," he went on, as if she weren't dying of embarrassment. "I can check your ribs when you're out. I brought your bag in, so you have clean clothes. Then we'll head to the arena. Does that sound like a plan?"

"Um…" she repeated, feeling stupid. Here she was, wondering if he was in bed with her because he'd read her mind about maybe sort of wanting some no-strings sex so she wouldn't have to think for a while, and he was over there making perfectly reasonable plans for the rest of the night.

God, she was an idiot.

Ian raised his eyebrows as he waited for a coherent reply. "Yeah," she agreed, afraid to move her other hand because the way he was lying—

she might brush *something.* "No, yeah—a shower sounds great."

"Do you think you'll be able to wash your hair yourself?" He sounded pretty normal, considering what he'd implied—that if she couldn't, he would wash her hair for her—but then his gaze drifted up and the next thing she knew, he'd lifted his hand and wrapped a curl around his finger and said, "Beautiful," like a prayer.

No, she must have heard him wrong. "It's a mess," she said, which was part knee-jerk reaction and part the truth. Her hair never did what she wanted it to.

"Why do you always wear the hat?"

"I don't wear the hat in bed," she defended— and then felt her own head to see if she had her hat on. Nothing but hair. "Right. No hats in bed."

He grinned at her. She couldn't help but notice that he still had a lock of hair wrapped around his finger. "Do you have a position on hats in the shower?"

She gave him as sharp a look as she could pull off, given the circumstances.

"No, then." He gave her hair a light tug, then let it slip over his fingers. There was something sensual about the movement of her hair over his skin. But she managed not to shiver. "Will you need help?"

There was a part of her that wanted to say yes.

Then Ian would have to help her into the shower and wash her hair and…

And she wouldn't have to think, wouldn't have to worry—at least for a little bit. She could get lost in the feeling of his hands on her body. It'd work. Hell, waking up with his hand in hers had nearly short-circuited her brain.

But there was a bigger part of her that wanted to shave her legs and her armpits before she did anything ridiculous such as attempt any level of nudity in front of Ian Tall Chief.

"I think I can manage."

He nodded as if this were the answer he'd expected. "I'll carry your bag into the bathroom."

He did more than that. He got the water running and the hotel soaps and shampoos where she could reach them and he laid the towels out, too.

"Pizza okay?" he asked as he stood back to let her into the steamy bathroom. "Figured I'd call it in and we'd pick it up on our way back to the arena."

That made her pause. She'd thought he was going to leave the room—not stay within earshot. "That's fine. I like sausage and peppers."

"Got it. If you need help, call," he said, closing the door behind her.

The mirror had already started to steam up and Lacy was itching to get into the shower. Suddenly she could feel the dirt ground into her skin.

But she stood for a minute, surveying the damage as best she could in the foggy mirror.

Oh, yeah—her hair was a mess. Bits of dirt and twigs were stuck on the right side and the left had the familiar slept-on-it-wrong flatness to it. But that wasn't all. She had dirt smeared along the right side of her face; the circles under her eyes were a dull blue.

God, she looked like *hell*.

And this was what Ian had been curled up next to in bed. This was the hair he'd been playing with.

This was what he'd called beautiful.

Well. He was full of crap.

Her rib pulled as she tried to get the white tank top over her head. She had to hold her breath and lean against the counter until the pain subsided, but she did it.

She got her bra off using her left hand. The jeans and everything else weren't too bad, if she sat on the toilet and kicked out of them.

Then she grabbed her face soap and her razor and climbed into the shower. The steam enveloped her, and she stood there for she didn't know how long, letting the hot water run over her.

She knew she needed to formulate some sort of plan. She had an empty bank account and a whole lot of weekend left to go. She needed to call Murph, her hired hand, and tell him what had happened, ask him to cull some of the heifers he thought would bring a decent price.

But that's not what she was thinking about as the water hit her skin, lulling her into a warm, soft daze.

Ian had been in bed with her. But on top of the covers. He'd touched her while she'd been passed out—but just to hold her hand. And he'd touched her while she was awake—but just her hair.

And she wanted him. But she didn't see how being selfish enough to have him would get her anywhere.

Honey, I know you can do better than this.

Her mother's voice rose up from the steam, unbidden and—for the first time—unwanted. Lacy didn't want to think about how her parents would be disappointed in her if she sought a little comfort in Ian's arms. She didn't want to think about what that said about her.

She didn't want every single thing she did to feel like it carried the weight of the world.

She pushed the thoughts of the box and the truth out of her mind and focused on the task before her. Washing with soap was not a big deal. But washing her hair? Ugh. Ian had been right.

She would not call him in, though. She could handle this.

Shaving her legs wasn't too bad, but she had to give up on her right armpit after almost cutting herself. Then she rinsed off and let the water beat on her back for a little bit longer.

She didn't want to get out because that would mean she had to make a decision about Ian—did she need his help getting dressed? Did she want something more than a little help?

Lacy Evans—the old Lacy, the girl she'd been before her parents died by the side of the road—would not even consider "something more," no matter what.

But she wasn't that girl anymore. Maybe she'd never really been that girl. Maybe she was her mother's daughter—her real mother's daughter.

After all she'd found out, she didn't know who she was supposed to be anymore, but she was sure about one thing.

She wasn't going to figure it out in Ian's arms. She turned the water off.

CHAPTER ELEVEN

One. Two. Three…

"The Cubs have made several off-season roster moves. With more on this developing story…"

Four. Five. Six.

Ian did push-ups at a punishing pace as he tried to focus on *SportsCenter*. Spring training was happening soon. He should be able to focus—it was *SportsCenter*, for God's sake. He loved this show.

But it wasn't enough to distract his thoughts from Lacy. In the shower. Nude.

Ordering the pizza hadn't distracted him, either. It'd only taken five minutes and Lacy was still in the shower with the water running over her naked body. He'd turned on the television. Loudly.

He made it to a hundred in record time before his arms began to scream in protest, yet he couldn't stop picturing her running a soapy washcloth over her bare breasts, down her stomach.

Sit-ups. A lot of them.

He couldn't stop thinking about how sweet and soft she'd looked lying in bed with him—how she'd had to feel her head to make sure she hadn't slept in her hat.

How she'd blushed when he'd asked if she'd need help in the shower. How he'd wanted to bury his hand in her wild head of hair and had somehow restrained himself to one curl wrapped around his finger.

Friends, he repeated in his head over and over. They were friends.

This was the natural reaction to the long drought he'd been in, right? Months since he'd last been with a woman combined with his natural attraction to Lacy, with her way of looking at him with part innocence, part lust...

This was not helping. He rolled over and went back to the push-ups.

Then the water shut off. He stood up and, breathing hard, listened.

She didn't call out his name, which was probably for the best, dammit all. He could hear her moving around. Good. She wasn't in so much pain that she needed his help. Wonderful.

"Ian?"

He was at the bathroom door in less than a second. "I'm right here."

"Do you..." She paused, and he could imagine the look on her face—that innocence, that stubbornness. "Do you need to check my ribs?"

"I think it'd be a good idea. You had a hell of an adrenaline rush earlier and you might not have noticed if there was something else wrong. You barely felt the broken rib at first, remember?"

The door cracked open before he was ready. Steam poured out. Her hair—lord. It was still wet and it hung down longer than he ever would have imagined. Big, fat droplets of water swelled at the end of soft ringlets and dripped down onto—

He wasn't sure if he was still breathing because she had on a plain white tank top that outlined her body with exquisite detail. It was like looking at a different woman. Gone was the prickly cowgirl who'd told him off on multiple occasions. And in her place—

His blood pounded in his veins as he snapped his eyes back to her face. Friends, friends, *friends*.

"Okay," she said, seemingly oblivious to his sudden inability to do anything but stare at her like a hormone-crazed teenager. "I got my tank top on, but it kind of hurt." Her mouth twisted to one side. "And I couldn't get my hair very dry."

He pushed the door open a bit and snagged a towel off the counter. "Here," he said, and there was no missing the way his voice had dropped down an octave. "Let me."

She turned around and he began to towel off her hair. "It's longer than I thought," he managed to say.

"It's the curl. It's much longer when it's wet.

Then, when it dries—*poof*!" She tried to use her hands to show him exactly how much her hair would *poof*, but she only got the right hand up about halfway to her head. "Ow," she muttered, dropping her hands back down. "And a hair dryer only makes it worse," she finished weakly. "I don't even own one."

"I'm impressed you got it washed."

"That makes two of us."

As he toweled her hair, it did indeed start to "poof" up. He dropped the towel on the ground and put his hands on her back.

She tensed and sucked in a tight breath. "Just feeling your ribs," he muttered, almost as much to himself as to her. "Tell me if anything hurts."

"Okay."

Slowly, he pressed his way down her back and then fanned his hands out along her ribs. She didn't gasp or anything, which was a great sign.

And then it hit him.

No bra.

He must have done something to clue her in to his realization because she suddenly said, "I couldn't get it hooked," as if she was confessing a crime. "And I figured, I'm going to sit in a truck by myself all night, anyway, so—"

"No, you're not." Because it was much, much safer to think about Lacy in a truck, fully clothed with many layers of tops and maybe a sexless jacket, just to be safe, than it was to think about the soft woman whose body was under his hands.

"I'm...not?" She cleared her throat. "Yes, I am. That's why I agreed to coming back to this hotel with you in the first place—so I can stay up and watch my bulls—"

"You're not sitting alone," he interrupted. Then he stepped back and settled his hands around her waist. He turned her around and backed her up against the door frame. She let him. Her eyes were huge. He didn't let go. "I don't know what kind of man you think I am, but I'm not about to let a woman who's so beat-up that she can't dry her own hair sit alone in a truck in the middle of what's essentially a crime scene and wait for the bad guys to come back."

"But—"

"What do you think you're going to do if someone shows up with less-than-honorable intentions? You'd be a sitting duck. No," he repeated, this time cutting her off before she could protest. His hands tightened around her waist. "I'm sitting with you and that's final."

He saw her swallow, and then she tucked her lower lip under her teeth. He could feel her body heat through the thin fabric of her shirt, but he wasn't going to drop his eyes and look. He might not know exactly what kind of man she thought he was, but he was in no hurry to prove that he was *that* kind of man.

"I'm going to feel your ribs now," he said, his voice serious. "And you're going to tell me if it hurts. Got it?"

She nodded.

He skimmed his hands up over her waist as he stepped into her. He wouldn't have thought it possible, but her eyes grew even wider as his hands slid around the back of her ribs.

Carefully, he pressed along the lines of her bones. Bones were easier to think about.

His hands moved around to the front, right under her breasts. He could feel the warm weight of her flesh against the back of his hand—so warm it almost burned. And he had to look because he wanted to make sure he wasn't pushing too hard where he knew she already had one fractured rib.

Her nipples were hard. Sweet merciful heavens above, the pointed tips were poking through the white fabric of her tank top and all he wanted to do was lean his head down and fill his mouth with her sweetness.

He didn't. He was possibly going to die of blue balls, but he didn't. "How does this feel?" he asked as his hand rested over her busted rib.

"Good." The way she said it sent what little blood he'd managed to keep in his head right down to his dick.

Because that wasn't the "good" of someone

getting a medical exam. That was the "good" of someone who wanted to be touched.

He could not keep staring at her nipples, rock hard and mere inches from his fingertips. The more he looked, the more he wondered how she'd react if he brushed his thumb over that tip. Would she moan? Shiver at his touch? Beg him for more?

Stop it, he ordered himself as he dragged his gaze up.

But looking her in the eyes wasn't exactly the smartest thing he'd ever done, either. She'd tilted her head back so it leaned against the door frame, exposing the long length of her neck. Her lips were parted and a soft blush played lightly over her freckled cheeks.

She looked like a woman who wanted to be kissed.

He moved his hands, dropping the one on her right side back down to her waist and nestling the other between her breasts.

No, *not* between her breasts. On her sternum. That was the only thing he was feeling here. How her sternum moved when she breathed. Her breasts—full and ripe with nipples that practically begged to be touched—had nothing to do with this.

"How about this?"

This time, she moved. She rested her right arm

on top of his left, her left on his right shoulder. "Real good," she whispered.

"No pain?"

She shook her head. Her eyes never left his.

"Lacy..." He let his hand slip down until it was back on the other side of her waist. He dug his fingertips into her flesh, just enough that she'd feel it. "My offer still stands."

She blinked. He wasn't sure she was breathing. Hell, he wasn't sure he was breathing, because if she said yes...

"Your offer?" She said it as if she didn't know what he was talking about. But as she said it, her back arched ever so slightly, pushing her breasts closer to his chest.

His lips quirked. "If you want a little distraction, I can give you that." He could give her a hell of a lot more than that. But he didn't want to spook her. "You've had a rough day."

"And you can make it better?" She all but purred it.

"I can't fix the rib, babe. I wish I could. But I can put a smile back on your face."

She arched an eyebrow at him. "How do you know I'm not about to kick you in the crotch?"

Somehow, that reaction was perfect. Prickly, but with some playfulness to it. "Because I know you."

A strange look of confusion washed over her

face. "Do you?" She sounded serious about the question.

"I know you well enough to know your body language. I've seen how you react to Slim and Jerome." He pulled her closer to him, his hands flat along her back. "This isn't the same."

"You sound awful confident." Her voice was barely a whisper.

Grinning, he leaned back against his side of the door frame, which put his head almost at the same height as hers. Then he spread his legs on either side of hers. She hadn't dropped her arms away from his. "I'll take my chances."

Then he waited. This was her move. It had to be.

"What if…" she started, and then hesitated. Ian waited. "What if I say no? To your offer."

He took a deep breath. A long time ago, he might have pouted and pleaded. But he wasn't that kid anymore. Who knew that manning up would hurt so damn much?

"Then we'll still be friends. I'll still help you with your bulls—help you're going to need now that you're busted up. No arguments, either, since I'm technically the one who busted you up."

She considered this for a moment and he thought she would argue. But then she said, "And…what if I say yes?" She stepped into the space between his legs. The spark of heat between them threatened to roar into a full-fledged blaze. "Then what will we be?"

His heart pounded harder. Other things got harder, too. He wrapped his arms around her waist and pulled her in closer so he could touch his forehead to hers. "Then we'll be friends with benefits. I'm still helping you out. *But*."

Her eyes widened again. "But?"

"But I'd peel you out of those jeans and carry you to that bed and I swear to everything that's holy, Lacy, I would make you forget about the rest of the world for a great long while."

She was panting now, short gasps of air. "You would?"

"I would." If he were a gentleman, he'd stop. He'd shut his damn mouth and let her imagination do the rest.

He wasn't a gentleman.

"I would start with kissing you, then I'd move down until I got to your fabulous breasts." He let his hands drift up from her waist, barely skimming over her ribs until he got to the fabulous breasts in question.

He desperately wanted to cup them in his hands, to let their full weight settle against him. But he didn't. He kept his touch light as he let his fingers drift over the undersides of each breast, but not touching her nipples. Not yet—even if it killed him. "I would take my time with these, tweaking and sucking until you were begging for me to let you come."

She gasped in shock or need, he didn't know which. Her pupils had dilated completely now. And he wasn't done. He wasn't sure he'd ever be done with her.

"Then I'd kiss you lower and lower until I could taste your sweetness. I'd go down on you *so* hard—sucking and licking and biting your hot little clit, touching and rubbing and stroking you until you came for me." He let his hands fall away from her breasts and slide down her hips. Then, using just his index fingers, he traced small circles on her hips. "I'd slip one finger inside of you, testing to see how wet I made you. I'd focus on getting to know you, what made you shiver, what made you scream. You'd tell me what you liked, how hard you wanted it— how hard you wanted me. Then I'd see how far I could push you to the edge of coming before I let you fall over. It would be slow and hot and the best kind of torture, Lacy. And when I was done with you, you wouldn't be able to think of a damned thing except when I was going to touch you again."

"Oh," she whispered. Her whole body shook in his arms. He alternated the pressure of his hands on her hips, which caused her to sway as she responded to his touch.

As carefully as he could, he slid his hands

down to her bottom and pushed her closer. He let his lips drift from her forehead, down the side of her face to her cheeks. She smelled like clean soap.

"Then I'd lift you on top of me and watch you ride as I thrust up into you and sucked your breasts and made you come again and again. Seeing your pleasure, feeling your hot, wet body tight around mine—" Hell, just thinking about it was going to pull his trigger. "I wouldn't let go until you were done, I promise you. But I wouldn't be able to help myself. Not when it comes to you."

She made a high noise in the back of her throat and it about broke him. She was so close—he was so close—he could make her come by driving his knee between her thighs and rubbing her through her jeans. And all she'd have to do would be to touch him, maybe take him in her mouth—he'd lose it in seconds.

That was a problem. It wouldn't be long and slow and the best kind of torture—it'd be quick and dirty and over too fast.

And that's not what he'd promised her, dammit. So he didn't. Every cell in his body was screaming for her and he ignored them all. He'd made his bet. Now he had to wait to see what play she'd make.

"It would just be you and me, Lacy. You can trust me with whatever you want, because I will always take care of you. Your secrets are safe with me."

He held himself against her, his lips touching her earlobe. But he didn't kiss her.

They stood there like that for he didn't know how long, locked together in an embrace that was both intimate and not. He could feel her regaining control of her body. First the shivering stopped, then her breathing slowed. Finally, she said, "Friends with benefits?" She leaned her forehead against his shoulder. "No strings?"

The disappointment in her voice felt like a slow punch to the gut. He pulled his hands off her ass and wrapped them back around her waist, careful not to squash her ribs. "No strings. It's all I can offer. When we're at the same rodeo, I'd spend every single second of my day thinking about what I was going to do to you the moment I could get you anywhere private."

He sighed, trying desperately to think of all the very real reasons that was as far as it could go. "But I can't commit to anything else and neither can you." He lifted his head and tilted hers so he could look her in the eye. "You've got a lot to deal with right now, and I've got things I've got to do, too."

He could tell that wasn't exactly what she wanted to hear, but at least she didn't look as if he'd rejected her. "And if I say yes—even if it's casual—would you be casual with anyone else?"

"No." He tucked her against his chest. "I don't do this a lot. You may not believe this, but it's been almost eight months since my last time. I'm averaging just one or two times a year."

That got her attention. "Really? I'd have thought you'd be picking up chicks every weekend or something. I mean, *look* at you."

He grinned at her when she said *chicks*. "Don't get me wrong. When I was young and stupid— well, I was young and stupid."

The words *I have a son* danced right up to the tip of his tongue. He was asking her to trust him with not just her health or her safety, but with her body and maybe a little bit of her heart—the least he could do was trust her with his deepest secret.

And he wanted to tell her. He wanted to show someone the pictures Eliot's parents sent every six months with a brief letter detailing Eliot's development and say, "That's my kid," instead of saving the photos and emails in a special file that was password protected so no one would accidentally find out about the boy.

I have a son. His name is Eliot. I didn't fight for him.

But the words died. As much as he wanted to tell her about Eliot, he couldn't. He couldn't bear to watch that blend of innocence and lust in her eyes die when she knew the truth about him.

He'd tell her soon, he promised himself. So instead of admitting that he'd signed his paternal rights away, he said, "But I'm older now and hopefully a hell of a lot smarter."

"How old are you?"

"Twenty-six." He got the distinct feeling she was stalling on making a decision. He also got the distinct feeling this hotel didn't have enough cold water to knock down the erection he was working on if she said *no*.

Friends, friends, *friends*.

The corners of her mouth curved up in a blink-and-you-miss-it smile. Then she was serious again. "Are you going to kiss me?"

Was that an invitation? Hell. She was going to kill him, slow and sweet. What a way to go. "No. Not until you tell me to."

And he thought for a second that was that. She wasn't interested in friends with benefits, even if those benefits were exclusive.

Then she lifted her hand and touched his face. Ian's eyes drifted shut. Her touch was something a hell of a lot closer to *yes* than *no*. He leaned into her and whispered, "Are *you* going to kiss *me*?"

Her thumb stroked over his cheek, scrubbing over the light layer of stubble. He held himself as still as he could because if he moved, he'd be kissing her and carrying her to the bed and going down on her until she screamed his name.

"Not…right now," she said in a voice so soft he wasn't sure she'd spoken.

"Maybe later?" That was his pride talking. Well, that and his dick.

"Maybe," she agreed. Then she surged up and pressed her lips against his cheek.

If he were really an honorable guy, he'd accept her peace offering—because that's what it was—and they'd go on with their lives. Pizza was waiting for them, as was Jack at the arena.

But he didn't let her go. He held her against him as tightly as he dared. There was no way she could miss his erection. There was no way he missed her hardened nipples pressing against his chest.

"You know where to find me," he growled in her ear. She gasped, but she didn't pull away. "When you make up your mind, you let me know."

She squirmed against him—not twisting out of his arms, not pushing him away. Instead her hips shifted back and forth, driving her body against his dick. "Lacy," he growled again, this time in warning. Because if she didn't stop that right now—

"We should—we should go." When she leaned back, he let her put some space between their bodies. "Is that okay?"

His dick all but wailed in protest. He brushed a wave of hair back from her face. It was dry now and soft as silk. "Yeah. Give me a minute." It'd be at least that long before he could walk again.

But he could get things under control. Just as long as she didn't ask him to hook her bra for her.

Of course, if she didn't, then that would mean she'd be braless as she sat next to him in the truck all night long.

Yup. He was doomed.

But what a way to go.

CHAPTER TWELVE

"THERE YOU ALL ARE," Jack said when Lacy and Ian drove up. He stood up from the folding camp chair he'd been sitting in and gave her a look that felt way too long.

Lacy's face burned painfully hot. Hell, everything burned hot. The places where Ian had touched her felt as if they were blistering.

"I, um— Thanks?" Could Jack tell she didn't have on a bra? Or that Ian had nearly made her climax by whispering a few words in her ear?

She tried to hold the pizza boxes in front of her breasts but nearly dropped them. Which of course only made Jack look at her harder.

"We brought dinner," Ian said, holding up the six-pack of beer and the six-pack of Sprite. Lacy felt a hundred times better when Jack turned his attention to Ian. He broke off a beer and tossed it to Jack. "We had to stop at a Walgreens to get supplies. Got you a supreme, extra pepperoni."

"I do love extra pepperoni," Jack said, giving Lacy a saucy wink. He sat back down in his chair, popped his beer and asked, "How you feeling?"

"Um, better."

"Have a seat," Ian said, motioning to the other camp chair. "And give me the pizza."

"I don't want to take your seat," she started to say, but Ian cut her off with a look that was an end to any argument. Her blood began to pound in her ears again, and all she could hear over the rushing noise was the memory of Ian whispering, "Your secrets are safe with me."

How could she not think about the way he'd promised to rub her clit when she sat and her jeans chafed against that very spot?

It had been the most erotic moment of her life.

She had never, in her life, been this sexually frustrated.

Or this embarrassed.

She tried to focus on what Ian and Jack were talking about, since it sounded as if it was about her animals. Jack was saying something about a conversation he'd had with Mort, and Lacy was pretty sure Ian was asking important questions— questions she should be asking, like what the security around the arena was going to be and whether anyone else had seen anything.

All she could focus on was not squirming in Ian's chair as he leaned against the pen, eating pizza and occasionally giving her a look that made her hold her breath.

"Lacy?"

"Huh?" She looked at Jack, who was standing. He also seemed to be waiting for a reply. "I'm sorry—what?"

Jack looked worried, but over his shoulder, Ian shot her a knowing grin, as if he could imagine exactly what had her lost in thought.

Thank God it was getting darker by the moment. Maybe they wouldn't see her blush.

"I said," he repeated, slightly slower, "that I'd be back here around ten tomorrow. I've got a few things to do in the morning."

"Oh, okay, sure." She wasn't sure why he was telling her that. Then her manners caught up with her. "Thanks for keeping an eye on the bulls. I appreciate it."

He gave her another one of those slightly worried looks. "You listen to Ian now—if he says you need to go to the doctor, you need to go, you hear? He knows his stuff. Don't try to tough this out."

She dropped her gaze. Which was worse—having Jack think she was mentally compromised or wondering if he suspected what she and Ian had been doing?

Which had been talking. And him checking her ribs. And barely even the lightest of light petting. She should not feel as if she'd done something embarrassing. She hadn't done anything except be unable to get her bra on by herself.

And be unable to tell Ian no. Or yes. She didn't know which was worse.

"I won't," she promised. "I'm okay. Really. We'll see you in the morning."

Jack nodded and left shortly thereafter. And then Lacy was, once again, alone with Ian.

He took the camp chair Jack had vacated, grabbed another slice of pizza, and popped another beer. "It's going to be cool tonight," he casually observed. "We'll have to climb in the truck before much longer."

She nodded. It was nearly dark now, and there was something about the darkness that put her more on edge. Darkness hid things. Darkness let people move around unseen.

And she'd be in the dark all night with Ian. Who was still acting as if they were friends and nothing more.

She didn't like that. She didn't like that he could seemingly turn his attraction on and off. Okay, so she might be a little jealous of that— she'd give anything to not have this heavy weight pulling at her inner thighs—but if he wanted her that badly, couldn't he at least act like it?

What if he was playing around? What if he wasn't interested in her, Lacy Evans, semiprofessional hot mess—what if he just wanted to get laid?

The thought made her mildly nauseous. But then, he'd been up front from the beginning—no strings, friends with benefits. There'd been none of those wild promises about how he couldn't live without her. If he'd said anything along those lines, she would have known he was in it for the sex. If he were trying to get laid—why insist that she had to tell him to start? Why not kiss her into submission when he had the chance?

But instead, after she'd said not yet, he'd let her go, helped her put her shirt and her boots on and held her hat for her until she'd wanted it. If he were playing her, he must be playing a hell of a long game.

"You're awfully quiet over there."

This simple observation made her startle, which pulled on her ribs. She grimaced. "I'm just, uh, thinking."

She thought she saw him smile. "About?"

What she needed right now was a lie. And a good one. "About how I'm going to drive home like this."

Ian grabbed another piece of pizza, and then nudged the box in her direction. "Eat, Evans." He waited until she had taken a bite, and then asked, "Where are you going to be next weekend?"

"Pierre, I think." Somehow, South Dakota felt almost as far away as Oklahoma. "You?"

"Same." She saw him stretch out his legs and tuck his arms behind his head. "I have a proposition for you."

She blurted out, "Another one?"

There was a pause, during which she got the feeling he was giving her a look that would definitely cause her to start squirming, if only she could properly see it. "I left my truck at home on the rez and flew to West Virgina," he finally said. "I rode down with Jack to his home in Texas for the week. I was going to ride back up with him to South Dakota, where my dad will pick me up and take me home so I can get my truck. Or..."

"Or?" Why did that one little word set her body on fire?

"Or I can come home with you. I don't like the idea of you driving across Tornado Alley with two bulls in a trailer by yourself."

Her heart began to pound. Just take Ian home with her? As if it was no big deal? As if no one would notice that she'd up and driven off with one of the bullfighters?

And then—well, then he'd be at the Straight Arrow. In her house—her parents' house. She'd never brought a boy home to meet her family before they died. She didn't know how she was supposed to feel about the idea of Ian being alone in her house with her.

She shivered. No, she didn't have a single freaking clue how she was supposed to feel about this "proposition" at all. "You don't have to like it," she heard herself say. "I can still do it."

She caught a flash of white. "*Can* and *should*

are two different things." Before she could protest further, he said, "You can think about it. We've got a few more days of sleeping in a truck to get through first."

Wait, what? He was going to stay with her for the next two nights?

He stood and stretched. "Come on," he said, holding out his hand to her. "I'm getting cold."

They climbed into the cab. Well, Ian climbed. He half lifted her into the driver's seat. "You got your pillows?"

"Yes." He'd insisted on snagging some of the pillows from the hotel and she had a fleece throw that her dad had always kept in the truck.

Ian reached behind her until he found the throw. "Second time today I've tucked you in," he said. She tried to get comfortable, but they were sitting in the dark. In the silence. There probably weren't enough drugs in the world to make this situation comfortable for her.

"Tell me about home," she said, because she felt they should be talking, but she didn't want to talk about her.

"Home," he repeated. "Home is grass and sky and cows."

The way he talked was softer now. Some of the words came out longer. "Your accent is so pretty." She shifted again. This was not helping. The sharp stabbing in her ribs had dulled to a throbbing ache. She tried to look on the bright side. At least if she was in this much pain, she wouldn't run the risk of falling asleep.

"Here." The next thing she knew, Ian had flipped the seat divider back and was gently pulling her into his arms. "Lean on me."

"Um…" He all but lifted her onto his lap, snagging the pillow that had been under her head and wedging it under his own. Then he settled his massive arms around her waist, careful to avoid her ribs. His hands were resting on her belly—under the blanket.

"There," he said when she was sitting between his legs, her back pressed against his chest muscles. "Think of me as your human heating pad."

"Ian." She was horrified to hear that her voice had dropped to a whisper again. Why did it keep doing that every single time he touched her? He didn't seem affected by her body pressing against his. She shouldn't be, either. She could be cooler than this, by God. She would be, even if it killed her.

"Easy, babe." This time, his voice was deep and low and right in her ear. The warmth of his breath seemed to trickle down the back of her neck, sending shivers over her skin all the way down her back. "You haven't told me I can do anything yet. Let me hold you so you don't hurt as much. That's all this is. Try to get some sleep."

"I don't sleep." He was considerably more comfortable than the driver's-side seat had been and yes, she could feel the heat of his body already warming her. But she couldn't quite bring herself to relax. The tension of keeping her back straight was not helping her ribs.

"Why not?"

How was she supposed to answer that? Tell him about the nightmares? How she usually woke up screaming and crying and reliving car accidents and abandonments and so much work yet to do, and knowing she was responsible for all of it?

No, she was weak enough right now. Busted up, unable to drive or take care of her bulls—hell, she couldn't even take care of herself.

"Don't need to," she said. Almost against her will, her back eased against his chest.

He shifted his head and she felt his chin rest on the top of her head. "You're a lousy liar, you know that? I hope you don't play poker."

It was time to change the subject. "Tell me about home," she said. She leaned her head back against his shoulder. "Tell me something about you. Something secret." That way, she might feel as if she had leveled the playing field ever-so-slightly.

Everything about him tensed up—she could feel it as his hands tightened against her and in the way his chest muscles went rock hard against her back. "I…" His words seemed to get stuck in his throat and then he moved—maybe burying his nose in her hair?

She just wanted to hear him talk, so she tried a different approach. "Tell me about growing up."

"Growing up…" He sighed, his breath ruffling her hair. The tension left his body. "My dad is a managing partner for a cattle ranch north of the rez—the America's Real Pride Ranch, although that wasn't what it was called when I was growing up. It was the D&J—Dave and Joseph. They got off the rez and scraped together enough money to buy some land and some cows."

His accent was so much thicker right now. So pretty. It seemed to suit him more than the generic Midwestern accent he often used. She let her eyes drift closed as she tried to picture a home that was nothing but grass and sky. The cows part she didn't have trouble picturing.

"I was working cattle from when I was old enough to sit in a saddle," he went on.

"Me, too."

"Then you know what it's like."

"Castrating calves and branding and manure and getting up early? Yeah, I know."

He chuckled. Lacy felt it in her whole body. "That's it. My mom died when I was still really little. I don't remember her much."

"I'm so sorry." Unexpectedly, her throat tried to close up. "It's hard to lose your parents."

They sat in silence for a moment longer. "It's okay, babe," he whispered in her ear.

"It's fine," she quickly insisted, but she knew it was a lie.

He knew it, too. He sighed heavily and held her a little tighter. "You want to talk about it?"

"No." Because she didn't. She didn't even have a clue about where to start. "Tell me about growing up with June. Did you know she was going to be a famous bull rider?"

"Junie? Hell, no. Our moms were sisters. That side of the family..." She felt him shaking his head. "Anyway, her dad is in jail and her mom was a drunk. So there'd be days when I'd wake up and find June on the couch. She'd have stolen a car or a horse and made it the ten miles across the rez to our ranch, and either Dad would let her in or she'd break in."

"Dude, really?"

"Really. So she was this irritating big sister, basically. Anything I could do, she could do better, and woe unto the person who told her she couldn't. That's why she rides bulls. Her dad said she couldn't and she had to prove him wrong."

"Tell me a story about you two growing up." Lacy shifted so she could rest her head against his chest and feel the rumble of his voice. "Tell me a nice story."

"Hmm..." He all but hummed it in her ear and

for some reason, it sounded like a cat purring. "Will you sleep if I tell you a story?"

"I don't sleep," she reminded him, but her body betrayed her with a yawn. "Besides, I'm supposed to be watching my bulls."

He shifted then, one of his massive hands leaving her stomach. He brushed her crazy hair to the side and then his fingertips traced her face. That warmed her almost as much as his chest did. "I will keep watch."

"It's my responsibility," she said defensively. She didn't know why. "Mine, and mine alone."

His fingertips stroked over her cheek. "And you are mine."

Everything about that should have set off warning bells. Her brain struggled mightily to come up with the reasons why she was absolutely not his responsibility—she was no one's responsibility because she was without a real family or a proper name.

But her body betrayed her yet again. Stupid body. Her muscles gave up the fight with her brain and she sank back against his chest, her eyelids drifting shut. *Safe*, she thought as she said, "Better be a damn good story."

"We raised cattle," he began, his voice low and his accent so thick she wanted to reach out and stroke it with her hands. "But on the line between our land and the rez, there lived a herd of buffalo. They belonged to the land, to the grass and the sky."

She could see it in her mind, the sea of grass and the blue sky and the dark shapes moving through as though hundreds of years hadn't passed the animals into the modern era. "How many?" she murmured, nuzzling against his chest.

"Over three hundred. The tribe had the official papers, but my father and Joseph kept an eye on them. Which meant June and I kept an eye on them. One day, she was driving me crazy—it was early summer and it was hot. We came upon a buffalo cow who'd been scraping her winter fur off on a barbed wire fence and she'd gotten tangled up in the wire."

"Was she hurt?"

"Naw. Her hide was too tough—nothing gets through their skin, really. So we were untangling her and Junie was driving me crazy. She's almost as stubborn as you, you know."

"I'm not stubborn," Lacy said with another yawn. "I'm just right all the time."

Oh, the sound—the feel—of his laughter was something real, something right. "That you are, my girl. That you are."

"Not your girl. Not your babe, either." She didn't know why she was arguing with him. Not when she was sinking into the heat of his chest.

She could feel his fingers moving again, this

time stroking her hair. "Do you want to hear the end of this story or not?"

"I do," she admitted. She also wanted him to keep stroking her like that. It felt so good, so lovely—her rib didn't even throb right now. That was probably the meds, but everything else was Ian. The warmth, the heat, the stroking… "What happened next?"

"I said she couldn't ride a buffalo and she said she could. So when the cow was almost untangled, June climbed up on that hairy back and held on and when I cut the last wire free, those two took off. The buffalo didn't buck or anything— she ran, shaking her back like June was this itty-bitty fly. I think June made it all of twenty feet before she lost her grip and went down."

Lacy tried to picture the woman she'd seen in videos riding No Man's Land clinging to the back of a pissy buffalo cow. "Was she hurt?"

"Who, June? Hell, no. She popped up out of the grass and said, 'See? I told you I could ride a buffalo!'"

Lacy chuckled sleepily. "All because you said she couldn't."

"Yup." He shifted underneath her and Lacy felt his lips press against the top of her head. "Sleep."

"No," she protested, and she didn't miss how childish she sounded. "More stories."

"Hmm," Ian hummed again. "And what am I going to get in exchange for all these stories?"

"I don't have anything worth exchanging. Nothing except the bulls." As she said it, sadness took hold of her. All she had was the bulls, but that no longer included Wreck. God, how was she ever going to make it now?

"That's not true, darlin'." His fingers moved from her hair to her cheek again and instead of the crushing panic of failing, she felt light. Free, almost. As free as she'd felt in a long, long time. "Let's say...you owe me one."

"Just one," she murmured. She could feel sleep pulling at her and she wanted to sink into its soft warmth and *be*. But she wanted to keep listening to Ian's voice, his unusual accent. "Don't stop talking."

"Babe, I'll talk all night if you sleep." He chuckled and she really was floating. "Old stories, then? Of Iktomi the Trickster and Coyote and Deer Woman?"

"Mmm," which was supposed to be "Okay" but didn't make it.

"Iktomi was the Trickster," he began with no other introduction. "He was a spider and a man at the same time..."

She drifted on the warmth that was Ian, his voice vibrating through her even when she no longer understood the words.

Safe, she thought.

She could sleep and it'd be okay. Ian and his voice would keep the nightmares away.

She knew he'd still be there in the morning.

CHAPTER THIRTEEN

"No."

The word—half cried, half begged—was whispered into the silence of the truck's cab, pulling Ian out of the half doze he'd been stuck in. Instantly he was on high alert, scanning the view outside the windshield for danger. The sky was that dim gray that signaled dawn was only a few minutes off. He didn't see anything wrong. No skulking shadows, no busted metal, no runaway bulls.

Lacy. She was lying on his chest—okay, good. She hadn't woken up and bailed on him. But something was wrong. She was shaking her head, her body twitching with fear.

"Lacy," he whispered softly in her ear. "It's okay. I'm here."

"No," she repeated, and this time, her voice was nothing but pain. Pain and sorrow so deep it hurt him to hear it.

Was he supposed to wake her up or let her ride it out? He couldn't remember. But when she whimpered again, he couldn't take it. "Wake up, babe. It's just a dream."

She thrashed her head again and he began to worry she was going to reinjure her ribs. "Lacy," he said more firmly. "Lacy, wake up."

She sat bolt upright and cried, "No!" Which was followed closely by a sob.

"I'm right here." He put his hand on her shoulder and tried to pull her back down.

She wasn't having any of it. "They're gone," she said. "They left me and she didn't want me and I'm all alone."

"Lacy," he said. He honestly couldn't tell if she was still asleep or not. "You're not alone. I'm here."

She startled. When she twisted around and looked at him, it hurt him to see tears streaking down her cheeks. "Ian?"

"I'm here, babe." He tried to tuck her back in his arms, but she didn't bend and he didn't want to hurt her. "You're not alone. I'm here."

"Ian." Unexpectedly, she fell back against him, her chest heaving with great gulping sobs. "I don't want to be alone anymore." She continued to weep.

"I'm here." He held her as tightly as he dared and rubbed his hands up and down her back. "I won't leave you. I promise." He kept repeating it, too.

This time, the storm passed more quickly than

it had yesterday. After only a minute, her sobs trailed off and her body stopped shaking so hard. The nightmares must have been brutal, he decided.

But that thought was erased right out of his head when Lacy's fingers tightened on the front of his shirt. Suddenly, she went from crying on his shoulder to holding him.

"I don't want to be alone anymore," she whispered. Her voice had a waver to it, but not the kind that went with crying. It was something different.

And just like that, they were right back to where they'd been yesterday, bodies pressed together as he told her every single thing he wanted to do to her.

"I'm here," he whispered back. His hands slowed, and he took his time feeling her body against his, feeling how she was responding to his touch. "I'm right here for you."

"I don't want to hurt anymore," she whispered, shifting so her face was tucked against his neck. Her breath was hot against his skin—hell, her whole body was hot against his as she stretched and shifted.

He went hard—so hard, he ached. "I can make you feel better," he promised her. But he didn't kiss her, didn't do anything but keep rubbing her back in slow, sensual strokes. That's all he could do. She had to be the one who—

"Like…" She released her hold on his shirt. Her hand skimmed up his neck until she was stroking the stubble on his jaw. "Like you promised you'd do? Yesterday?"

"Yeah." Okay, maybe not exactly like what he'd promised—they were in the narrow confines of a truck cab instead of in a hotel room with a nice, wide bed. But he could work with this, if only she'd give him the go-ahead. "You and me, babe. Let me take care of you."

He couldn't help it. He dug a hand into her mane of wild hair, letting the rough silk tangle around his fingertips as he shifted his hips against her. His dick throbbed with need, but he wasn't going to—not until she—

"I don't want to hurt anymore," she whispered, her gaze locked on him. Her eyes were wide, her pupils huge, and she was breathing heavily. "I want…" She touched her fingertips to his lips.

Ian held his breath, his heart pounding. A curl sprang free and he brushed it out of her face. "Are you going to kiss me?" he asked, praying the answer was yes.

"No," she said, her voice a ghost from a dream. In the space between those two cruel little letters and what she said next, Ian was pretty sure he was going to die of sheer sexual frustration. But then she said, "I want you to kiss me."

"Done." He cupped her face in both his hands and pushed her up to his lips.

And he kissed her. Soft and gentle at first, because he wanted to make sure this was what she wanted. He wanted to show her he could take care of her, he could put her first—even when he wanted nothing more than to bury himself in her body and let the climax he'd barely kept under control run free. He let his lips settle against hers—soft and gentle.

She pulled back and glared at him. "What the hell was that? *Kiss me*, dammit."

He couldn't help the grin that took hold of his lips. "You sure?"

"For the love of everything holy," she muttered as she tried to straddle him—but she must have pulled her ribs because she grimaced. "Ow…"

"Easy. Let me—" He picked her up and turned her around so her back was against his chest and she was facing the windshield. "You're going to hurt yourself."

"I want—"

"You want," he said fiercely in her ear, "exactly what I'm going to give you, don't you?" And he finally, finally allowed himself to cup one of her breasts in his hand—the left one, so he wouldn't risk hitting her busted rib. "You want me to touch you, don't you?"

Oh, yeah—she wasn't wearing a bra. He pinched her nipple through the layered shirt. She gasped and squirmed, driving her ass against his dick.

"Here," he said, letting go of her long enough to pull the dusty blanket up over the both of them. The odds of someone walking by at this time of the morning and seeing them in the dim light were laughably slim, but he wasn't leaving a thing to chance. She'd given him permission, and by God, he was going to make the most of it.

Once he had the blanket tucked around her shoulders, he slipped his hand under her shirt and cupped her breast again. Heaven help him, her nipple was already hard.

He could make it harder. He rolled her nipple between his finger and his thumb and was instantly rewarded when she arched her back, thrusting her breast up into his hand. "Oh, yes," she moaned in a high-pitched voice. "Oh, Ian…"

"You feel so good in my hands," he growled in her ear. Then he wrapped his lips around her lobe and sucked lightly, still tweaking her nipple as he did so. "Do you want me to touch you? Touch your clit?"

"You—you promised you would," she said in short, hot gasps. "You promised."

"I keep my promises, Lacy." He kept stroking her breast with his left hand while he let his right hand drift down over her gently rounded stomach, down over the front of her jeans. She tensed as he plunged his fingers between her thighs, skimming over the seam of her jeans. "You like that, don't you?"

She nodded. The disadvantage of this particular position was that he couldn't see her face—and couldn't kiss her while he was working on her body. He used his chin to push her hair to one side so he could at least press his lips to her neck. She made a high whimpering sound when his teeth nipped at her skin. "If we were back in the hotel room," he whispered before he let his teeth work over her again, "I'd strip these jeans off of you and do this to your clit."

"Oh," she managed to say as he bit down with a little more force. He pulled at her nipple and stroked at the seam in her jeans.

"You like to hear what I'm doing to you, don't you?" Even though it was buried underneath several layers of stiff denim and her panties, he could feel her warmth building under his touch. "I could get you off like this, couldn't I? Just light little touches, rubbing right here, right… here…"

He pressed his finger against her and she bucked in his arms. "Oh, yes, oh, please," she said, her voice high and tight and so hungry for more that it sent his temperature spiking. The world outside the cab fell away until all that remained was Lacy and Ian and the way he touched her.

"But you need more, don't you, you beautiful thing? You need me right against you, don't you?" Gently, he switched to her other breast, careful to focus only on the nipple, not on the underside. The last damned thing he wanted to do right now was hit her ribs and have the pain pull her out of the moment.

"Ian," she gasped and he heard the frustration in her voice.

"Undo your jeans for me," he ordered, lifting both his hands away from her body. "But don't push them down."

"But how—"

How were they going to have sex? "This isn't about me," he told her, stroking his hands down her thighs and back up over her hips. "Now undo your jeans or else."

He felt her shoulders tighten. "Or else what?"

"Or else I won't let you come," he promised her. "I'll work you up into such a state that you'll do anything for the release, anything I want you to, and I won't let you."

She paused for only a moment before she did as she was told, quickly undoing her button and pushing the zipper down. "Like that?"

"That's a good girl," he said, pushing the denim aside and sliding his hand over the fabric of her panties.

They weren't silk or satin, her panties—he hadn't expected them to be. But they were soft and thin and already wet with her desire. "I feel how much you want me," he whispered. He palmed her, thrusting his hand down as far between her thighs as he could. "God, you're so wet already. You need to come so badly, don't you, babe? Tell me how badly you need to come."

"*So* bad," she whimpered, her hips shifting back and forth as she tried to grind down where he was cupping her. "Please, Ian, *please*."

He could find her hot little clit and press down and she'd fall apart, he knew. He could give her that final push.

And then it'd be over. She'd come down off her high and probably do something foolish like start thinking again. And he couldn't let that happen. Not when he'd promised.

So instead of pressing down, he made a V with his fingers and stroked over the edge of her panties. He lifted his other hand back up to her left breast and circled her nipple with his thumb and finger.

"You—are—killing—me," she got out through clenched teeth as she closed her thighs, trapping his hand. "Ian."

"Such a prickly woman," he teased. "I love that about you. Now open up for me and I'll let you come."

"When?"

"Soon, I promise." He wedged his leg under hers and used it to spread her wide.

"Soon isn't—soon enough," she moaned as he circled closer and closer to her clit.

"Patience. You are so hot for my touch." Then, as he kissed her neck again, he closed the V of his fingers and rubbed over the panties, pressing just hard enough that she shimmied but not hard enough for her to come. "I could keep you like this all day."

"Gonna—regret it," she threatened as he lifted his fingers away from her silky heat and lightly tapped against her clit. It was the barest of touches, but she was so turned on it made her suck in air as if she'd been drowning.

"How wet are you?" he mused, as if he weren't as turned on as she was, as if he wasn't on the verge of coming in his pants like a hair-trigger teenager. *Keep it together*, he scolded himself as he slipped one finger under the elastic of her panties.

His finger tangled with soft, tight curls and, against his will, he groaned. "Lacy. You're going to kill me."

"Ian," she whimpered. She'd clamped her hands down on his forearms and was lightly pushing him.

He'd worn number fifty-four in college. He'd racked up thirteen sacks his last season. When the hit had come, his femur had snapped like a damned twig.

It was only the memory of that pain that kept

him from exploding in his pants. Lacy's ass was grinding against him, pushing his awareness of her body higher and higher. He didn't know how much longer he could take it.

He stroked over her curls. His eyes fluttered shut as her wet heat surrounded his finger. "Oh, so wet for me," he whispered in her ear before he bit down on that place where her neck met her shoulders. "Show me your secrets, babe."

She made a high noise in the back of her throat and he wanted to kiss her, to taste her need. But they were still sitting in the cab of a truck with only a blanket for privacy. Later, he promised himself. Later he'd get them back to a bed and he'd start her up all over again.

He traced the seam of her body and found her opening. Her body offered no resistance.

"Oh, Lacy," he groaned as he slid his finger into her welcoming body. "You feel so good."

"I do?" There was something uncertain in her voice.

"So good," he reassured her. He could not let this train be derailed right now. He had to keep her in the moment. He'd promised, by God—and it was a promise he'd keep.

As he stroked into her, he slid his other hand under her panties, parted her curls and found her clit, tight and hot for him. "Let me take care of you," he said as he rubbed her in small circles, timed to the movements of his finger. "Show me what you like. You like that?"

"Oh—yes—" Her head thrashed from side to side on his chest, her wild curls springing everywhere.

He was surrounded by Lacy. Her body bearing down on his hands, her weight on his chest, her hair around his face—the scent of her sex and the sounds of her pleasure filling the small space—all of this was her.

He thrust two fingers into her and was rewarded with a moan of need. "Ian, please," she begged as she tried to twist around, her hand grabbing for his jeans. "Please, I just—please."

"No." He had to let go of her to grab her arms. She looked up at him with confusion in her eyes. "No, Lacy. I'm doing this for you."

"But... I owe you one."

He almost gave in to her right then and there. He almost jerked her pants down and unbuttoned his fly and pulled her on top of him and pumped into her until they were both shouting.

And it would be wrong. It was the sort of thing he used to do all the damn time; quick and indiscriminate screwing in the backseat—or front seat—of a car.

It was exactly the type of sex that had led to his son. And Lacy deserved more than to be knocked up and left behind.

In his last desperate attempt to hang on to his

self-control, Ian kissed her hard. He would subdue her one way or the other. She moaned into his mouth and he pulled away. "You can owe me two. I'm not screwing you in the cab of this truck. If I make love to you, it's damn well going to be in a bed with a door and lock. Now turn around or *else*."

"Oh." She was panting again. The confusion was still there, but she nodded and let him spin her back around.

This time, he wasn't slow or teasing or patient. Especially not that. He plunged two fingers into her body and rubbed her clit as if it was his last act of salvation. After only a few strokes, she was grinding down on his hand again. He curved his fingers forward inside of her and felt a tighter spot. Lacy's body tensed. "That's it, isn't it, babe? That's your secret spot. That's what you need."

She made a noise of pure need, high and tight, and it drove him wild. "Come for me, Lacy," he growled in her ear.

He circled her clit one more time, and then pressed down on it, hard, as he twisted his fingers inside of her.

She cried out as her muscles tightened down on him. Her thighs clamped shut, trapping him within her. He felt the spasms shake her as her deep, satisfying groan ripped free. He buried his face in her neck and kissed her as best he could while she rode the waves of pleasure.

"So beautiful," he murmured as the last of the tension left her body. "God, Lacy—*so* beautiful."

She went limp in his arms, her breath coming in heavy gasps. "Oh—Ian," she said weakly. Her hips shifted and he eased free of her body's embrace. "Oh, that was *wonderful*."

But he didn't let go. He cupped her sex and breathed deeply. He was so close to his own climax he would have blue balls for a week. As it was, he was having trouble coming up with the kind of sweet pillow talk she probably needed. "Glad to hear it."

She snaked her left hand back between their bodies and rubbed at his dick. "Won't you let me…"

Outside, the noise of metal squealing cut through the air. It was followed by loud cursing.

Lacy went stock-still. "Damn," he muttered, pulling his fingers free of her pants. "Get buttoned up. Stay here. If anyone asks, you just woke up."

"I'm not stupid, you know," she hissed back, sliding off his lap and fumbling with her zipper under the blanket.

He didn't respond to that. Instead, he opened the passenger-side door and slid out, landing softly on the hard-packed dirt. His erection was gone now, but the heightened awareness Lacy had left him with worked in his favor. He moved toward the noise. Which was not the same direction as Lacy's bulls. In fact, Ian was moving backward, away from her animals.

He clung to the side of the truck and peered around the bed. Two cowboys, their shapes dull gray in the dim light, were staring at the side of a different truck. "Well, hell," the shorter one said.

"A-yup," the taller one added.

Ian knew those voices. He stepped out of the shadows and said, "Randy? Garth? What are you doing here?"

CHAPTER FOURTEEN

"AND YOU GUYS just got here?" The way Ian said it wasn't a question.

Lacy shifted uncomfortably from foot to foot and it had nothing to do with the sudden appearance of the two men. The movement wasn't a smart idea. Every motion either pulled at her rib or made her jeans chafe at her crotch. Her clit, as Ian had so easily referred to it, was tender and throbbing and made standing damned near impossible.

It would have been a good feeling—a great one, even—if she could have pulled the covers up over her head and let Ian's hard muscles curl around her body. If she could have stayed lost in him for a little while longer...

But no. Instead, she was standing in the early-morning light, listening to Ian grill two cowboys named Randy and Garth. Lacy couldn't remember which cowboy was which.

"Dude, seriously—we left Wisconsin last night after we got off work and drove straight through," Randy/Garth said.

"You can call our boss," Garth/Randy confirmed. "We were at work until five. What's this all about, anyway? Why are you two here at the butt crack of dawn?"

At this, Lacy shot a worried look at Ian. It was a short leap from a man and a woman in an unexpected place alone and them being alone together. One wrong word and these cowboys would put one and one together.

This was how rumors worked. Not that she'd figure that by Ian's attitude. How could he stand there—leaning against the back of her truck, one foot kicked up, his hands in his pockets—when it'd been less than fifteen minutes since...

Well. Since he'd had his fingers inside her body.

Ian had made her feel very good—and for a few minutes, anyway, she hadn't thought of nightmares or death or bulls. She'd been in his arms, chasing a kind of freedom she'd only caught shadows of before. Nothing she'd ever done to herself had come close to what he'd done to her. And it had been glorious.

Except now, she didn't feel quite the same and she didn't have the luxury of time to figure out if that was a good thing.

She just knew she wanted him to do it again. She caught Ian looking at her and blushed. Furiously.

The woman she'd been before her parents'

deaths would not have let Ian touch her like that. She wouldn't have offered to do the same in return. She would have turned her back on him from the moment he'd offered his no-strings-attached kind of fun and that would have been that.

Except it hadn't been. And now there was no going back.

She crossed her arms. Ian's eyes widened. He shook his head the tiniest bit, and she remembered that she still didn't have her bra on. So she uncrossed her arms and jammed her hands into her pockets.

"There was an accident yesterday—except maybe it wasn't an accident," Ian explained into the expectant silence.

"What happened?" Randy/Garth said.

Ian looked at her. Hell. "One of my bulls got loose." Her voice cracked on the last word and she had to look at the ground and swallow a few times.

"He had to be put down," Ian said for her.

"Damn, that sucks." Both Randy/Garth and Garth/Randy turned to look at her. "Anyone hurt?"

"No."

At the same time Ian said, "I cracked one of her ribs tackling her out of the way. This is Lacy Evans. Owner of the Straight Arrow."

She glared at Ian, hard. What the hell was he doing—trying to make her look weak?

"Wait." The taller one took a step closer. "Don't you own the bull that nearly ran me down?"

She tried to remember if she'd heard the name of the rider Ian had saved. Randy seemed like a better fit than Garth. Randy was the taller cowboy. "Rattler is mine, yeah."

"Which bull died?"

"Wreckerator."

"Well." Randy took a step back. "That's too bad."

"You said it was maybe not an accident?" Garth asked.

Lacy looked at Ian. These were his people. If he trusted them, then she'd have to.

And he apparently trusted them. "The panel that gave when the bull got out? Turns out it'd been cut."

Both men whistled. "Damn, Chief," Randy said. "That's low-down."

"We don't know if it was random or if someone targeted Lacy specifically. If you guys hear anything…"

"Yeah, yeah," Garth said, scuffing his toe in the dirt. "Damn. I don't like to think of people in our rodeo family pulling crap like this. I don't like it."

Ian shrugged, as casual as could be. How did he do that? She was all out of sorts, and he looked as if he'd done nothing more than sit in a truck all night. "If you hear anything, let me know. The cut panel isn't exactly common knowledge," he added. "So keep it under your hats. Got it?"

"Got it," Randy and Garth said at the same time. Then Garth said to Ian, "You got a plan?"

She didn't like it a damned bit. Wreck had been *her* bull. Slim Smalls was out to ruin *her* name. And Jerome what's-his-face had been the one to pin *her* to the side of the trailer.

This was *her* fight, dammit. She would not stand around like some helpless arm candy while the all-knowing, all-capable men mounted a plan of action to save her from the big bads of the world.

"No," she said.

"No?" Ian asked as they all three looked at her.

"No," she repeated with more force. "Look, I appreciate the help but I don't even know you two, and you," she added, turning to face Ian, "you can't take over."

If she'd been expecting him to be insulted, she was sorely disappointed. If anything, he looked amused. "I can't?"

"No, you can't. You guys are acting like there's some sort of evil conspiracy to destroy me." True, it did feel that way and had, ever since her parents had died. But she couldn't let that fear rule her.

Randy and Garth exchanged uncomfortable looks. "Coffee," Garth said decisively.

Randy was already climbing into the driver's side of the truck. "We'll be right back. With coffee." Garth climbed up and within seconds, they were backing out of the lot, leaving Ian grinning at Lacy, and Lacy wondering what the hell she was doing. She needed help; she knew that. She'd spent most of the past month alone and somewhere between terrified and panicked about how she was going to make it all by herself.

And Ian had offered to help her. He already had helped her.

So why was she telling him to back off? Was this about the sex? If she hadn't even gotten his pants undone, was it really sex?

He kept on grinning at her and she kept on glaring at him until the crunch of tires on gravel had faded away and they were alone again.

She was upset and she didn't understand why. Anger was a real, tangible thing she could hold on to, and hold on to it she would. "You've got a real superiority complex. Is there anything you think you can't handle?"

He lifted his eyebrows in a gesture that pretty clearly read as no. "You're probably hurting right now. When Randy and Garth get back with some coffee, you should—"

"I don't need you to save me," she all but shouted. "I am perfectly capable of saving myself. I don't need you to tell me when to eat and sleep and take meds. Or how to take care of my animals and run my business." He opened his mouth but she cut him off. She drew herself up as tall as she could—which still left her several inches shorter than him—and did her best to look down her nose at him. "I'm a grown woman. I don't need you. I can take care of myself."

Which wasn't 100 percent true, and they both knew it. Wreckerator would have trampled her if he hadn't gotten to her first. And Jerome— who knew how far he might have pushed it if Ian hadn't been there?

But she didn't want to need him. She didn't want to have to hope and pray that every time something went wrong Ian would be there to save her.

She didn't want to be the kind of person who needed to be saved.

And damn his hide, Ian didn't reply. He didn't tell her she was ungrateful after all he'd done for her, and he didn't even tell her she was prickly. "Are you done yet?"

"No. Yes. I don't know." The wind was suddenly gone from her sails and she felt foolish. She *should* be grateful that a man like Ian had an interest in her, that he was willing to help her out. That he liked her enough to offer a physical relationship, even if it was no-strings-attached.

She turned away and headed back up to the pen where Chicken Run and Rattler were still dozing. The chains were all fastened. No one had cut them while she'd slept. She didn't even know if Ian had gotten any sleep. Gah, she was an idiot. The sane person would have been grateful for the rest, for the orgasm, for the help.

Which really only left one inescapable conclusion.

She wasn't exactly sane.

She rested her forehead on the top of the pen railing and listened to the sound of her animals snort as they started to stir. Wasn't it bad enough things were already a total mess? Did she have to keep making them worse?

She heard Ian walking behind her, saw him kick up a boot onto the lower rung of the pen right next to her. She tensed as she waited for him to acknowledge what was so obvious—she wasn't worth his effort, his attention.

Yet he didn't. He stood there, close enough that she could feel the heat of his body on this cool morning but not so close that she could touch him without being really obvious about it. She wanted to rest her head against his shoulder and tell him she was sorry.

She didn't, of course. She couldn't let him know how badly he'd turned her around, what with all his thoughtful gestures and hot hands and trying so hard to take care of her, even if she wouldn't let him. She couldn't show weakness. Not even to him.

Never mind he'd already seen her pretty damned weak.

"Who left you?" he asked in a low voice.

She stiffened. "What?"

"When you woke up, you were going on about how she didn't want you and they left you and you were alone." His voice was even, but he'd started tapping on the top of the railing with his fingers.

She had done that, she remembered now. She'd fallen asleep in his arms and had nightmares and woke up crying. He must think her such a fool.

She couldn't look at his fingers. So she stared at Rattler.

"Your dad died, I know." His voice was still gentle. She wondered if this was how he talked to a spooked animal. "Did your mom do something after that?"

Gah, she couldn't have him thinking ill of Linda Evans. Mom might not have always been the warmest of mothers, but the woman had loved Lacy all the same. "No."

He waited. No coaxing, no explaining. No telling her why she was wrong or crazy for not accepting his help. None of that. He just waited.

She took a deep breath. She could say this out loud. It'd been months, after all. She could do this without falling apart. "They died together. Car accident. On their way home from my college graduation."

Those were the facts, as plainly stated as could be. Nothing emotional about them.

Each word felt as if it'd ripped away part of her soul. Part of her knew she should have died with them. Dad had been driving the family Suburban with the horse trailer full of her belongings and Lacy had the truck. She'd gotten a bit ahead of them and had stopped at a McDonald's to wait. But Mom hadn't answered her phone or replied to Lacy's texts about where to meet up.

She'd sat at that McDonald's for an hour, trying to fight a growing sense of dread with milk shakes. Finally, unable to bear it any longer, she'd gotten back in her truck and retraced her path.

That was when she'd come upon the emergency vehicles blocking the road and she'd known they were gone.

She'd begun to shake. If only she hadn't insisted that they drive separately in a fit of immature independence. If only she'd stuck closer to them instead of racing down the road. If only she'd done anything other than slurp down milk shakes for the last hour.

She'd thrown up in the ditch and she hadn't had a milk shake since.

Then Ian's arm was around her, gently pulling her against his side. "You're not alone. I'm here, Lacy."

That made everything both better and worse. "You shouldn't be hanging out with me," she warned him even as she let her head fall against his shoulder. God, it felt good. "My streak of bad luck's a mile wide right now. Everyone and everything I care for…" Her voice cracked so she stopped talking.

He sighed, his big chest moving against hers. "I can take care of myself, Evans. You don't have to push me away because you think it's safer for me. And before you say it, I'm fully aware that, under normal circumstances, you're more than capable of taking care of yourself." He turned her so she was facing him and cupped her cheek in his palm. "You graduated—what, last May?"

She shook her head no. "August."

"Okay, August." He grinned widely. "I knew you were smart. So you've been doing pretty damn good on your own for eight months. If what I'm saying or doing somehow implies that you can't function on your own, that's my problem and I'm sorry for that. It wasn't my intention.

"But," he went on, his voice gruff, "even you have to admit that things right now aren't normal. You're hurting in more ways than one, and I can't bring myself to stand aside and let you flame out because you're too proud to admit you need help."

"I don't want to need help," she whispered.

That got a sly grin out of him. "Can't say I blame you. But them's the facts—you've got a busted rib and there's something else going on here beyond a losing streak. So let me help you. Let me keep my promise to you that I won't leave you alone." Something in his eyes changed and he looked sadder. "I haven't always been the kind of man people could rely on, and I know it. I've let people down and I've let myself down. But I'm trying to change that."

"This isn't about sex, is it?" She hoped not, not when he was holding her tight and looking her in the eyes and making her feel as if maybe things were starting to go her way.

His lips curved up into something that would have been half a grin if it hadn't been so damned lost looking. "I learned the hard way that thinking with my dick gets me nothing but trouble."

There was something in the way he said it that spoke to much more than a messy breakup, and she remembered asking him to tell her something secret, something no one else knew about him—and he hadn't.

"What kind of trouble?" she asked, if only because talking about him meant they were no longer talking about her.

"Not important right now," he replied as easy as pie. "Right now, we have to get through a rodeo, and you have to decide if you want me to come home with you. And it isn't about sex," he added, giving her a stern look. "It's about you trying to do the work of three people by yourself with a busted rib. If you keep reinjuring it, it won't heal right and it'll hurt for the rest of your life."

In the distance, the sound of tires on gravel began to echo around the arena. Rattler shook himself awake, and Lacy realized she hadn't even peed this morning, much less brushed her teeth. And she still wasn't wearing a bra.

"You let me know," Ian said, pressing a kiss to her forehead before he let her go. "It's your call, either way."

Great. Good to know. Except now she had a decision to make.

Would she take him home? And if she did, would she welcome him to her bed?

CHAPTER FIFTEEN

IAN GOT OUT of the truck and stretched. His butt was numb and his eyes were about to cross permanently. But they'd made it to the Straight Arrow before the sun set all the way.

"So this is home?"

She'd been painfully quiet on the drive up. True, she'd been asleep in the passenger seat for the first half. When she'd agreed that maybe it would be best if Ian helped her get the bulls home, she'd insisted he sleep the whole night. She was not about to entrust her life and her animals' lives to a man who'd gotten a total of six hours of sleep over the two previous nights. She'd made *that* clear in no uncertain terms.

So last night, he'd slept and she'd stayed awake. She'd stayed on her side of the truck and he'd stayed on his. He hadn't anticipated missing the warmth of her body curled up against his, but he had. He'd asked if she was comfortable and she'd said she was fine so he'd let it go. She wasn't sending out "touch me again" signals, so he'd gone to sleep.

The night had been quiet enough. Then, around five thirty this morning, they'd loaded up the bulls and headed north.

"Yup." Lacy didn't look at him when she said it.

It didn't take a genius IQ to figure out what this was about. Two nights ago, he'd wrapped his arm around her and she'd slept deeply—and then hadn't been able to look him in the eyes the rest of the day. It'd only been at night, when they'd climbed back into the cab of her truck for the third night of watching that she'd even replied to his questions with more than single-syllable answers.

This wasn't about the nights. This was about the mornings. The one morning in particular.

This was about sex.

The hell of it was, he wasn't sure which part of the sex was the problem. Was it that they'd fooled around at all? Or was it that they'd nearly been caught?

"Nice place," he remarked as she hauled herself out of the truck. She wobbled a bit and Ian fought the urge to rush around the truck and slide an arm around her waist. "Who else is here?"

"Murph, the hired hand. He worked for my father and stayed on." She cleared her throat and looked at the ground. "He owns a small piece of land between our ranch and Slim Smalls's property. Otherwise, it's just us." She swallowed.

"Me, I mean. Our property lines run from half-way up the side of the Laramie range to 17, the road we turned off of about twenty minutes ago."

That was more than she'd said to him in the past twelve hours. So Slim Smalls was her next-door neighbor? Maybe after they'd gotten the bulls unloaded and settled in, she'd let him in on what the feud was about. He wasn't going to push her right now, though. He was many things, but he liked to think that stupid wasn't one of them.

"Pretty land," he said again, keeping to the smallest of small talk.

"Different than your ranch?"

Ian turned to look at the low mountains of the Laramie range that were standing tall to the east of the Straight Arrow. "The rez is a lot flatter. Not as many trees. Let's get the bulls unloaded. Is Murph around?"

Even in the late-afternoon light, there was no missing the furious blush that lit up her face. He knew the answer before she said the words. "It's just us."

He didn't grin, even though she wasn't looking at him. He didn't know what was going to happen. He knew what he'd like to happen—but he wasn't going to push it.

"Then let's get it done."

In short order, he had the truck and trailer backed up the way Lacy wanted it, and they had the bulls out. The animals were more than glad to be back on solid ground—Rattler nearly clipped Ian in the head with a surprise buck of his back legs.

Then he and Lacy stood there for a moment, the sun setting in the west. It made the mountains behind them glow fire orange. "Beautiful," he said.

"Most beautiful piece of land in Wyoming," she agreed. But she didn't move.

Ian needed a shower and a hot meal and a bed. Hell, even a couch would do. Three nights and a solid day in a truck was more than enough for him. He wanted to give her all the space she needed, but a man had to eat. "You got anything resembling dinner in the house?"

She crossed her arms under her chest. At some point, she'd started wearing a bra again, which was a crying shame as far as he was concerned. Her breasts were lush and full and his hands itched to feel their soft weight again.

He cleared his throat and turned to face the low ranch house. Food. That was the only thing he was hungry for. Really.

"Come on." She got the trailer uncoupled from the truck so quickly that Ian didn't even have the chance to offer to help, much less crank the jack for her. He grinned, this time not even bothering to hide it. She was, hands down, the most stubborn woman he knew.

They drove back to the house and parked in

a lean-to shed behind it. Ian grabbed both their bags while she unlocked the house and turned on the lights.

The house had a late-sixties feel. There wasn't anything fancy about it—this was not one of the grand old ranch mansions from the late 1880s, when cattle barons ruled the West. But the place was clean and well-cared for, and the kitchen had stainless steel appliances that looked newer than Ian's truck.

"Nice place," he offered into the silence. "You grew up here?"

"Yup," she replied. Back to the single syllables, he noted with a smile.

"Where should I put the bags?" Which was the least suggestive way of asking where he was sleeping tonight that he could come up with. He held up both duffels.

"This way." She led him through the living room, which featured a huge sectional sofa in a deep blue fabric that faced one of the bigger televisions Ian had ever seen.

"That screen is huge," he noted, because it seemed like something someone would be proud of.

"My dad really liked watching movies after we got our work done," she said as she led him down a long hallway.

They went past a closed door. "What's in there?"

She pulled up and he saw the tension ripple

across her shoulders. "My dad's office." Her voice was tight and clipped. "It's…off-limits."

"Fine with me," he replied, trying to sound casual even as he stared at the back of her head. Something was definitely off.

"My parents' room," she went on, opening the next door. "You can put your things here."

Ah. Well. He walked into the room, which was surprisingly pink? A deep rose carpet was on the floor and a blue bedspread with pink flowers was over the bed. The rest of the room was less surprising. The walls were light blue, the furniture— including the massive king-size bed—was oak and the view was of the still-orange mountains. Another decent-sized television was mounted over a fireplace.

The room didn't look as if it had been touched much in the past eight months. Ian would be willing to bet that, if he opened a dresser drawer, it'd still have socks in it.

"Bathroom is through that door," Lacy said, pointing on the other side of the fireplace. "I, uh, haven't gotten around to cleaning things out." She said it as if it was something to be ashamed of.

"No worries. After three days in the truck, this looks like the lap of luxury." He wasn't lying, either. The bed looked good. "You have work for me to do tomorrow, right?"

"*We* have work to do. You sure you're okay

with that?" She looked around at the pink carpet. "With this?"

With me. She didn't say it out loud, but she didn't have to.

A new thought occurred to him. What if she wasn't being distant because she wasn't interested? What if she was just unsure?

Maybe he hadn't given her enough to think about, what with him being the gentleman here.

Only one way to find out. "I am." He held out her bag to her. When she took it, he added, "I'm going to shower before dinner."

Her eyes widened as he started unbuttoning his shirt. "I'll—uh—"

He pulled his shirt out from his waistband and yanked it and the undershirt over his head.

She hadn't moved. Her jaw was open as she gaped at his chest. Ian fought the urge to flex. Instead, he started unbuckling his belt and turned his back on her. "See you in a few," he threw over his shoulder as he walked into the bathroom.

Let her think on *that*.

Lacy stood in the kitchen, frying pork chops without really being aware of what she was doing. All she could think about was the casual way Ian had started undressing in front of her.

Good heavens, she was in so much trouble.

The old Lacy would leave Ian in his bedroom and keep to hers. The old Lacy wouldn't have brought Ian home at all. The old Lacy would have never let Ian hold her while she slept or touch her while she was awake.

She realized she was staring at the office door. What was left of the old Lacy was hanging by the thinnest of threads, and the thing that would snap that thread was in there, less than twenty feet away from where she stood.

The old Lacy wouldn't. But the new Lacy? Well, she was still figuring that woman out.

She shifted from foot to foot. That heavy feeling between her legs was building again, had been building ever since Ian popped the first button on his shirt. It was an unavoidable fact on top of other unavoidable facts.

She wanted him. And if he wanted her back…

The bedroom door opened and Ian strode out. Her breath caught in her throat as he walked toward her. Oh, God. He looked good. Better than good. His hair was still damp and he wasn't wearing socks or boots. He had on a regular gray T-shirt. He didn't look like a cowboy right now. Somehow, that made a huge difference.

"Looks great," he said in appreciation as he stood next to her. "Thanks for cooking." Then, as if it was no big deal, he draped his arm around her shoulder and pressed a kiss to the top of her head.

She looked up at him in a state of shock.

"There's, uh, beer and soda in the fridge and some lemonade..."

"Lemonade sounds good," he said, the corner of his mouth curving up into a smile. He pulled her hat from her head. "You don't wear this in the house, do you?"

"No." She couldn't look away from him, couldn't pull away from him. Her body? It wanted his.

She wanted him.

He brushed his fingertips over her forehead, pushing a freed curl away from her eyes. His fingers stayed on her skin, curving over her cheekbone and along her chin.

Her eyelids fluttered at his touch and she thought, *Kiss me.*

Ian stepped away. "Lemonade?"

"Yeah. No." What was she doing? Hell, she didn't even know. "Wait."

Which, to his credit, he did. "Yes?"

"What are we doing here?"

"Having dinner?" He sounded confused, but he had a curious grin on his face.

"You know what I mean." *Don't make me tell you*, she silently prayed. She was pretty sure she didn't have a hope in hell of saying the words out loud.

"Having dinner," he repeated with more certainty. But as he said it, he stepped back into her and cupped her face in his palms. "After that, you're going to take a hot shower." His lips touched her forehead before they drifted down to her temple. She closed her eyes and let herself savor his touch. Dinner would be good, a hot shower would be great. Especially if… "And then we're going to go to bed."

She swallowed and forced herself to look at him. "Alone?"

The look in his eyes made her shiver. "I'm not going to guess at what goes on inside your pretty head, babe. I got the feeling you'd reconsidered the benefits part of our friends-with-benefits arrangement. But if that's not the case…"

Hot embarrassment burned her cheeks. "I wasn't sure if you still wanted, you know—*me*. After I yelled at you in front of your friends. I can be a real bitch sometimes. Most of the time, actually." She couldn't look at him and talk. He was so perfect and she was just so…Lacy. So she dropped her gaze.

He wrapped his arms around her and pulled her into a fierce hug. "You were well within your rights to put me in my place. I wasn't trying to step on your toes."

Wait—was he apologizing? He was, wasn't he? Well, that was unexpected.

He sighed and she wanted to sink into the warmth of his chest and just *be*. She didn't want to think about what people might say or what was in the office or how badly she'd burned dinner. She wanted to be in the moment with Ian.

He stroked her hair and she realized she desperately needed a shower before he began to stroke anything else. "I've got this powerful urge to take care of you," he went on. "There's something about you—you're tough and prickly, but you're also delicate and vulnerable and beautiful."

The embarrassment was bleeding over into disbelief. Was he trying to feed her lines? "I'm not, you know. Pretty, that is. Never have been, never will be."

He lifted her chin and looked her square in the eyes. "Just because you can't see it doesn't mean you're not beautiful."

Her pulse was racing as he stroked his thumbs over her cheeks. "And then, I couldn't—in the truck. If someone had seen us..."

He touched his forehead to hers. "We're not in the truck anymore."

She blushed again. She must look like an over-ripe tomato at this point. "I'm really bad at this. I didn't think you still wanted me."

"Don't apologize. But be honest about what you want, Lacy."

Honest? About what she wanted? She barely knew what she wanted—much less how to put it into words. "I don't know if I can do that."

"It's not that hard, babe. This is me being honest with you. I want you. I have from the very first moment you threatened me about a bull. You spark something in me, and it kills me to pretend that you're one of the guys. You are *anything* but that." His lips touched her temple again and moved over her cheek. "You're *everything* but that," he breathed against her skin.

He wanted her. God, wasn't that something? She'd never been wanted before. It was stunning how different those words made her feel. She desperately wanted to believe them. *"Really?"*

"Really." He shifted and let his lips move over her other temple. "Same rules as before. You want me, you have to tell me. Otherwise, I'm *just* here to help out a friend. So tell me what you want, Lacy."

"You." Her heart was pounding so fast she felt faint. She was doing this, really doing this. She turned into him, felt his breath on her lips. "I want you."

There. She'd said it—out loud, even.

A ghost of a kiss pressed on her lips and he said, "Shower. *Now.*"

CHAPTER SIXTEEN

"WHAT?"

"You owe me one," he said with a sly grin. "So I'm cashing it in. Shower." He began to march her back down the hall. "Dinner will reheat. Which bathroom do you use?"

"I have one in my room…"

He kept his hands on her shoulders. "Go."

She led the way back through her room, with the impossibly tiny-looking double bed. Her collection of Breyer model horses lined the top of her dresser and her ribbons for riding and shooting looked faded and dusty. She was almost embarrassed by the girlishness of her room, but all Ian said was, "I like it," low and close in her ear. "Shower?"

She nodded and led on, past the bed with the red comforter and the heart pillows her mom had made for her ninth birthday and past the bookshelf where the *Little House on the Prairie* books she'd read with her mom were neatly organized.

Her bathroom was tucked into the back, behind her closet. She had a bathtub and a single sink. She tried not to think about when she'd last cleaned the sink.

Ian pulled her up short and turned her in his arms. "Okay?"

"Okay," she replied, and she wished she could sound more confident or sexier.

He began to pop the buttons on her shirt. Lacy stood there in a state of confusion. He was undressing her, which was both sexy and unnerving. She focused on taking deep breaths and trying to think back to the way he'd made her feel in the truck. Sexy. Desirable.

He got the shirt unbuttoned and pushed it down over her shoulders. Then he pulled her white tank top off, going slowly so her ribs wouldn't pull. He traced the edges of fabric down between her breasts. "When did you get the bra back on?"

"Two days ago. In the ladies' room at the arena." Which was why the shower was a good idea. She hadn't had one since that afternoon in Ian's hotel room.

"Damn, babe," he murmured, spreading his fingers wide and cupping her breasts. "I've been dreaming of what you looked like." His hands slid around her back and easily unhooked it.

The bra fell away and except for her jeans, she was bare before him. "Oh, Lacy," he murmured. "Wow."

This was really happening, wasn't it? Then his thumbs flicked over her nipples and a shiver went through her, electric and hot. Oh, yes. Yes it was. Finally, she wasn't the odd girl out, the one too butch or too bitchy to get a boyfriend.

Except, of course, that Ian wasn't her boyfriend. This was no-strings-attached.

It was better that way, she decided as he leaned down and kissed the top of her right breast. She could enjoy herself and not worry about what came next.

She arched her back, lifting her breasts up to his touch. But he stepped away. "Hot shower," he said in a no-arguments voice.

She winced. "Do I reek that bad?"

He laughed as if she'd told a joke. "Hell, no," he said as he stepped around her and cranked on the water. "But you're nervous and you're already sore. This will help your muscles loosen up."

Embarrassment flamed at her cheeks again. "You make it sound like we're going to be doing acrobatic things."

He didn't respond immediately as he adjusted the water. Then he turned back to her. The look in his eyes sent another shiver through her.

"Take your jeans off," he ordered as he leaned against the bathroom wall.

"What are you going to do?"

"Watch." He crossed his arms over his chest.

She could not tell the difference between panic and excitement. The two emotions bled into each other, swirling around until there was no way to tell where one feeling started and the other left off.

Steam filled the bathroom as she undid her zipper and pushed her jeans down her hips. She kicked out of the pants and socks, which left her in nothing but a pair of simple blue cotton panties. She wished she had something sexier—that she'd prepared better.

She forced herself to look at Ian. A muscle in his jaw twitched and even to a novice like herself there was no mistaking it—he was barely holding himself back.

"Take off your panties," he said through clenched teeth.

So she did. She slid them down her hips and legs and tossed them to the side with the rest of her clothing.

As Ian's gaze burned into her skin, he let out a low groan. She dropped her gaze to his jeans. Yes, she did that to him. The realization gave her a certain amount of confidence. She might not know exactly how to seduce a man, but she could have that kind of effect on Ian.

The heavy weight between her legs began to throb with need. She needed him to touch her as he had before, needed to feel him inside of her. This time, there wouldn't be any interruptions.

"Get in the shower," he ordered her.

Her uncertainty got the better of her. "What about you?"

"I'll join you in a few minutes. I have to go get my towels."

"Oh." Him—and her—in the shower? *Together?* Her blood pounded in her ears—and in other parts.

Something that was far too sensual to be called a grin curved his lips. "You're cute when you're surprised."

She stepped over the rim of the tub and let the hot water run over her chest as he stared. "Damn," he said again. "I'll be right back." Then he pulled the curtain shut with more force than was necessary and was gone.

Lacy didn't waste a second. She quickly shaved her armpits and ran the razor over her legs. Before she could attack her bikini line, however, Ian said, "I'm coming in," and the curtain was pushed aside.

She couldn't look. Not yet, anyway. So she closed her eyes and listened.

She heard Ian step into the tub and the rasp of the curtain as it was pulled shut. The water sounded quieter, probably because his big body was taking up more space.

"Have you ever done this before?" he asked seconds before his hands touched her shoulders. She jumped.

She wasn't sure which "this" he was asking about—the sex, or the showering with someone else. Didn't really matter. The answer was the same. "No."

"Hmm." His hands skimmed down her arms and settled around her waist. She felt something warm and hard nudge against her hip. She almost reached over and touched him, but didn't. "Do you trust me?"

"Yes." She didn't even have to think about that question. She'd trusted him enough to sleep in his arms for two nights in the truck, to take her back to a hotel room when she was wounded and vulnerable. She trusted him enough to bring him to the Straight Arrow. This—being here in the shower with him—wasn't much different.

"Then look at me, babe." He cupped her face in his hands and lifted her chin so she couldn't possibly look at anything but his face. The water streamed through her hair.

He was right there, close enough to kiss. "You are so beautiful, you know—and don't you dare tell me you're not," he added when she opened her mouth.

"I've never felt beautiful before."

"You will," he promised as he lowered his lips to hers. She knew he was telling the truth, too.

But, like the first kiss in the truck, it wasn't a kiss that made her forget everything else. It was sweet—but not what she needed right now.

"Ian," she said, her mouth moving without the

express permission of her brain. If they were going to do this, she needed to be swept away.

"Easy, babe." Then he tilted her head back even farther. The water ran over her scalp and despite the fact that she was naked in the shower with a man, it felt good. "Turn around," he said after her hair was good and wet.

She did as he said—without looking down. He chuckled and said, "You're something, you know that?"

"So I've been told."

He picked up her shampoo. "Your hair does things to me," he said as he massaged the shampoo into her hair.

The pressure on her head was just right and the hot water sheeted over the front of her body. "I have trouble believing that. It drives me nuts. Totally unruly."

"Oh, yeah," he said, his fingers sliding through the soapy curls. "I like that about it. Wild and untamed. When you sent me that picture?" He whistled low in her ear. "You really don't know how crazy you make me, do you?"

As he said it, he shifted and she felt his erection push against her backside.

She could do this. She was in all the way. She took a deep breath and reached around behind her. Her fingers closed around him—barely.

Oh, God—were they even going to fit together? Ian moaned in her ear. "I like it when you touch me," he said, his voice deep and throaty. Then he pulled back before leaning forward so that her hand slid over his entire wet length.

He groaned again and that surge of power went through Lacy. She was doing that to him.

He raked his fingers through her hair and tilted her head to the side. He pulled one hand free of her curls and cupped her right breast, teasing her nipple between his finger and thumb as he kissed her ear, then the side of her neck and her shoulder, all while he slowly thrust into her hand.

She was just getting well and truly lost in the sensations when he pulled away. "Turn around," he said, his voice husky with need—for her.

This time, she did not close her eyes and she did not look away. As she turned, she took in the full magnitude of his body.

"Oh, my God," she whispered. He was—well, he was huge. Her grip hadn't been lying. But his erection fit him—it matched the broad, muscled chest and the thick thighs. "You really are built, aren't you?"

He snorted and ran his finger under her chin, lifting her face up and tilting her hair back under the water. As the water ran over her hair and his fingers worked the last of the shampoo out, she thought he would let her observation slide.

Then he said, "You're a virgin, aren't you?"

"Is it that obvious?" She tried to smile, as if it was a funny joke, but she didn't quite make it.

That made him laugh as he turned her back around. "You keep acting like you're sure you're about to chase me out of this shower, and I'm over here mentally running through football game tape to keep from bending you over and taking you right now, right against the wall. Conditioner?"

She went very still. The line between desire and panic was thinner now because there was a part of her—a part she was more aware of than she'd ever been in her life—that wanted him to do just what he'd said.

"You'd—you'd do that?"

"Not for your first time," he said, massaging the conditioner into her hair. "I told you—it's going to be you, me and a bed. This…" His hands trailed down her back as he bent his head forward and skimmed his teeth over the spot where her shoulder met her neck. He cupped her bottom and squeezed. The intimate touch sent another spike of desire through her. "This is the warm-up."

"Oh. Okay."

He let go of her and picked up the washcloth and the soap. "Can I ask about the virgin thing?"

"Sure, I guess. I assume you're not."

She expected him to chuckle but instead he paused. "No. And I haven't been with a virgin since my first time."

"Oh. Okay," she repeated, because what was

she supposed to do with that sort of information? Be thankful he didn't have a thing for virgins? Or be weirded out that he had so much more experience than she did?

He didn't say anything as he washed her back. It was half bathing, half massage—and all good. She let her chin drop to her chest as the hot water ran over her front and Ian worked on her back. Muscles she hadn't realized were knotted began to relax. She sighed in pleasure.

"Well?" he said, crouching to scrub the backs of her legs.

"Well what?"

"The virgin thing, Lacy."

"Oh. That. It's not complicated. I was raised to wait until I was married, and no one ever took it upon himself to try and change my mind."

He stood and turned her around. She tilted her head back and let the water run over her hair. "Did you date?" he asked.

She sighed. "You really have to ask, huh? I would have thought all my supersmooth moves here would have answered that question already."

Ian burst out laughing, and Lacy felt herself smiling along with him. It was better that he knew and it was out in the open, she realized. She didn't have to pretend she was something she wasn't.

"I...I like the way you touch me, too," she said as he ran the washcloth over her again and again.

"Then we're doing it right." Seconds later, his mouth closed over her left nipple.

The shock of his mouth against her made her stumble backward and her foot slipped on the wet tub. Ian's mouth came off her breast with an audible *pop*. She tried to catch herself, but Ian's arms were around her waist and he pulled her into his chest. "Easy, babe," he said, an amused smile on his face as every part of her front pressed against every part of his.

"Sorry. Not very good at this," she said sheepishly.

One of his hands slid lower and cupped her bottom again, while he brought the other up and brushed her wet hair away from her face. "Don't apologize. You aren't going to chase me off. In case you missed it, I'm naked. Where am I going to go?"

She grinned up at him. "Second shower of the day, huh?"

"Totally worth it." His tongue traced her lips. She sighed into his mouth and wrapped her arms around his waist and let herself sink against him, skin to skin.

Then a panicked thought occurred to her and she pulled away. "I don't—for protection, I mean. Do you have?"

"Yeah, I've got condoms." Ian crouched back down on his heels as he washed her legs again.

"Explain to me again how me owing you one means I get bathed?"

"Because it gives me the opportunity to do this," he murmured as he pressed his mouth— Oh, God. He looked up at her as he slipped his hand between her thighs. When his fingers stroked over her, he said, "Open up for me," in a tone that was part command, part plea.

If his touch didn't feel so good, she'd be panicking. Was this what sex was—the small space between excitement and terror? Was he really going to put his mouth *there*? "What—what do you want me to do?"

Oh, that smile—that was positively wicked. "Can you put one foot on the edge of the tub and brace yourself with your arm?"

She did as he said. "Like this?" But that was as far as she got before he swept his tongue over her. Every single nerve in her body tightened. *"Ian."*

"You taste so good, Lacy." She swore she could feel his voice vibrate through her center.

With her free hand, she grabbed hold of his hair. He growled against her skin as he sucked and licked her. "That's it, babe. Let me do this for you."

She held on to him for what felt like dear life. His hands and mouth were all over her, touching and rubbing and sliding against the folds of her flesh. She gasped and panted. "Ian—I'm not— I'm going to— I can't stand much longer."

"I think you can." He locked one arm around the back of her thigh and held her up. His other hand— *Oh*. He slipped a finger into her, stroking in and out as his tongue traced circles around her clit. "Watch, babe. Watch what I do to you."

"Ian—Ian!" She didn't know if she was trying to pull him away or hold him closer.

He looked up and their eyes met and he smiled. Smiled with his mouth against her as he slipped two fingers inside and curved them and—and—

All her muscles tensed as she tried to scream, but no noise came out. All she could do was watch Ian unleash her orgasm. And all she could think was, *Yes*.

Then, almost as quickly as it happened, she came back down to earth. Her legs started to shake and she felt limp.

Ian stood and pulled her into his arms. "My God, do you have any idea how beautiful you are when you come?"

She knew she was blushing, but she didn't care. She hadn't thought it was possible, but that was even better than what she'd felt in the truck. "I can't believe you did that."

"Babe," he said, reaching around her and shutting the water off, "we're just getting started."

CHAPTER SEVENTEEN

LACY WAS SHAKING so much she had to take it slow getting out of the shower. Ian took that as a compliment.

He could still taste her honey sweetness on his tongue as he followed her out and grabbed her towel. "Here." Even though his dick ached and he was having trouble thinking straight, he started at her legs and worked his way up, buffing the towel over her backside.

She sighed, a sound of pure satisfaction. Then she turned in his arms and said, "I can touch you, right?"

"It usually works better that way," he said with a grin, even as his pulse picked up another notch. He didn't know how much longer he could play it cool. Yeah, it'd been a long while, but this need he felt—it went way beyond wanting to relieve a little sexual tension. He moved the towel to dry her hair.

But before he could, she leaned over and licked his chest. He watched in shock as her tongue swept over his pecs, right around the edge of his tattoo. Her hands flattened against his sides as she moved up, covering his neck, his jaw—until she finally got to his mouth.

The towel fell to the ground as he growled into her. He'd touched her; he'd gone down on her—all the things he'd promised to do. Now? Now was the part where he buried himself in her warm, relaxed and very willing body.

He pulled her against him and tangled his hands in her hair as her tongue tentatively touched his lips. He thought he was still in control until her fingers closed around his dick.

He moaned into her mouth. Days of sexual frustration peaked as she moved her hand up and down his shaft. He tore his mouth away from hers. "Bed. Now."

One of her eyebrows lifted in amusement as she stroked him again in direct defiance of his order. "You've gotten to do everything to me. I haven't gotten to do anything to you yet."

He could not stand here and let her continue to pump him. After days of being with her? After that shower? He wasn't that strong.

He had other ways of making her listen. He made sure his hands were under her butt before he lifted so he wouldn't torque her ribs. When he picked her up, she made a little squeaking noise. "First off, I haven't even started doing *everything* to you," he told her as he carried her out of the bathroom and toward the bed. She gasped in shock. "Second off..."

Any other time, he would have thrown her onto the bed and pounced. But this time, he set her down and laid her out before him. "Second off, you have no idea what you do to me."

He covered her body with his, careful to keep himself propped up on her right side as he kissed her. She kissed him back, looping one of her legs around his. She ran her hands down his back, grabbing at his butt and pulling him into her.

Yeah, foreplay was over. He pulled away long enough to grab the box of condoms he'd set on the bedside table and roll one on. "I'll go slow," he promised.

"We'll—" She swallowed hard and looked down. "We'll fit, right?"

"We will." He stroked her sex, all wet and ready for him, and was rewarded with a low moan. "Okay?" Her eyes widened as she nodded. "Say it, babe. Say you want me inside of you."

"I do," she gasped as he slid a finger into her tight passage. "Don't want to wait anymore."

"That's it—tell me what you like. Be honest with me." He pulled his finger out and positioned his dick at her entrance. "I want this to be so good for you."

She gripped him by the shoulders as he pushed into her—slowly, as he'd promised. She clung to him tightly. He watched her face. She didn't gasp or jolt in pain. Instead, eyes wide, she said, "Oh—that's—okay."

"Okay?" He grinned. Not a ringing endorsement, but for her first time, that wasn't a bad thing.

"Here—let me—" She shifted, her body tightening around him.

He groaned and said, "Lacy, you're going to kill me." He couldn't help it—he flexed, pushing himself deeper.

"It doesn't hurt," she said, her voice full of wonder. "I thought…"

He cut her off with a kiss. "Lacy, there's more to this than not hurting and I can't hold myself back much longer."

"Oh. Okay. Go on." She dropped her head back and lay still.

Grinning, he kissed her as he began to thrust. This time, she did gasp—in surprise. "Oh!"

"Yeah, that," he said, fighting mightily to keep his control. "God, you feel so good, Lacy."

"Yeah?" Her breath was coming in shorter gasps. She shifted her hips again, taking him deeper. "You—you feel good, too."

"Good." He hefted himself up on both his hands so he could thrust harder. "Like that?"

"Yeah." She made a high noise in the back of her throat—a noise he already recognized as her getting closer.

Couldn't have that. He'd barely gotten going.

He slowed way down, pulling out and pausing. "What? Don't stop, Ian—don't— Oh!" He slammed his hips forward, driving all the way into hers.

"I told you," he growled as he did it again, slow and hard, "that I was going to make you come again and again, and I will always keep my promises to you."

Her head fell back, eyes closed. She moaned while he drove into her again and again. He could feel her body tightening around his. "Look," he ordered her, leaning back so she could see where their bodies joined. "Look at us. We fit, babe. We *belong*."

"Oh, God," she whispered as he slammed home again. Then suddenly her back lifted off the bed. "Ian!"

He fell forward and pumped into her. Everything fell away as he buried himself in her. Rodeos and bulls and ribs and children and everything he'd ever screwed up—all of his sins were burned away in the clear heat of this act with her. "Lacy—*Lace*," he said as his climax roared out of him.

She cried out again as he came, clutching his shoulders and breathing hard.

Spent and suddenly exhausted, he barely managed to roll to the side so he wouldn't crush her. He was gripped with a strange urge to tell her things—that the sex had been something different, something *more* than he expected it to be—but hell if he could make sense of the mess that was his head. Besides, he realized as rational thought started to return, if he started spouting stuff like that, she'd wonder what the hell was wrong with him. This was no-strings. Telling her more? All about the strings.

So he kept his mouth shut and pulled her into his arms.

"Ian…" Unexpectedly, she curled into his side, her face pressed against his chest.

He lay there, trying to catch his breath and get his mind in order as he stroked her hair. The feeling of her body in his arms—okay, yeah, it'd been months since he'd last allowed himself to enjoy everything a woman chose to share with him.

But damned if he'd ever felt like this—as if he'd been sideswiped by a bull going at top speed. Lacy had chosen him to be her first. It really shouldn't be that big of a deal and yet, now that he'd taken care of her? Washed her and dried her and made her forget everything but the way their bodies fit together?

He'd always felt that pull to take care of her. He hadn't expected sleeping with her to make that pull feel this much stronger.

Sex was fun. He liked it; he was good at it. When he was a teenager, he'd been careless. And it wasn't just that the carelessness had led to Eliot. Ian had cheated on girlfriends in high school. In college, at least he hadn't had a girl-friend to cheat on, but that was only because he'd had his pick. His position on the football team had only increased his appeal and he used it. Shamelessly.

It wasn't until it all fell apart on him that he'd realized he couldn't go on screwing his way through college. So he'd stopped. For the past six years, he'd only given in to his baser urges when he couldn't stand the loneliness anymore. And even then, it'd been about him. He'd been lonely. He'd been horny. Yeah, he'd made sure his part-ners were satisfied, but in the morning, he'd al-ways felt anxious and crappy instead of relieved.

Lacy sighed in his arms. This—this was not crappy. This was something so different he had trouble naming it.

"Is it always like that?"

"Not always. Sometimes it's better, sometimes it's worse. Sex is never predictable." Just as he hadn't predicted the depths of his feelings right now. He wanted to hold her close and stand be-tween her and the world, keep her safe, and the whole time, he wanted her to be prickly and vul-nerable and innocent at the same time.

She traced the triad tattoo on his chest with her index finger. He tensed—would she ask about it? And if she did, would he tell her about Eliot?

"I didn't know it would be so...*so*."

He chuckled. "I hope that's a good *so*." Sighing, he slid his arm out from under her. He had to get up, and so did she. "Be right back."

He washed up in the bathroom and took care of the condom. When he came back out, Lacy was sitting up in bed, her knees tucked up to her chin. She looked impossibly young, in this room with all its trappings of her youth. That strong urge to protect her hit him again.

But he didn't want to come on too strong. She was watching him as he picked up his clothes where he'd abandoned them at the foot of her bed. "Your turn."

He got his jeans on while she cleaned up and tried to guess which Lacy he'd get when she came out—defiant? Shy? Both?

He'd put his money on both and was not disappointed. She strutted out, gloriously naked—but there was no missing the way she couldn't meet his gaze.

He stood and said, "Dinner?" in as casual a voice as he could muster. That didn't stop him from pulling her into his arms and against his bare chest.

"Dinner," she agreed, leaning into him.

A high buzzing noise cut through the house, causing Lacy to jump. "The doorbell!" She looked down at her complete lack of clothing. "Um…"

"I'll get it." He snagged his shirt and yanked it over his head. "Get dressed."

She rolled her eyes at him. "As if I was going to waltz around naked," he heard her mutter as he headed toward the front door.

He opened it to see a weathered older man leaning toward the locks, keys in hand. "Help you?" Ian said in his best bouncer voice, even though he was pretty sure this had to be Murph, the hired hand.

Murph jumped back in surprise. He took one look at Ian and his face hardened into a mask of rage. "Who are you? What are you doing here?"

Ian held up his hands in the universal sign of surrender. "Easy—I'm a friend of Lacy's."

Murph was not impressed by this statement. "Where is she?" he snarled, advancing a step on Ian. "What did you do to her?"

Ian was not prone to fits of embarrassment, but right then, his cheeks shot hot. He wasn't afraid of Murph—the old coot was probably pushing sixty—but he didn't want to give away any of Lacy's secrets. Nor did he particularly want to admit to having been the one who broke her rib. "We're friends," he said in as calm and steady a voice as he could manage. At least Murph hadn't pulled a gun on him—but the day wasn't over yet. "I'm here to help out."

"Murph?" Lacy called out. "I'm here—I was in the shower! I'll be right there!"

"Is this guy supposed to be here?" Murph yelled back.

"Yes! Give me a second!"

Ian knew it might take several seconds, depending on what she decided to wear. The hot shower and the sex might have relaxed her, but jerking her arms through a shirt could still leave her gasping for breath.

He took a risk and stuck out his hand. "Ian Tall Chief. You must be Murph. Lacy's told me a lot about you."

"Funny," Murph said, not shaking hands. "She hasn't mentioned you at all."

Ian cocked an eyebrow at the older man and let his hand drop. "We were about to eat dinner. Care to join us?"

Murph didn't reply. Instead, after another few moments of glaring, he leaned forward and said in a low voice, "You hurt her, there's no place you can go I won't find you."

He had to give it to Murph, he was doing a bang-up job of intimidation. "Good. She needs someone watching her back."

This caught Murph off guard. He looked at Ian in confusion as Lacy hurried into the room, fastening the last button on her shirt. "Murph— oh, you've met," she said, completely missing the tension in the room.

"Ian, right?" Murph said. He took his hat off his head. "We met."

Lacy must have caught a whiff of disapproval

because her head popped up. "Ian's a bullfighter on the circuit," she explained.

This did not appease Murph. He shifted his gaze to Lacy, who colored prettily.

Ian wanted to jump in and tell Murph where he could shove his judgment, but he figured that was the quickest way to a fistfight. This was Lacy's house, Lacy's hired hand. So Ian kept his mouth shut and let her handle it.

"He's been helping me since Wreck," she said, lifting her chin. Her eyes flashed with defiance. "I wouldn't have been able to get the bulls loaded if he hadn't been there." Murph stared at her as if she'd spoken Latin. "We're both going to be at the same rodeo in Pierre next week, so he offered to drive home with me."

"She said she had work for me to do," Ian added. "I grew up on a ranch."

Murph's gaze darted between the two of them. "Well, we could use a hand getting those cows ready for the trucks—they'll be here on Wednesday."

Ian wondered if Lacy had told Murph about her rib. No, he decided. She wouldn't want anyone else to know she was hurting.

"Good. The carcass hauler cut me a break on...on Wreck," she finished, trying so hard to sound strong.

Which only made him want to pull her back into his arms. He did no such thing.

"I sure am sorry, girl," Murph said. He sounded sincere about it. "He was a good bull."

"He was a pain in the ass," she said with an awkward laugh. "But this changes things. You're staying for dinner?"

Murph shot another look at Ian, one that clearly said the older man was going to leave Ian alone with Lacy as little as possible. Ian ignored him.

"Thank you kindly," Murph said. "Tell me what happened."

LACY WAS NOT hiding in her bathroom. Really she wasn't. She just didn't know what she should do next. Should she go out there naked? She didn't normally sleep naked. But then, she didn't normally have a man waiting for her in her bed.

She was being ridiculous, especially after everything they'd done together. The old Lacy would have hidden in the bathroom like an idiot. The new Lacy would wear what she wanted to bed and it wouldn't be a big deal.

Except... Murph had been doing his best impression of a dad, scowling at Ian anytime he got within three feet of Lacy and making her feel as if she was thirteen again. True, her father wouldn't have been quite that rude about the whole situation, and yes, Ian had handled it perfectly. Just as he'd been doing for weeks now, he treated Lacy as if she was one of the guys. She felt stupid for remembering how she'd thought that meant Ian wasn't into her.

Now she knew better.

She turned off the light and tried to open the door with confidence. Then she saw Ian, shirtless, sitting in her bed, her quilt bunched up around his waist, her heart-shaped pillows in his hands. She was stunned for a moment at how good he looked—how he seemed to fit right in. She wished she felt that comfortable anywhere.

"I gotta say, I didn't figure you to have pillowsized candy hearts—complete with messages—on your bed," he said without looking up.

"My mom made them for my ninth birthday," she said, glad he wasn't looking at her in her long sleep shirt and panties as she walked to the bedside. She slid under the covers next to Ian, catching a glimpse of black boxer briefs. Somehow, the fact that he wasn't naked made her feel better.

"She made you pillows that say I LUV U and BE MINE?" He handed her a pillow, and then leaned over and rested his head on her shoulder.

"Yeah." Lacy looked down at the I LUV YOU pillow. Once, it'd been bright red. Mom had even gotten it to be sort of flat and heart shaped, like the real candy hearts. But the fabric had faded and years of sleeping on it had made it lumpy.

Mom had loved her. "She used to say…" Lacy could still see her walking into the room when it was time to go to sleep. Mom would sit on the edge of the bed and smooth Lacy's hair away from her face. That was their moment together, that quiet time right before Lacy went to sleep. "She used to say I was the answer to her prayers."

Linda Evans had never much said the words "I love you." Instead she'd made pillows and bought plastic horses and every night, told Lacy that she was the answer to her prayers.

Lacy hadn't realized what Mom had really been saying until it was too late.

She leaned her head against Ian's. She could tell that he had questions—hell, she had questions—but he was giving her space. She changed the subject while she still could. "I'm sorry about Murph. He's protective of me."

"No problem." Ian slid down under the covers, so Lacy set the heart pillow aside and turned out the light.

It shouldn't seem this natural to curl up against him, but it did. "He only threatened me a little."

"He did *what*?" She was going to have words with that man.

Ian's chest moved underneath her arm. "He didn't pull a gun or anything, so it's good. I take it he's known you your whole life?"

"Yeah—well, since I was two." She sighed, letting Ian's warmth surround her. "But then, so has Slim Smalls and he'd throw me to the wolves if he got the chance." Ian stroked her hair and she felt her body relax. "I wish I knew what he wanted with this place. Or with me."

"Don't know. But I'm not going to let him get away with anything that puts you in danger again." His other hand covered hers as it rested on his bare chest. "At the risk of sounding like I'm taking over—which I'm not trying to do—I do have a plan for some friends to keep an eye on you when I'm not around." He leaned up and kissed her forehead. "Although I'm going to be around as much as I can."

Her heart pounded faster. Because as good as that sounded, it wasn't exactly a ringing endorsement for "no-strings-attached."

She was on her unbroken side, with her leg over his and her arm on his chest. He stroked her hair with one hand and the other was tucked under his head. The physical closeness was something she hadn't realized she'd needed. Her parents were not overly affectionate in public— the most handsy she'd ever seen them was when they watched movies. That was when Mom would curl up next to Dad and he'd put his arm around her shoulders.

Being able to touch another person—to hold them and to know they were holding her back?

She thought she'd be able to sleep tonight. The pain in her ribs was better and Ian was here, her human heating pad.

He turned to face her. "I know the land is your

home, Lacy, but when that bull had you in his sights, it scared the hell out of me. And there's not much in this world that actually scares me."

She gave him a weak grin. "I'd tell you that's a load of bull crap, but I did see you take down Rattler. I believe it."

"I don't want anything to happen to you," he told her, his voice a breath on her lips.

"You happened," she reminded him.

He rolled into her. "Is that a good thing?"

"Best thing that's happened to me in months," she told him truthfully. "And I haven't seen any of it coming. Not just you. My parents' deaths, the…" She swallowed. *The box*, she wanted to say. *The box with the adoption papers in it.*

But she didn't. She couldn't. Which was almost as ridiculous as being unable to decide if she was sleeping in her nightshirt or not. She could share her body with Ian, but not this. Not yet.

"I won't let you lose another bull," Ian told her, misinterpreting her silence. "Rattler's a great bull. Meanest beast I've tangled with in a long time."

"You say the sweetest things." Why couldn't she tell him about the box? He'd never known her before, not like Murph did. He'd only known her after. He wouldn't think any less of her.

This wasn't the 1950s anymore. She had nothing to be ashamed of. Her birth parents had given her to good people who had loved her and raised her right. She'd had a good life.

All of these things made perfect sense.

And she still couldn't bring herself to own up to a truth that still felt as new and raw as it did the day she'd opened that damned box.

So instead she hugged Ian as best she could without jostling her ribs. "Tomorrow," he said, his voice gentle as he cupped her cheek and lifted her face to kiss her. "Don't think I've forgotten about the rest of my promise."

The only thing he'd said he'd do to her—and hadn't yet—had been pulling her on top of him and watching her ride. Lacy shivered at the thought.

"Tomorrow," she whispered back.

"Sleep," he told her.

Yes. She would. And tomorrow...

Maybe tomorrow she'd tell him about the box.

Maybe.

CHAPTER EIGHTEEN

"How's your girlfriend?"

Ian shot Jack a hard look before he turned his attention back to the rider and bull in the chute. "Dude, she'll punch you if she hears you say that," Ian warned him.

Jack chuckled. "So it's going well, then?"

"She's okay."

Jerome Salzberg nodded and his bull flew out of the chute. Ian danced out of the way of the bull's hooves but kept close enough that he could step in when Jerome bit the dust.

Which he did after only six and a half seconds. Ian heard a small crunch as Jerome landed on his pretty-boy face and rolled. That was probably his nose, Ian thought with satisfaction. That's what Jerome got for being too cool to wear a helmet.

As much as Ian might like to see the jerk get a few more bruises, he couldn't let a rider get trampled. He jumped between Jerome and the bull and waved his hands, ready to dodge if the bull took it personally.

The animal wasn't in the mood to fight. Instead, after tossing its head at Ian and Jack, the bull trotted out of the arena.

"Thanks," Jerome muttered. His nose was bleeding. It was almost as satisfying as if Ian had punched him.

"Yup," Ian said. While they were in the arena, he could be a professional.

"Just okay?" Jack said, picking up the conversation after Jerome had made it to the fences. "You're kidding, right?"

"Dude," Ian snapped as he found Lacy standing on top of one of the chutes. Her bull Chicken Run was in the chute and it looked as if the Preacher was due up. "Get your mind out of the damned gutter. I drove her home and spent the next four days working my ass off." Jack snorted, but Ian ignored that. "She's got about eight hundred head of cattle and one hired hand—plus a broken rib. I don't know how the hell she's kept her ranch going for the last eight months."

"You really worked?"

Ian would have said a few choice words, but the Preacher had gotten his grip and Chicken had exploded out of the chute. The bull gave it a good shot, but the Preacher hung on until the buzzer. Even better, when he let go and went flying, he landed behind Chicken.

Jack did the waving this time as Ian circled around to make sure the Preacher's escape was covered as the bull left the arena. "Wooee!" the

Preacher said when his score of eighty-four was announced. "Making a good run for Vegas this year."

Ian nodded, trying to keep an eye on Lacy without ignoring the Preacher. She was hopping down off the chutes and probably following Chicken back to the paddocks. "You've got a hell of a shot."

The Preacher chuckled as he followed Ian's gaze. "You gonna be up there with us?"

Wasn't that the ten-thousand-dollar question. "Working on it," Ian told him. If he could make it to Vegas, he could contact Eliot's parents.

Of course Ian knew he could contact them, anyway. But if he was going to meet the son he'd given away, he wanted to be someone the boy could be proud of. He wanted Eliot to know that he came from good people, people who could do anything they made up their mind to.

Once the Preacher was out of the arena, Ian walked back over to Jack. "Seriously, man— what are the odds we'll get called up to Vegas?" They were amassing points but he didn't know if it'd be enough.

As if on cue, Jack rubbed at the leg that'd been broken two years ago in a bad wreck. "Seriously? Maybe fifty-fifty."

"Dammit."

"You're young. You've got time," Jack said, his Texas drawl heavy. He tried to stretch out his bum leg and winced. "Either we'll get there or we won't. All we can do is take it one rodeo at a time."

"Zen is a really weird emotion on you, man."

"You should try it sometimes," Jack retorted.

Garth was up now, but he didn't make it more than four seconds. His landing was rough and the bull was pissy. All three of them wound up running for the fences, where they sat until the rider on horseback could get the bull roped and out of the arena.

"Hey," Garth said as they waited, "how's your girlfriend?"

"Dude, seriously? We're *just* friends." Ian could feel his cheeks getting hot, though. "Friends," he repeated with more force.

"Yeah, sure," Garth snorted. "I know I'd sleep in a truck for days on end to watch a 'friend's' bulls."

"Don't you have someplace else to be?" Ian snapped. "Ropes to pull, bulls to step on you?"

Garth shot him a smarmy look and hopped down. "I gotta keep an eye on those bulls. I'll tell your girlfriend you said hi."

"She'll wipe the floor with you!" Ian called after him.

"That, I believe," Jack said. "You got the plan set up?"

"I don't think anyone's going to try anything here—not on my home turf." Not too many people had made the three-plus-hour drive out from the rez today, but tomorrow? Yeah, it was going to be a party.

"I've got the boots on the ground lined up for when she's in Cheyenne next week and we're in Lincoln," he went on. "But I want whoever's behind this to think she's going to be on her own. I want to draw them out."

That had been the part of the plan Lacy had liked least. She didn't exactly cotton to the idea of playing the poor, helpless damsel. But Ian had convinced her it was the best way to draw the real culprits out into the open.

"Got it," Black Jack said, hopping down. "Hope like hell it works."

"That makes at least three of us," Ian said, dropping back down to the dirt.

"You going to spend the week working for your not-girlfriend again?"

Ian shot him a hard look as the rider up in the chute had to reset. The bull was a kicker. "Yeah. My dad's going to drive me back to the rez Saturday night. I'll pick up my truck and head for her place on Sunday. She needs the help," he added before Jack could make any other cracks. "She's selling off some of her cattle to pay for the carcass removal last weekend. And she's *not* my girlfriend. I'd do this for any of my friends. I'd do this for you."

That was the deal. They were friends with

benefits, no-strings-attached. The line between where they were now and anything resembling a real relationship was clearly drawn. That's all this could be.

Not that Jack bought it. "Whatever gets you through the night, man."

The next two nights, to be specific—two nights of sleeping sitting up, with Lacy curled against his side. In a truck. Fully dressed. With no privacy to speak of.

The things he'd do for a friend.

THE STRAIGHT ARROW sat off in the distance, bathed in the low light of dusk. The Laramie mountains were washed in gold and red. Lacy's house sat down in the shadows, looking small and dark.

Ian had a flash of—well, not fear. But worry. Everything was okay, right? Lacy had texted him before she went to sleep last night—but it'd been one of those quick, "Hey, wish you were here," texts. She'd made it home and gotten her bulls unloaded—but what if something had happened today? What if Slim had come by and stirred up trouble?

Dang it, Ian should have left home after breakfast. But his father had wanted to talk about the rodeo and his chances of making it to the bigs and his plans for after the season. Was Ian going to come back to the Real Pride Ranch? Or did he have something else lined up?

He hadn't particularly wanted to come up with an answer right then. He'd wanted to load his stuff up and get to Lacy. He'd thrown his duffel into his truck as his dad had said, "You know we'll always be here for you. That's what family is."

"Yeah," Ian had replied, climbing behind the wheel, desperate to get away, "I know."

It'd been one of those times where he'd wished he could tell someone—anyone—about Eliot. Ian hadn't been there for Eliot because he wasn't Eliot's family. And Ian couldn't admit to his own father that he'd failed so badly at fatherhood. Hell, he hadn't even failed because failure implied an attempt. Ian hadn't tried.

He'd signed the paperwork and walked on.

He shook his head. He was tired. His head hadn't hit a pillow until about two this morning and he'd been up at seven. Dad was a crack-of-dawn guy. Sleeping until seven was sleeping in for Dave Tall Chief.

As Ian got closer to Lacy's house, he realized she was sitting on the front porch. Something unclenched his chest at the sight. What would it be like if this were how it was? Him coming home at the end of the day to a good woman? Or them coming home together?

He parked alongside the house and walked up

to where she sat in a love seat glider. She held a glass of iced tea and her hair was wet from the shower. She looked like something out of a country song. "Hey, babe."

He dropped his duffel and hauled her into his arms. She looped her arms around his neck and kissed him. It shouldn't feel this good to come home to her. This wasn't the sort of thing he should get used to.

Which did not explain why, when the kiss ended, he buried his face in her hair and said "I missed you," as if he hadn't seen her for a month of Sundays instead of less than twenty-four measly hours.

Except that it'd felt longer than that. For three days, he'd had to act as if there was nothing between them. And this?

He kissed her again, tasting her tart sweetness as she sighed into his mouth.

This was something. Dammit all.

This time, she broke the kiss. And instead of that little smile she usually wore when he kissed her, he saw the worried look in her eyes. He went on high alert. Dammit, he should have left home this morning. "What's wrong?"

"Nothing," she said too quickly.

"Did Slim try something? I knew I should have—"

"No," she cut him off. "Haven't seen him." But she didn't look any less concerned.

He touched the small furrow on her forehead. "Something's bothering you, babe."

"I…" She swallowed and dropped her gaze. "There's something I feel like I need to tell you."

His heart picked up the pace. She wasn't going to end this, was she? If she hadn't wanted him to come, the decent thing would have been to have that conversation two nights ago, while they sat up in the cab of her pickup truck. "Okay…"

"It's not bad," she hurried to add. "I mean… I'm glad you're here." She exhaled heavily and took hold of his hand. "Come with me."

Ian snagged his duffel and followed her into the house. He dropped his bag on the couch as she pulled him toward the hallway. At first, he thought she might be leading him back to her bedroom, but instead, she came to an abrupt stop in front of the office door.

It was still closed.

He waited for her to do something—open the door, explain what was going on—but instead she stood there, staring at it. Then Ian realized he could feel her shaking. "Babe?"

"It's not a big deal," she said—except the shaking was getting stronger. "It's just—I haven't told anyone, and since, you know, we're sleeping together, I thought I owed you the truth."

How was he supposed to take that? She'd told him about her parents, how they died. He remembered the first morning she'd woken up in his arms—the way the nightmares had eaten at her. There was something else—and that something else was no longer off-limits. "And the truth— it's in the office?"

She nodded. But she didn't make any move to open the door.

So Ian reached around her and turned the knob. The door swung open and revealed what some Realtor might have called a den—heart-of- pine paneling on the walls, wooden duck decoys and a few stuffed deer heads on the walls. But the massive oak desk in the middle of the floor and the dull gray metal filing cabinets along one wall gave it away. This was a ranch office.

The desk was piled high with stacks of paper that defied gravity. Maybe the collection of pho- tos in frames was somehow holding everything up? In the center sat an old metal ammunition box. The lid was open. He had no idea if it had ammo or not. He looked around—ah. There was the rifle, over the filing cabinets.

"Your dad's office, huh?"

He'd hoped she'd make some witty comment about what gave it away—the dead animals? But she didn't. She barely managed to nod.

He put his hand on the small of her back—a simple touch to let her know he was right there for her. "Those are some nice ducks," he said, trying to figure out what could have paralyzed her this badly.

She took a ragged breath. "I made that one in art," she said, managing to point to a thing that was almost duck-like. "Sixth grade."

"It's nice." That got a sarcastic smile out of her. "What? It's probably a duck, right?"

He could see her visibly relax. The smile reached her eyes and her shoulders moved down. "Right. If it walks like a duck and talks like a duck…" Then her smile faded.

"Must be a duck," he finished, trying to sound encouraging. "What else is in here?" Because surely ducks weren't what was inspiring this level of anxiety.

She looked around the room. "Memories, I guess." She stepped into the room and picked a framed photo off the filing cabinet and held it close. "I… I never saw it, you know? I can't believe I didn't see it. It was right there the whole time…"

"What was?" He lifted the photo. It was one of Lacy as a kid, maybe eight or nine years old, sitting on the back of a paint pony. Her parents stood on either side of her. Snow blanketed the ground and everyone had huge grins on their faces. It was the perfect picture of a happy family. "Was the pony a Christmas present?"

She nodded. "Do you see it?"

All he saw was a happy family. "No, babe. What am I missing?"

She reached over and touched the picture of herself. "The hair."

True, her hair was a sight to behold. It was supercurly and was shaped into some bad mullet cut from the late eighties. "You know I love your hair, Lacy. And I've got some great pictures of when I had long hair."

"No," she said with more force, pointing to her parents. "I mean, I can see why I never noticed the skin. We were all outside so much and my mom wasn't one of those sunscreen people. I don't ever remember putting any on. But the hair—why didn't I ever notice the hair?"

Ian looked again. Lacy's dark brown borderline 'fro—and her mom's stick-straight hair that, in this faded photo, looked as if it was probably light brown. And her dad's hair was darker—but even cut to his shirt collar, Ian could tell the man's hair was straight.

"What are you saying?" But he knew. He realized what she'd said—she'd never noticed her skin, never noticed it was *darker* than her parents'.

Darker skin. Curly hair.

"I was going through their things," she said, her voice barely a whisper. "Trying to pay the bills, trying to find the contracts. And I found the box…"

As if he were on autopilot, Ian turned and

looked at the ammo box on the desk. He asked, "What's in it?" as if he couldn't guess.

"I didn't know," Lacy whispered.

Ian walked over to the cluttered desk and looked down into the ammo box. There, on top, was an official-looking document from the state of Illinois. An adoption record. Lacy Evans was officially the daughter of Dale and Linda Evans.

Underneath that was a medical record, he guessed. At the top were two columns. The first read "Mother," and underneath that was "Race: Puerto Rican." The second column said "Father" and underneath that was "Unknown."

Ian blinked at the two documents, but the type stayed the same.

Just because he hadn't seen Eliot's versions of this paperwork didn't mean that he didn't recognize it for what it was.

"Why didn't I see it?" Lacy whispered. He looked up at her. She was as pale as he'd ever seen her, and that included when he'd broken her rib.

"You're adopted." He didn't bother to phrase it as a question, not with the evidence in his hands.

She couldn't even nod.

"You're part Puerto Rican," he went on. Okay, so she was obviously deeply upset about this news. And he got that, he really did. Being Lakota was such a central part of his identity—he couldn't imagine waking up one day and finding out he wasn't, that he wasn't even an Indian.

But a secondary emotion built underneath the worry he felt for Lacy—hope. He could tell her about Eliot and she'd get it. She'd understand. He could share the weight and take some of hers from her.

"The hair, I guess." She made an odd noise, something that was part laugh, part scream. She looked as if she was swaying. "I should have known."

"Babe," he said, dropping the documents back into the box and rushing to pull her into his arms. "It's okay."

"I don't know who I am," she said, collapsing against him. "I thought… I thought I was this girl, you know? I was always odd, always different. I didn't look like anyone else. I didn't act like anyone else. But I was me. I was Lacy. And now…"

"You're still *you*." He tilted her head back. "This doesn't change that. You're still the toughest woman I know—you're still smart and stubborn and beautiful and sweet all at the same time. You're still the same woman I'm falling for."

Now, he thought. He had to tell her about Eliot. Show her he trusted her with his secrets, that he could hold hers close. "Lacy, I have something to—"

She cut him off. She wasn't listening. "How could she?" she demanded in a burst of anger so powerful it knocked Ian back a step.

"What?"

"How could she give me up?" Lacy demanded. "My real mom."

"Babe," he said in what he hoped was a soothing tone. "Your mom—" he said, pointing to the woman in the picture with the horse. "Linda Evans—she was your *real* mom."

"No. No! Don't you understand? That woman—" she shot a hard look at the box on the desk "—*she* was my real mom. Everything else was a lie. She didn't want me. She gave me away like I was nothing. How could anyone give their child away like that?" As quickly as it had come on, her rage left and her eyes filled with tears. "Why didn't she want me?"

I have a son. I gave him up.

What hope he'd felt died away. There was no way in hell he could say those words to her, not now. Not while she was like this. Not when she would think he was some careless, heartless man who hated his son.

So he didn't. Instead, he focused on calming her down. "Babe," he said with more force. "You don't know she didn't want you. Maybe she wanted you so much—but couldn't keep you. Maybe she had a hard life or she was young and scared and knew she couldn't give you a good home."

"You think?" she sniffed.

"I'd bet money, Lacy. I know…" But the words simply wouldn't come. He couldn't bear the thought of her looking at him and seeing a heartless bastard who hated his son. "I know," he said again, this time more sure of himself. "She didn't give you away because she hated you. She gave you up because she loved you."

"You can't know that," she sobbed. "You can't."

"I do." Wasn't that why he'd signed away his paternal rights? Yeah, he'd been young, and sure, he'd been selfish. He hadn't wanted to quit school and give up his dreams of being a pro football player to be a father to a son he hadn't even known existed before the papers arrived. And Leasha hadn't wanted to depend on a man who cheated on her while they were dating to provide child support. They weren't ready to be parents—certainly not together.

How could Ian make Lacy see how much better it was this way? She'd had the love of two parents who'd taken care of her, who'd left her a huge ranch with a cattle business. She'd had a roof over her head and things like ponies for Christmas.

"Now they're dead," Lacy sobbed. "They're gone and she didn't want me. No one wants me."

"I want you," he said, both because it was the truth and because she needed to hear it.

She looked up at him. Her eyes were blood-shot and teary and her nose was red. "You do?"

He kissed her—kissed the woman she'd thought she'd been and the woman she still was. "I want you," he told her as he bent over and swept her legs out from under her. Cradling her to his chest, he carried her out of the office, pausing only to pull the door shut with his foot. "I want you so much it scares me, Lacy."

"I don't know who I am," she wept as he carried her down the hall of her childhood home to her bedroom, the one with books and toy horses and all the other signs that people had loved her—that her birth mother had loved her enough to give her up and that her parents had loved her so much they'd made little pillows so she'd never forget.

"You're Lacy," he told her as he stripped her clothes off and then his. "You're Lacy and I want you."

He repeated those two truths as he laid her out on the bed and joined his body to hers. He kissed away her tears as he buried himself in her again and again until she wasn't weeping anymore, until she was crying out his name, until she came in his arms.

And afterward, with her body curled up against his, she slept as he stroked her hair. He

knew he needed to sleep, too, but he couldn't
She had trusted him with her deepest, most painful secret. She'd depended on him being there
for her.

Trustworthy. Dependable.

All of the things he hadn't been when he'd fa-
thered a child. A child that would turn six in a
few short days.

How was he going to tell her about Eliot?

CHAPTER NINETEEN

ALTHOUGH SHE DIDN'T expect to, Lacy slept soundly. She and Ian got up at five the next morning and worked cattle. Then they came home, showered together and ate dinner. There wasn't a lot of talking, but that wasn't a bad thing.

She felt okay. The day was okay. *She* was okay. How weird was that?

It didn't last. That night, Ian said, "We should go through the rest of the box."

The thought of going back into that box took everything that had been okay about the day and blew it to smithereens. "Why?" she asked suspiciously.

Ian gave her a look. "There might be something important in there. Something about your birth mother or something from your parents— it's a pretty big box and there was more in there besides two pieces of paper."

"I don't…" She managed not to finish the childish statement. She didn't want to. But she wasn't a child. "Okay."

So Ian went into the office and brought the

box out to the dining room table and started unpacking it. It didn't take long before he unearthed an envelope with her name on it in her mother's handwriting.

"Here." He held it out to her.

She couldn't bring herself to take it. Maybe it was cowardly, but she didn't want another major shock. "You read it first."

Ian looked as if he wanted to argue, but he didn't. He opened the envelope and slid out several sheets of light blue stationery—her mother's favorite kind.

As he skimmed the writing, Lacy wondered if she should still call Linda Mom or if she should call her Linda or what. They'd been Mom and Dad for so long it felt almost dishonest not to call them that. But they weren't her real parents.

Her heart pounded as the familiar panic started to build. She could not deal with this, any of it. She'd hoped that maybe, in the months since she'd found the box, she'd learn to be rational about this. But no. The panic was attacking and all she wanted to do was hide until it was over.

Ian covered her hand with his. He gave it a gentle squeeze as he kept reading. Lacy felt herself breathe again. She wasn't doing this alone. Ian was here. He'd been there for her last night and he was here still. The fact that she was someone else hadn't sent him running for his truck.

Maybe, just maybe, it was going to be okay.

"You should read this," he said, sliding the papers across the space between them. But he didn't let go of her hand. If anything, he held on tighter.

Okay. She could do this. "Is it bad?"

"Just read it, babe."

She didn't like how much her hand shook as she picked up the papers. She didn't like being this weak. But then Ian slid his other hand under the palm of the one he was already holding and linked his fingers with hers.

Right.

She began to read.

Dearest Lacy,

You turned fifteen today and we still didn't tell you. We planned to—we always planned to tell you that you were adopted. But we put it off. We didn't want to confuse you when you were little and we didn't want to upset you as you grew older and every year your father and I decide that this is the year we'll tell you and then we look at you celebrating another birthday and nothing changes.

We don't have a good excuse why we didn't tell you, except we didn't want to make you doubt how much you were ours. We don't know much about your birth parents. The adoption agency had no information about your birth father. The adoption was closed but we were able to get a medical history for your birth mother. We understand that she was very young—fifteen. The same age you are now. And yes, she was at least part Puerto Rican. She was healthy—and so were you.

If you're reading this, you've found the box with the adoption papers in it. You might even hate us for not telling you the truth but the truth was, you are our daughter. I know I never told you this before, but it hurt too much. I wanted a child so badly but I couldn't carry a pregnancy to term. I lost hope after the fourth miscarriage. It was a dark time in my life and in my marriage to your father. He's the one who suggested we look into adoption. He filled out the paperwork and dealt with the agencies. And one day, we got the call that changed everything. You'd been born and you needed a family.

You are our daughter. The greatest joy of my life has been watching you grow up into the beautiful young woman you are today. Your father and I are so proud of you, sweetie. You were then, and you have been ever since, the answer to our prayers.

There were a few other sentences before the letter ended, but Lacy couldn't make them out through the tears that streamed down her cheeks. "She always said that—every night. I was the answer to her prayers," she told Ian. Talking made her cry harder, but she wasn't running from it.

"And your birth mother was only fifteen," Ian said, tapping the sheet of paper. His voice was gentle. "She was a kid, Lacy. She gave you the best life she could by giving you to your parents."

She tried to say something, but her voice wasn't working. Her mom had written that letter when Lacy had been fifteen. But her birth mom had had Lacy at fifteen.

Fifteen. That was when her mother had set her down and talked about the birds and the bees and waiting for marriage. Was that because Linda Evans had been afraid Lacy might go down the same path as her birth mother? Was that why Linda had always said, "I know you can do better" to Lacy when she'd done something disappointing?

Fifteen. Lacy kept coming back to that number. At fifteen, she'd been in the throes of awkward puberty, unable to even pull off adorkable. There would have been no way she could have taken care of a baby—and that was with two loving parents at home. Her mother wouldn't have let her quit school—college was expected.

Instead, her birth mother, as Ian kept calling her, had given up Lacy. She understood now what Ian had been saying yesterday.

"I'll never even know her name."

"You don't have to," Ian replied. "You just have to know that she wanted the best for you."

"Do you think she thinks about me?"

"Yes." His mouth opened as if he wanted to say something else, but he closed it and cleared his throat. "I bet, especially on your birthday, she thinks of you and hopes you're well and happy and loved."

An image of a woman with wild, curly hair lighting a candle and saying a prayer in a church popped into Lacy's mind. There was something peaceful about the image. She managed a weak smile. "I hope she had a good life, too."

"You can probably find her," Ian said, a note of caution in his voice. "If you wanted. Adoptions are a lot more open now. It's a thought."

"I don't know..." She picked up the letter. *All of our love, Mom* was how her mom had signed it. She traced the letters with her finger. "Maybe not right now."

Ian nodded. "When did you find the box?"

"A few months after they died." The letter from her mom, explaining the whole thing, had been in the box, too, just a few layers deeper. If she'd been able to get it together, she wouldn't have spent so much time lost in the hell of not knowing. The answers—as many as she would get—had been right there all along. She dropped her head into her hands. "God, I'm an idiot."

Ian chuckled and stroked her hair. "No, you're not. You're dealing with a lot."

That was true enough but she still felt like an idiot.

"Come on," Ian said, standing and pulling her up. "That's enough for one day."

"One day at a time, right?"

"Right."

Later, after they'd snuggled under the covers and Ian was stroking her hair again, she said, "Thank you."

"For what?"

"For...for being here, I guess. Except for Murph, I've felt so alone these last few months. Thank you for letting me share my secrets."

"Your secrets are safe with me. Always."

They lay there for a little bit longer. His fingers drummed a steady beat along her arm. She had the weird feeling he wanted to say something, so when she heard, "Lacy..." in a tone that was more worried than anything else, she paid attention.

She leaned up on her elbow and looked at him in the dim light. "What is it?"

"I know this was supposed to be no-strings, this thing between us."

"Oh. Yeah." Disappointment bloomed in her heart. "That was the deal, right? No hysterical adopted women." She was pretty sure she was not the definition of *fun* right now.

"That's not what I'm saying." He brushed her hair back and cupped her face. "I'm saying… maybe it could be something more than that. Maybe *we* could be something more than that."

She blinked down at him. "*More?* This isn't one of your white-knight attempts to save me from myself, is it?"

He snorted. "Yeah, you're feeling better. No, it's not that. It's… I like you, you know? I like being with you. I want to spend more time with you. I want you to know that you can depend on me."

It was such a foreign concept—a guy as hot, as thoughtful as Ian and he wanted to spend his time with *her*? "You mean, like, dating?"

"Yeah. Dating. A relationship." His hands slid down her bare back, pushing her up to his mouth. "More of this."

"I'm a hot mess," she warned him, because after the past few days? How could he want her still?

"Don't worry," he said, pulling her down to his lips. "I like you like that."

FOR THE FIRST time in her life, Lacy had a boyfriend. Sort of. Much as she was still trying to get used to terms like *birth mother*, *boyfriend* didn't seem to fit Ian. He was no boy.

Semantics aside, being an official couple meant after she did the rodeo in Cheyenne and he did his rodeo in Lincoln, they would meet up back at the Straight Arrow and spend another week together. Then they'd travel to the next rodeo in Des Moines and Ian would come home with her again. It wasn't quite going public with their relationship, but it was something.

She wouldn't be coming home to the empty house with the box in the office—they'd gone through the rest of the box together and Lacy was okay with it.

Ian was still living out of his duffel bag, but spending four or five nights out of the week in bed with her was pretty damned close to them living together. And while they'd discussed dating, no one had made mention of anything more permanent.

She thought back to her mom's letter. Would Linda Evans still be proud of Lacy if she knew her daughter was shacking up with a bullfighter?

For the most part, Lacy managed not to think about those sorts of questions. She had a ranch to run, bulls to load and Ian to fill the rest of her time.

Thursday afternoon, Ian helped her load up her bulls for the hour-long trip to Cheyenne, and he kissed her goodbye. "I'll see you in a few hours."

"I wish you were coming with me now." She had to take the bulls on Thursday so they could get acclimated before the rides on Friday. Ian

didn't have to be in Lincoln until Friday, so he
was going to come down and keep an eye on
things tonight.

Ian seemed to think whoever was behind the
attacks would be more likely to hit again if they
thought Lacy was on her own. He'd made arrangements with friends of his and had an elabo-
rate cloak-and-dagger plan to hide in the shadows
so he could catch bad guys in the act.

It all seemed a tad unnecessary to Lacy, but
she did want to get to the bottom of the sabotage.

"I know, babe. Mitch and Paulo will be waiting for you," he told her as he held her tight.
"They're good guys. You can trust them."

"You better be right." Because she was nervous about facing the rodeo without Ian by her
side.

Her rib had healed up a good deal and she was
confident she could handle loading and unloading the bulls, but she did not like the idea that
she was supposed to be a sitting duck. And she
did not like the idea of putting her trust in two
men she'd never met before.

So, filled with trepidation, she arrived at the
Cheyenne arena looking for two cowboys named
Mitch and Paulo.

She'd just gotten the bulls into the corral when
a single cowboy popped up. "Well, *hello*, gorgeous," he said—and waggled his eyebrows sug-
gestively. The cowboy was long and lean with

a beak-like nose that held up a pair of glasses. He leaned an arm in a cast against the corral and looked her up and down, a knowing smile on his lips.

Lacy stiffened. She was not about to put up with another Jerome-style incident. "Really? That's your pickup line? Back off. I'm not a buckle bunny."

"Ooh, you're feisty—I like that." The cowboy winked at her while she debated punching him. "He needs that."

That pulled Lacy up short. "Excuse me?"

"Ian. He needs someone who won't take his crap." The cowboy gave her another once-over and held out his hand. "I'm Mitch Jenner."

She gave him the side-eye and pointedly did not shake his hand. "I was told there'd be two of you."

"Two Mitches? My poor Momma wouldn't have been able to take it!" He chuckled. Then he leaned in closer. "Paulo is around. Don't worry. He won't be seen until he needs to be."

"Gosh, how comforting." This was the cowboy she was supposed to trust? He was a walking horndog. She had to stop leaving her pistol in the glove box. Instead, she pulled out her phone and snapped a quick picture, then sent it to Ian with the text, Is this Mitch?

For some reason, this made Mitch Jenner laugh. "I like you. So tell me—how did a fine, upstanding woman like yourself wind up with a hunk like him?"

She looked at him. Unlike Jerome, Mitch hadn't advanced on her or tried to touch her. And—had he called Ian a hunk?

Her phone chimed. Yep—tell him to be nice or else.

Are you here?

Yup, was the reply. Paulo and I are watching. Try not to punch him, okay? Go to dinner.

She scowled at her phone, and then looked around. She didn't see Ian. "Please tell me Ian's the one who broke your arm."

"Oh, no—I wrecked on No Man's Land. And the very next night, June Spotted Elk went out and rode the damned animal." Mitch sighed dramatically. "*So* not good for my ego. Otherwise, I'd be back out on this circuit right now, trying to get back up to the bigs. Paulo took the year off to take care of me." Everything flirty and snarky about Mitch Jenner softened unexpectedly. It didn't last. "That's neither here nor there. Tell me about you and Ian!"

Okay, something else was going on here but she had no idea what. "Tell me why I shouldn't shoot you?"

Mitch had the nerve to look amused. "Oh, I

do like you. We're going to get along famously. I'm under strict orders to make it look like I'm hitting on you."

"What do you mean, make it *look* like that? Aren't you hitting on me?"

Mitch smiled at her, but it didn't seem to reach his eyes. "Ah. I thought Ian explained the situation—but I see that he did not." Before Lacy could ask what the heck he was talking about, he continued. "No worries. Trust me, girlie, I have no designs upon your person. Ian and I are old friends. He's a good guy—for a jock, anyway—and he's very good about keeping secrets."

She faced Mitch, her hands jammed on her hips. "What are you talking about?"

This time, Mitch didn't have a flirty comeback at the ready. "Easy," he said, holding his one hand up in surrender and backing up a step. "He didn't tell me anything more than you were a stock contractor who was having a run of bad luck—the kind that might be blamed on someone else."

"That's it?"

"Just that you were stubborn and that if anyone hit on you, I should let you shoot them." Mitch rubbed his good hand along his jaw. "He didn't tell you anything else about me or Paulo?"

"No," she said suspiciously. "Just that you were good guys and I could trust you. Should he have told me something else?"

"Not necessarily. But it proves my point—he's good at keeping information close to the vest. Now," he said with great finality, "let's discuss the evening's plans. I'm to flirt shamelessly with you and whisk you away from the corral. Now, we can hit the bars after the rides, but I don't think that's quite your speed and I'm not such a great dancer these days," he added, lifting up his cast. "Let's say dinner?"

She glared at him. "I swear to all that is holy that if you say Ian told you to make sure I ate dinner, you're both in deep trouble."

The corner of Mitch's mouth curved up into a smile that gave her all the answer she needed.

"Lord." At what point had she agreed to this harebrained idea? She looked around the arena again, but it was her, Mitch and some bulls.

"Honey, they're hiding," Mitch said. "Come on, it'll be fun. I happen to be very bad at keeping other people's secrets. I can tell you all about June and Travis Younkin's wedding," he said in a promising voice, as if he were holding out a piece of candy to her. "Ian and I stood up with Travis."

I do not think she cares for Mitch.

IAN STARED DOWN at the text from Paulo and grinned. The man might not say a whole hell of a lot in English, but he did just fine typing. I bet not, Ian texted back. Lacy had a low threshold for BS and Mitch was an expert at it. Everything okay?

Sim was the short answer in Portuguese.

Yes.

Ian put his phone in his pocket. This was killing him, not being with her. Instead, he was hidden in the shadows on the west side of the grounds. Paulo was somewhere on the other side. If they were lucky, no one had seen them get here.

Ian watched as Lacy sparred with Mitch before finally nodding. They climbed into her truck and drove off, just as they'd planned. Now, if Randy and Garth had done their job of making sure everyone knew Ian was in Lincoln and Lacy was on her own here, all Ian and Paulo had to do was watch and wait.

Ian hated waiting.

His phone vibrated again. He pulled it out, hoping to see a message from Lacy. Instead, he had an email from Eliot's parents. His heart skipped two beats.

Hi, Ian. Hope this update finds you well. Eliot just had his six-year checkup. The doctor says he is doing really well. He's in the 90% percentile for height and 80% percentile for weight and as healthy as a horse, the doctor says. Eliot's ready to start kindergarten this year. Because his birthday was so late, we decided to keep him home one more year but he can't wait! He's already looking at cool backpacks.☺ He really appreciated the football you sent. I've attached some pictures from his birthday party for you. Best, Rayanne.

Ian made a mental note to keep his eye out for a cool backpack or pencil case to send to mark the big occasion of starting kindergarten. Milestones like that needed to be celebrated.

After a quick look around to make sure no one else was about, Ian scrolled down and looked at his son. The boy grinning out from under a birthday crown over a cake with six candles arranged around a superhero logo was unmistakably a Tall Chief. Ian was willing to bet that, if he compared the photos of Eliot to his own photos from that age, they'd be almost identical. His own little Mini-Me.

The next picture was of Eliot, a huge grin on his face, holding up the football Ian had ordered online and had shipped direct with the message "From your buddy, Ian," because he really didn't know how Eliot's parents were dealing with the adoption issue.

Lacy's parents had never told her the truth, but Eliot's adoption had been semiopen. That meant that every Christmas and birthday, Ian sent presents and in return got a short update from Rayanne with pictures. But it also meant that he didn't get anything else. He was not a part of their lives.

He scrolled to a shot of Eliot and his dad, Chris, in a big yard. Chris and Eliot had big smiles as they tossed the football around. Ian didn't know what Rayanne looked like—it was always Chris in the picture. He looked like a nice guy—white, middle-aged, balding but still in good shape. Chris had a big smile and was often holding or playing with Eliot in the pictures. He was the kind of guy you'd want your kid around, Ian figured. Stable, loving, happy.

Still, the photos of Chris and Eliot together hurt Ian in ways he was never ready for. Chris was playing football with Eliot—not Ian. If things had been different, it would have been Ian with Eliot, throwing the football around—not in a backyard in suburban Las Vegas but in the wide-open grasslands of the ranch. And all those other photos that Ian had saved in a secret file? It would have been Ian with Eliot on his lap, reading him stories. It would have been Ian holding Eliot by the hands as Eliot took his first steps.

But it wasn't Ian. And it never would be.

It was better this way. It always had been. He'd signed away his parental rights because he would have been a lousy father. He'd wanted something

better for his son. And by the looks of it, Chris
was it.

That rationale didn't prepare him for the last
picture of Eliot holding up a drawing of what
was probably supposed to be Eliot and the football on a field. In awkward black crayon letter-
ing over a bright blue sky, it read, "Thanks Ian
Your Buddy Eliot."

Ian clutched at his chest as if someone had
shot him, his eyes filling with tears. Buddies.
This was the first time Eliot had ever said anything to Ian directly—even if it was a drawing.
He had a powerful urge to ask Rayanne to send
him the drawing or save it for him or *something*.
If he had a fridge, he'd put it up on there. Maybe
even frame it.

His boy—his *son*—knew who he was. They
were buddies. That was as good a place to start
as any.

Ian sat there, staring at the photos and rubbing the adoption triad tattoo over his heart. He
wanted so much—and he had the right to ask
for none of it. He wanted Eliot to know what it
meant to be Lakota, to know his people and their
ways. He wanted his boy to have his spirit jour-
ney and to feel the presence of the ancestors in
a sweat lodge. He wanted his son to be proud he
was a Tall Chief, from a long line of Tall Chief
men who worked hard and played hard.

That was what Ian had given up when he'd

signed those papers so that Chris and Rayanne could take Eliot home and be a happy family. And *that* was what Ian could never change.

His boy was six. He was happy and well. Ian thought of him all the time.

How was he going to tell Lacy about Eliot? He'd hoped that getting more clues to her past would make it easier to talk about this, but he wasn't stupid. Even though they'd gone through the box and looked at all the papers, the box had gone right back where he'd found it on the desk. He hadn't missed the way she tensed up every time she walked past the office door, or the way she'd ask him to go in there and look for something instead of doing it herself.

And if he hadn't picked up on those clues that the existence of the adoption papers still bothered her, there was no missing the way she sometimes woke up gasping for air or how she'd pull him into her and make ferocious love to him, as if the physical act could erase everything else.

She could tell him she was fine with being adopted, with discovering she was part Puerto Rican, with her birth mother giving her up because it was for the best. But Ian knew she was struggling and he had not forgotten that burst of anger, when she'd wondered how anyone could give away their child as if they were nothing.

Just as he had.

His heart in his throat, he scanned the arena grounds again before he hit Reply.

Hi, Rayanne. Thanks so much for these. Eliot's getting so big! Listen, there's a chance I might be in Vegas this fall with the rodeo. You and Chris can discuss it, but I'd like to meet Eliot, show him what I do. If you think that'd be okay for Eliot. I don't want to confuse him. Thanks again for the pictures. Give Eliot my best from his buddy. Ian

Then he put his phone away and thought as he stared at the empty lot.

He had a job to do. He *had* to get to Vegas.

He had to tell Lacy.

And somehow, he had to make sure she didn't hate him for what he'd done.

CHAPTER TWENTY

LACY SLID INTO the booth at the Cheyenne Denny's. She used to eat here with her dad all the time. Cheyenne was only an hour from home and the town's rodeo was famous. Some of that familiar sadness tugged at her. She missed her father so much.

Mitch slid into the other side of the booth and turned his full attention on her. "So tell me about you and Ian."

Hand to God, he sounded almost like a gossipy old church lady. "Not much to tell. He's helping me out."

After a second's pause, Mitch nodded slowly as if he were trying to drag more information out of her. "And…"

She managed a bored look. "And that's it. How about you? How'd you meet him?"

Mitch exhaled heavily and picked up his phone. "I was dating June but we broke up so she could be with Travis, and Ian had to threaten to rearrange my face. We've been friends ever since." He held his phone out.

Lacy found herself looking at Mitch and Ian

and Paulo all standing together. Mitch and Ian were wearing similar black jackets and bolo ties set with a turquoise center. "That's us at June and Travis's wedding. Paulo didn't stand up, in case you were wondering."

"I wasn't really." She studied the photo. She'd seen Ian in his bullfighter outfit and she'd seen him as a working cowboy. She'd even seen him in his college T-shirts knocking around the house, and of course she'd seen him in nothing at all. But she'd never seen him cleaned up. He was even more handsome than she remembered. And it'd only been a couple of hours since she'd seen him last.

Mitch leaned over and swiped the screen. The next shot was Mitch and Ian and two people who could only be June Spotted Elk and Travis Younkin.

She angled the phone to better see the resemblance between June and Ian.

"The wedding was huge," Mitch said, seemingly content to talk about this rather than keep pressing her for details on her love life. "Half the Lakota nation must have been there. Totally amazing, really. Very different than what I was expecting. I'm an only child raised by a single mother. So to walk into a ceremony where hundreds of relatives were there to celebrate with them was—well," he said, actually looking sheepish, "it was overwhelming. And that was before we got to all the Lakota traditions—you have to see the cakes!"

Lacy tried to pay attention as Mitch swiped past the medicine man who'd blessed the ceremony and shots of other riders she knew—the Preacher and Garth and Randy—and what looked like thirty sheet cakes in all kinds of wild patterns.

There was a shot of Mitch holding up a small quilt, a puzzled smile on his face. "Get this—you know how normally people give the bride and groom presents? Well, in their culture, it goes the other way! Everyone got presents to take home, and I don't mean party favors. Blankets and quilts and towels—it was crazy!"

But Lacy wasn't really looking at the quilts and Mitch—she was looking at all the other faces. The brown faces of Ian's family—his tribe. What would it be like to have a family like that? So large that you had to have important ceremonies like weddings inside a school gym?

Lacy remembered one of Ian's stories about June, how she'd crash with Ian for days on end. What would it be like to have family like that, a big family you could count on when everything else went to hell?

Did Lacy have a Puerto Rican family like that somewhere out there? Would they know her? Recognize her? Did she look like her birth mother? Or would even asking that question lead to more heartbreak than she was capable of handling?

"You're awful quiet over there," Mitch observed as their food was delivered.

"Sorry." She handed back his phone and stared at her fried chicken. She had zero appetite. "I'm an only child, too." Possibly. At the very least, she'd been raised that way. She forced herself to pick up her fork but she couldn't bring herself to start eating.

Mitch was silent, which was unusual enough that Lacy looked up. He was giving her a long look. She didn't like it, not one bit. So she changed the subject. "You think they'll catch anyone tonight?"

Mitch shrugged. "If it's a stock contractor, something might happen tonight. But if it's another rider, most of them won't get into town until tomorrow."

"What are we supposed to do in the meantime? You're not going to babysit me the whole time, are you?"

"Of course not." The look on his face, however, said something else. "Tell me about your bulls. Is it true that Ian wrestled one to the ground?"

Now, almost six weeks after that heart-stopping moment, she could smile about it. "Yeah. I about killed him for it, too. I need that bull—Rattler. He gets a few more points, he could get called up to the Challenger circuit. It's something my dad and I were working toward for a long time."

Mitch whistled. "Some of those bulls in the Total Championship Bulls Challenger rake in hundreds of thousands of dollars."

"I know." Money she could use. She needed to pay off bills and to hire a few more hands and make sure the hay barns were full up before another winter hit. If she didn't have that kind of money coming in...

Lacy was operating on exactly no cushion right now. It was so tempting to focus on Ian instead, on dating her first boyfriend—on him helping her out at home. But it didn't change the fact that she couldn't expect him to just work for her for nothing, even if they were sleeping together.

Mitch opened his mouth but his phone chimed. Seconds later, hers did, too.

She had a washed-out photo of two men next to a fence paneling. Seconds later, Ian sent the text, Got them. Get here.

"We need to go," she and Mitch said at the same time. Mitch dug out two twenties and left them on the table. They didn't bother waiting for the change or for to-go boxes.

Less than fifteen minutes later, they pulled into the arena grounds. Mitch killed the lights as he eased up to the corrals, then they both got out and ran the rest of the way. Well, Lacy ran. Mitch followed behind as best he could.

Please let everything be okay, she prayed. Up ahead, she heard the sounds of a scuffle, then, "Hey—hey!"

Lacy ran harder. She rounded the side of her trailer and saw Ian and another cowboy grappling with two men underneath one of the streetlights that dotted the arena's grounds. Her bulls were both still up in the corral—thank God—but the fight was agitating them. Chicken was trotting around and bellowing while Rattler was starting to buck his hind legs. If they both got going, the corral wouldn't be able to hold them.

The smaller man broke off from the fight and started to run away. "Get him!" Ian shouted as he hauled the other cowboy up. The guy Lacy hoped was Paulo took off after the runner, while Ian and his combatant spun in the light to reveal...

"Jerome? Jerome Salzberg?"

At the sound of his name, Jerome lashed out, catching Ian on the side of the face. Lacy screamed as Ian staggered back a step but he didn't go down. "That's the best you got?" Ian snarled, ducking out of the way of a second punch before driving an uppercut into Jerome's midsection.

With an audible groan, Jerome doubled over in pain and then fell to his knees. Lacy ran up. "What's going on?"

"Bitch," Jerome spat out. He swung a leg up as if he was going to stand.

"Stay down," Ian growled, planting a foot on Jerome's back and shoving. Jerome sprawled on the dirt. It wasn't an out-and-out kick, but the threat was implicit. "Or you're going to have a hell of a lot more trouble getting back up."

"Are these bolt cutters?" Mitch called out behind them.

"We got a couple pictures of them in action," Ian said, sounding surprisingly calm. "Wait—Paulo?"

"Here," came a thickly accented voice from several feet away.

"Get your hands off me," a high, thin voice snarled.

A chill went down Lacy's back. She knew that voice—she'd know it anywhere. Seconds later, Slim Smalls himself was shoved into the circle of light with a tall, dark cowboy behind him.

"The police are on their way," Ian said more to Slim than to Lacy. "We got pictures of you and your boy here cutting the chains."

"You can't prove a thing, Geronimo."

If Slim thought this would get a rise out of Ian, he was sorely mistaken. Ian rolled his eyes. "We catch you in the act and you think you can insult your way out of this?"

In the distance, sirens wailed. Chicken and Rattler shifted nervously.

"You don't have enough to convict us," Slim said again.

Lacy looked around. Mitch was still standing over the bolt cutters and the cut chain, his cast arm at an awkward angle. Jerome was facedown in the dirt and Slim looked like a cornered rat.

"I don't know about that," she said. "But how much you want to bet the head office isn't going to look favorably upon one of its stock contractors sabotaging bulls?" She looked down at Jerome. "Or one of its riders."

"He told me to," Jerome sputtered.

"Shut up, boy!"

"I'm not taking the fall for you, Uncle Slim."

Ian's eyes met Lacy's. Had she heard right— Slim had family? She didn't have a family but a snake like Slim had nephews willing to break the law for him?

Salt in the wound, that's what it was.

Slim shot her a look of pure hatred as Jerome said, "His idea. He asked me to do him a favor."

"Shut up!"

"Dude," Ian said decisively, "I don't give a rat's ass who started it. I don't even care why. You're gonna pay for the bull that had to be put down, though."

"You can't have the Straight Arrow," Lacy told him as uniformed officers—wearing cowboy hats, of course—rushed up to the scene. "You'll never get it."

Slim didn't reply. He clammed up and refused to speak to the policemen, except to say, "I want to call my lawyer."

It took the better part of the night to call the promoter and file their statements with the police and turn over the photos and leave messages at the head office. It was closing in on one by the time Mitch and Paulo drove off together, leaving Ian and Lacy alone, again, in the arena in the dark.

"How's your face?" she asked, touching the slight bruise that was forming along his jaw.

"Barely a scratch," he said, pulling her into his arms. "He didn't pack much of a punch. You?"

"I…" She shook her head, trying to get her thoughts to fall into some sort of order. "I didn't realize Slim had a family. That Jerome was his nephew. But that still doesn't explain why."

"Sometimes there's no good why."

"Easy for you to say."

Ian grinned at her, as if he'd expected her to say that. "He wanted the ranch. People do dumb things for land." He snorted. "I'm Lakota. Trust me on that one." When she laughed, he added, "I don't know about you, but I'm beat. You want to get a room?"

Lacy looked back to where Rattler and Chicken

were finally sleeping in their corral. They'd re-chained the panels. In theory, the bad guys had been caught, justice would prevail and she didn' have to sleep in a truck anymore. Plus, if she were in a room with Ian, then they could wake up tomorrow morning together before he drove on to Lincoln.

All of those were totally rational things tha any sane person would agree to.

"Yeah," Ian said. "That's what I thought. I cal shotgun."

She smiled up at him, a weird mix of emo-tions she couldn't put into words. "I've never had someone I could depend on—outside of my parents, I mean."

He leaned down and touched his forehead to hers in a gesture that felt almost reverential "You've got me now."

Lacy had never been in love before. Her crushes were usually quick and relatively painless—and completely unrequited. So she didn't know if this was love or not. But these feelings she had for Ian were something new and powerful, something that excited her and scared her a little.

This wasn't what the old Lacy would do, this thing with Ian. But she wasn't that girl anymore. She was something new—something powerful. And she wanted to be with him for however long it lasted. The rest of the season or...

Well. No use getting ahead of herself. First things first. "Truck. Sleep."

Ian snorted as he pulled her toward the truck cab. "Who said anything about sleep?"

CHAPTER TWENTY-ONE

"HEY," JACK SAID, his tone urgent as he came hurrying back to where he and Ian were set up. They had an hour before the Saturday night goes and Ian was trying real hard not to check his phone for texts from Lacy every three seconds. "Mark Soleus is here. Look alive."

"Who?"

Jack shot him a pitying look. "The promoter for the Challenger circuit. The bigs, man. Stand up and tuck your shirt in."

Whoa. Ian moved fast. He got his shirt straightened and his hat on his head as Mort came around the corner with a smaller man in a very large hat.

Ian recognized the promoter—he'd been at the rodeo where June had been called up to the bigs. That'd been the rodeo where Ian had realized that bullfighting was a perfect fit for his skill set.

Mark was in charge. And he was heading straight for Ian and Jack.

"Jack," Mark said, offering his hand. Black Jack shook it. "Good to see you back in the game. How's the leg holding up?"

"Real good, Mr. Soleus." Jack sounded nervous, which made Ian nervous.

Please, Ian thought. He needed to get to Vegas. He wanted to see his son.

"This is my partner, Ian Tall Chief," Jack said.

Mark looked him up and down as he might judge a prizefighter. "June Spotted Elk's cousin, right?"

"That's right," Ian said, giving the man his best handshake even though it rankled him to be June's cousin first. Still, he wasn't about to say anything that might screw up his chances of making the TCB this year. "Good to meet you."

Mark nodded and Jack nodded and Mort, feeling left out, nodded extra hard.

"I'm going to get the bad news out of the way first," Mark began. "Unless someone gets injured, you guys aren't going to make the Challenger Finals this year."

Damn, Ian thought.

"Damn," Jack said.

"But," Mark went on, "the Future All-Stars night that runs before the Finals has been a big hit with our target demographics of younger viewers and women." He eyed Ian when he said this. "And June herself continues to be a big draw. So, even though it's still four months off, we're offering you two the job of working the Future show, if you're agreeable."

Jack looked at Ian, who finally took his chance

to nod. "I think we'll take that," Jack said. "We sure do appreciate you considering us for the job.'

"Jack, you know the drill. We'll have some PR lined up—especially for Ian. You and June should anticipate doing interviews together..." He waved his hands in the air as if he was looking at a theater marquee. "The first family of bull riding!" He looked to Ian for approval but Ian must have been giving him a hell of a look. "Or something. We'll have marketing work on it. It's part of the deal."

"Understood. Absolutely not a problem." If that was what it took to get to Vegas, to be in the middle of a big arena where Eliot and his family could watch from the stands, then that was what it took.

"My assistant will forward the contracts," Mark said. They all shook hands and nodded some more before Mort and Mark Soleus left them.

"Not bad, right?" Jack said. "It's a good step. Hell, back when I was starting out, you were either in or out—wasn't much in between."

"Yeah, it's good. Remind me to thank June when I see her."

It didn't matter if Ian was getting to Vegas exclusively on the merit of his talent in the arena or if it was only because he was June's cousin. Hell, at this point, if someone said he was only getting in because injured ex-football players were trending on Twitter, he'd still take it.

He could buy tickets for Eliot and his parents, have them waiting at Will Call. He could ask them to come down behind the chutes after the show.

He might finally get to meet his son.

He wanted Lacy by his side when he did.

Now he had to make all that happen.

AFTER A WEEKEND of hanging out with Mitch and Paulo, Lacy was ready to load her bulls up for the hour-long drive home to the Straight Arrow. They were good guys, just as Ian had promised—Mitch talked too much, and Paulo didn't talk at all—but they weren't Ian.

Working together, they'd gotten the bulls in the trailer when the promoter, a guy named Jim, who had worked with her father for years, approached them. Jim had even been at the funeral. "Evans," he said in a gruff voice.

"Yeah?"

Jim took off his hat and rubbed a hand through his gray hair. "Slim's denying everything, but the head office isn't waiting around. They've canceled his stock contracts."

"That's good."

"There's no proof that he or Salzberg were involved in the incident in—" he looked down at his notepad "—Oklahoma?"

"Yeah, Clinton."

"Anyway, without proof—like the pictures your friends took—the head office won't be able to chip in on that bull's expenses."

"Okay…" She looked at Mitch and Paulo, as if they would know what was going on. Paulo stood there, but Mitch shrugged in confusion. "I figured that."

"Slim had a couple of bulls he provided for the TCB. To make up the loss of your bull and to fulfill Slim's contracts, I'm authorized to tell you that Rattler will fill one of the slots left vacant, starting next week. Can you be in Moline?"

She blinked at Jim, unable to decide if he was serious or if this was part of Fate's extended practical joke. "Moline? As in, Illinois?" When Jim nodded, she looked at Chicken. "What about my other bulls, Chicken Run and Peachy Keen? I can't be in two places at once."

As Jim flipped back through his notepad, Lacy began to panic. This was good—great, even. Rattler moving up to the next level was a bigger paycheck. Bulls at that level got branding and marketing. She could work toward plush Rattlers that kids would buy.

But Rattler wouldn't start out earning enough to make up the shortfall for the other two bulls—or the loss of Wreck. She'd still be struggling.

"Sorry," Jim said. "That's the best I can do. Neither of your other bulls are close to the ranking level for the Challenger. Let me know what you decide."

Lacy couldn't do anything but stare at Jim as he walked away. "What—what am I going to do?" she heard herself mumble. "I only have the one trailer..."

Mitch and Paulo shared a look. "We've got a trailer. We'll help you next week, but you should ask Ian."

"But he doesn't go to all the same rodeos I'm contracted for," she protested. As she said it, she really began to panic.

Part of the reason Ian was coming home with her was because they could ride to the rodeos together at least some of the time.

If she and Rattler were up at the TCB level all the time, Lacy and Ian would never ride together. Sure, he'd gotten the Future All-Stars, but he wouldn't be making the jump to the TCB this year.

He'd have no reason to come home to her, to stay with her. She was healing up. He might decide that, since she was better, he'd absolved himself of his guilt in breaking her rib in the first place. She wouldn't blame him.

"Honey," Mitch said, "*ask* him. Ian is the kind of guy who takes care of his own. You should realize that by now."

She wasn't his own—was she? They'd barely decided to be dating. That did not make her his

responsibility. As much as she needed the help
asking for more felt like another layer of failure
"But we're just—"

Mitch cut her off. "People like to say that
rodeo is one big family, but if you don't fit into
the family the way you're supposed to, it's like
they take it personally. That's why it's important
to find people you can count on. Sometimes we
have to make our own families."

Mitch's words settled around her in a strangely
comforting way. For the first time in a long time
she thought about family. Not the one that had
died on the highway, and not the one she'd probably never know. But a family of her choosing.

Something more. That's what Ian had said
even after she'd come apart completely. She was
the hottest of hot messes but he stood by her.
Was this what he was talking about? A family
of sorts?

She wasn't the same Lacy Evans she'd always
been. She was someone new, someone who had
a semi-live-in boyfriend and a complicated past.

Did she have a new kind of family, too?

Only one way to find out.

LACY WAS WAITING for Ian when he got to the
Straight Arrow Sunday. There was something
about seeing his truck driving from a long way
off, the plume of dust kicking up as he got closer.

He was coming back to her. She didn't know

how much longer this would last, them playing house together. She wanted to hold on to it, to him—to a little slice of normal. She wanted to fall asleep in his arms and know he'd be there in the morning.

She wanted him to stay. And she didn't see how it was going to happen.

"Hey, babe," he said as he got out of the truck. "How was the rest of your weekend?"

Lacy waited until he'd gotten to the porch, until he'd dropped his duffel and pulled her into his arms, until he'd kissed her before she said, "Rattler got called up to the bigs. They canceled Slim's contracts. Rattler gets to fill one of his slots."

"Really? That's great!" He picked her up and spun her around before kissing her again. It was so tempting to get lost in his touch, his body. A few nights without him and she already needed him more, again.

"You'll be in Vegas—we'll go together." He set her down and grinned at her, smoothing her hair back from her face. "Vegas, baby. You can meet my family. June and Travis will be there and—"

"But it's not great," Lacy interrupted. The truth was going to hurt. She steeled herself for another bracing dose of reality. She pulled herself out of the warmth of his arms and stepped around him. It'd be easier to get this out if she wasn't looking at him, wasn't touching him.

"Don't you see? I have to go with Rattler to Moline next weekend. You're going to be in Bismarck and Peachy and Chicken are supposed to be in Boise. I can't afford to get another trailer or the hired help to get Peachy and Chicken to where they need to be and I can't afford to not take Rattler and..." She forced herself to breathe, but that wasn't the best idea. The air got caught in her throat and her eyes began to water. "And I can't ride with you anymore. We'll never be going to the same place, not for the rest of the season. I know I can't keep asking you to work the Straight Arrow for nothing, especially not since I'm healing up. You've worked off the vet bill from Rattler and whatever debt you think you owe me for the rib."

"I see," he said in a voice that made it pretty clear he didn't. "Anything else?"

"It was supposed to be no-strings," she whispered. "This is why. Fun while it lasted. It just... didn't last as long as I wanted it to."

Ian came and stood next to her. He didn't touch her, which made everything worse. But if he was going to throw his duffel right back into his truck and drive off into the sunset, she wouldn't cry until he was gone. She promised herself that.

"What do you want me to do here, Lacy?"

"I don't know," she admitted, blinking rapidly.

"Do you want me to go?"

"No. But I can't ask you to stay."

Ian turned to her. She wasn't looking at him, but she could see his body pivot. "Why not?"

"It's not fair to you. You've got stuff you've got to do. That's what you said, back at the beginning."

"Last time I checked, life wasn't fair." Was he laughing? At her?

She turned to see that, yes, he did have a smile on his face. It made her mad—and the anger felt good. It was something she could hold on to without coming apart at the seams. "I know that. The last year of my life has been one reminder after another. But I'm not your pity case. You don't have to put your entire life on hold to take care of me. The rib is healing. Slim was busted and cut out of the circuit. I'm not in danger anymore. Why is that so hard to understand?"

Just once, she wanted to be mad at him and have him get mad back. Because that lopsided grin? It made her madder. This must be what wet hens felt like, she figured.

He put his hands on his hips and shook his head slowly. Finally, she thought. Finally he would see sense.

He looked up at her and damned if that smile wasn't still firmly in place. "You are, hands down, the most stubborn, infuriating, maddening woman I've ever fallen for," he said.

All the air felt as if it *whooshed* out of her chest. "What?"

"I'd thought," he went on, completely ignoring that whole "fallen for" comment, "we'd gotten this settled last week. I seem to recall telling you I wanted something more like a relationship with you and—correct me if I'm wrong—I seem to recall you agreeing. Enthusiastically."

"Well, yeah—but that was before things changed."

"What's changed? Okay, sure—I'm going to Vegas, and so are you. Rattler got called up. Slim got busted. So?"

"So? Everything's changed."

"No," he said, stepping into her. "This hasn't."

And then? *Then* he kissed her. He pulled her into his arms and pressed his lips against hers and swept his tongue into her mouth and—and—

Lacy forgot everything else. The rest of the world might keep on spinning, but she stood rooted to the spot as Ian kissed her. This was what she wasn't ready to be done with yet. She didn't know if she'd ever want to be done with it—with him.

When the kiss ended, she wavered in his arms. He brushed a curl away from her face and said, "Circumstances have changed. But that doesn't change what's happening between us. I'm not going to walk away from you because I can't catch a ride to a rodeo. I don't know that I could walk away if I tried. You want to hear something?"

"Okay," she said weakly, letting him hold her up.

"I missed you this weekend."

She blinked up at him. That was not the declaration of love she might have been expecting. "Oh?"

"I don't miss people, Lacy. Growing up, I wanted out. I was—not a good boyfriend, back then. I never cared enough about someone to miss them before. But I missed you." He sighed, as if admitting this were harder than he expected it to be. "It's a hell of a thing, caring for you."

"Even when I'm infuriating and stubborn?"

"Even then. So. You tell me what you want. Not what you think is best or right or fair—what *you* want. Do you want me to go?"

"I want you to stay," she whispered. "But I don't know how to make it work."

"If I can get you a trailer and some hired hands, will that help you see that I want to stay with you?"

"I can't afford it. Maybe in a couple of months…"

"I didn't ask if you could afford it. I asked if that would help."

She nodded, a strange new feeling taking hold of her. This was hope, she realized. For the first time in a long time, she was hopeful that something was going to work out.

Ian smiled down at her, his face strong and

handsome. He was too good for her, really. She should tell him that, but she couldn't. She was too selfish. She wanted him too damn much. "Good. I have a couple of favors to call in."

IAN'S IDEA OF "calling in favors" turned out to be calling his dad, Dave Tall Chief. In less than a week it was settled. A couple of hands from the Real Pride Ranch were to show up every Thursday morning and load up Peachy and Chicken and take them to the Ranger rodeo they were contracted for. A cousin of Ian's, Tony, would be one of the hands. The hands would also help Lacy load Rattler, but she insisted on being the only one to take her bull to the Challenger rodeos. For this, Ian's friends and family agreed to take a small cut of Rattler's take-home checks from the Challenger rodeos for the duration of the time they helped. Lacy didn't have to pay up front for the hired help or for the use of the trailer.

And that, basically, was how Lacy got to know Ian's family. His dad, Dave, came out the first week to meet with Murph and discuss the arrangements. If Dave Tall Chief didn't approve of his son shacking up with her, he gave no sign. Instead, he told embarrassing stories of Ian as an ornery little kid.

Then there was June Spotted Elk. She was riding in the Challenger circuit, and she was waiting for Lacy at Moline. "I'm June," she said before Lacy had even gotten out of the truck. "Are you seriously dating Ian?"

"I'm Lacy," she said, trying not to feel star-struck. "Yeah, I am."

"He's not a total jerk about it?"

Lacy gave June a tight smile and said, "He's not a jerk about it at all."

June gave her a hard look that bordered on making Lacy's skin crawl. But she stood her ground.

"And you actually *like* him?" June said it as if it was the most alien thing she'd ever heard of. In other words, she sounded exactly the way Lacy had always imagined a sister sounding.

"Yeah. Is this going to be a problem?"

At that, June smiled—almost the same smile Ian had when he was amused by Lacy's smart mouth. "Never thought I'd see the day…"

Lacy decided to change the subject. "Did you really ride a wild buffalo once?"

"He told you that, huh?"

Lacy nodded. Behind her, Rattler stamped in the trailer. He wanted out—and Lacy couldn't blame him. Moline was a hell of a long way from Laramie.

But June wasn't budging. She braced herself for some sort of sisterly threat—*don't break my cousin's heart* or something like that.

Instead, June said, "Mitch said you were good for Ian. But don't let him jerk you around."

Lacy tried not to scowl. There was a touching sentiment somewhere in there. She'd clearly gotten the Friends-and-Family-Seal-of-Approval.

But underneath that was something else—some sort of implication that Ian was, in fact, the kind of guy who would jerk a woman around. If Ian hadn't told her himself that he hadn't always been the best boyfriend, Lacy would have wondered if June knew something else, something that Ian hadn't told her.

But Ian had been up front with her about his failings, about how he was trying to do better. She wanted him to stay with her and he wanted the same. On his way home from Bismarck this weekend, he was going to stop at his father's ranch and load up his belongings. He was moving in on a more permanent basis. They might not have the weekends as long as rodeo season was going on, but they still had the rest of the week together.

"Don't worry," she promised June. "I won't."

"Good." June smiled widely and nodded, sending her swath of long, black and very straight hair falling forward over her shoulder. Lacy was suddenly gripped with jealousy over June's hair. "You know," June said in a casual voice, "there aren't too many women at these things..."

It was Lacy's turn to grin. Sure, getting in

good with Ian's relatives was a plus. But when was the last time Lacy had had a female friend? One who understood bulls and rodeos? "After I get Rattler out, you want to grab some dinner?"

"That'd be awesome."

So that was how Lacy came to be folded into Ian's family. His cousins were helping get Straight Arrow bulls to the rodeos. She was hanging out with June. She met Travis Younkin and hung out with Mitch and Paulo when they could make a rodeo and—and she had people she could count on, people who accepted her as she was. People who liked her.

And after all that, then she went home to Ian.

It wasn't the family she'd been born into, nor was it the family that had raised her.

But as the summer progressed and they settled into a routine, it began to feel like *her* family. She spent every moment of the workweek with Ian, working by his side during the day and spending her nights in his arms.

She didn't want it to be over.

CHAPTER TWENTY-TWO

Hi, Ian. Thank you for sending the Rocket Raccoon backpack for Eliot! He felt supercool (his words) for the first day of school—a picture is below. Chris and I talked about it and we think it would be fun to come see you perform (?) in the rodeo. We appreciate the offer of the tickets as well—we checked online and the event is already sold out! Eliot is excited to finally meet his buddy Ian. It'd be best to meet up before the show, if that's possible. The show will end way past Eliot's bedtime and if he doesn't get to meet you first, he won't be able to sit still! See you in a few weeks, Rayanne.

IAN STARED AT his phone in a state of complete, total numbness.

"Ian?" Lacy said, twisting around to look at his phone. "Did you hear me?"

"Huh?"

"I said, is everything all right?" She paused the movie they'd been watching. "Are you okay?"

Okay? No. He was *not* okay. He was ecstatic

and terrified and the world was getting a little dark on the corners.

He was going to meet his son. This was, hands down, great news.

But—oh, and the *but* was huge.

He hadn't told Lacy about Eliot yet.

"Ian?"

He looked up at her, fully aware that, on some level he probably looked like a fish trying to breathe air. He had to tell her. He had to. "I…" Dammit, after all this time and he still couldn't get the words out.

Lacy sat up, her eyes wide with concern. "Ian, you're scaring me. What's wrong?"

"I have something to tell you."

Lacy—sweet, beautiful, *adopted* Lacy—sat there on her couch, her forehead creased with worry as she waited for him to string together more than three syllables. "Okay. Is it bad?"

"I— No. See— Okay." She put her hand on his shoulder, but that didn't help.

He stood up and began to pace. He should have told her earlier; that much was clear. Oh, God— he hoped she wouldn't hate him for this. "When we go to Vegas, I want you to meet my family."

"But I already did. I've met your dad and your cousins and…" Her voice trailed off. "Unless you have a—a different family?" The way she said it—as if he had a secret wife in Vegas—did not bode well.

"I—" Ian was not a coward. He faced down bulls and offensive linemen and angry ex-girlfriends without even blinking an eye. Fear was an unfamiliar feeling—but there was no mistaking it this time. He was afraid. He did not like it.

He held out his phone, with the message from Rayanne still on the screen. "Here."

She took the phone and read Rayanne's note. "I don't understand. You're—what? Pen pals with a kid? Like, a fan or something? Why is that freaking you out?"

"The picture." He hadn't even seen it yet, but he knew the photo of Eliot would say what he couldn't.

As she scrolled down, Ian felt as if he was going to be sick. This wasn't fear, he tried to tell himself. He didn't want to be afraid of telling her about Eliot. He was proud of the boy. He'd done the right thing by his child.

"He's cute," she said. Then she gasped. Her head shot up as she stared at Ian, then back at the picture of Eliot in his first-day-of-school outfit. "He—does he look like you?"

"Yeah."

This time, when she looked at him, Ian saw exactly what he'd been trying not to be afraid of. Lacy was somewhere between pissed and disappointed. Both. He didn't know which was worse.

"Why does *he* look like *you*, Ian?"

"Because he's my son."

There. He'd said it. The words were out. There'd be no more hiding the fact. This was what he'd wanted, right? Someone else who knew about Eliot, who could look at the pictures and read the letters and be proud of the boy?

But the way Lacy's eyes widened in shock—no, *horror*? Not what he wanted. Not even a little bit.

"So he—what? He lives with his mom? This—" she looked back down at the screen "—Rayanne?"

"Yes. No. I mean—" He exhaled, trying to find even a drop of his normal swaggering courage. He didn't find any. "Rayanne is his mom and Chris is his dad. But she's not his birth mom. They adopted him."

Lacy didn't react. She didn't even blink. He wasn't sure she was even breathing. He waited for her to say something, to do anything—but nothing. She stared at him as if he'd sprouted wings.

And suddenly, Ian was talking. All the things he'd never said to anyone came spilling out. "I was twenty and I was at college when the papers showed up. I hadn't talked to Leasha—that's Eliot's birth mom—in months. I didn't know she was pregnant. I didn't know she was struggling. She was only eighteen and had dropped out and we'd broken up because I'd been cheating on her, anyway.

"I was young and cocky and thought I could do whatever I wanted. I was this football star and I had this huge NFL career ahead of me—I couldn't give that up to take care of a kid with a woman who hated me. What was I supposed to do?"

"So you just signed the papers," she said in a scary-flat voice.

"I called the adoption agency first. I asked what was going on. They explained that Leasha had already picked Rayanne and Chris. She'd gone through the whole process. All I had to do to give my kid a good family—a good life—was sign the papers severing my parental rights."

Finally, she blinked. Which did not help anything because a tear slowly trickled down the side of her face.

"It was the right thing to do, Lacy. Don't you see? I couldn't take care of him. I was young and stupid. I would have been a terrible father. But I couldn't give him up, not entirely. The agency said Leasha didn't want an open adoption, but if I wanted, Rayanne and Chris were okay with some communication. They'd send me updates twice a year and pictures. And I send presents for Christmas and his birthday. And I sent that backpack for his first day of school. I sign it 'Your Buddy, Ian.' I've got a bank account where I save a little money from every paycheck for him for when he grows up—he's going to go to college, you know? That's how I take care of him. I never forgot him, Lacy."

"You have a son."

"I do."

"What's his name?"

"Eliot. Eliot Berger." She looked back down at the picture of his boy. "They live in Las Vegas. I asked them to come to the show. So I could meet my son."

"You have a son named Eliot," she repeated.

"Yes."

This time, when she looked up at him, there was nothing but hurt in her eyes. "And you didn't tell me."

"I WAS GOING TO," Ian pleaded. He looked as if a bomb had gone off in the living room—pale and wide-eyed and scared.

Lacy couldn't look at him. But the other alternative was staring at his phone, at the photo of a little boy who looked so much like Ian it was physically painful.

A little boy he'd given away.

"You have to understand, Lacy—no one knows about him. No one. My dad doesn't know—June doesn't know. I know. Leasha knows. Rayanne and Chris know. But that's it. For the past six years, I haven't told anyone about him. He's been this secret I've guarded with my life."

"I told you my secrets," she heard herself say

as if she were speaking from the far end of a very long tunnel. "I told you everything."

And he hadn't done the same. All that talk about sharing—he'd held the biggest secret of all back from her.

"I was going to tell you when I realized what was in that box," he went on, talking faster than she'd ever heard him talk before. "I thought I'd finally found the one person who'd understand what I did, I did out of love for Eliot. You wanted to know how anyone could give away their child like they were nothing. Remember? And I was afraid you'd think that's what I'd done. That you'd hate me, too." He fell to his knees in front of her. "He's not nothing to me. He's my son. I gave him the best life I could. You understand that, don't you?"

"Sure," she said. It made sense. Hothead jock sleeping his way through college knocked up a girl he didn't care a thing about. Girl didn't want to live with the painful reminder of her mistake. Hothead jock didn't want to give up being a hothead jock. And some nice people in Las Vegas got a smiling, happy son out of it. Everyone wins.

She understood in the same way she understood that her birth mom was all of fifteen when Lacy was born and that the right thing had been giving her to Dale and Linda Evans. It was all for the best.

But the betrayal felt fresh all over again. He'd given his son away. And he hadn't told her.

She didn't know which part was worse.

"I broke my leg about six weeks after I signed the papers. I wasn't going to be a football player. I wasn't going to be a father. I was right back where I started, on my dad's ranch. I was filled with so much guilt that I stopped dating, stopped sleeping around."

"Except for me." How else could she describe their first agreement—no-strings? Friends with benefits? That sounded like sleeping around.

"You're different."

She let out a laugh so joyless it was more of a bark of pain. Different? That was her in a nutshell.

"I'm different with you," he protested. She'd never seen him beg before. It was unsettling. "I've been trying to make something of myself. And being a bullfighter—that's something. Getting to Vegas my first full year out? That's *something*. Something a kid would think is cool. I want him to know me, to know where he came from. To be proud of me."

Ian put his hands on her legs and looked at her with pleading eyes. "I'm finally going to meet him. I want you by my side." He took in a ragged breath. "I want to be someone you can trust, someone you can depend on. I want to take care of you. All those things I didn't do six years ago."

She looked at where his hands rested on the tops of her thighs. "And if they'd said no? They weren't going to come? Were you going to tell me anyway?"

Eyes wide, his mouth opened, and then shut and she knew the answer.

"Right," she said softly. She stood and stepped around him, then walked down the hallway to their room—her room.

"I didn't want to upset you," he called after her.

She paused at the doorway, but she didn't look back. "I don't need to be saved from myself. And while I need many things from you, being protected isn't one of them."

"Babe," he said in a strangled voice, but she wasn't listening.

She shut the door and lay down on the bed.

She'd trusted him with everything—her secrets, her livelihood, her heart. She'd made him her family. She'd dared to think that she'd finally found a place where she made sense in this world. And, fool that she was, she'd thought he'd done the same.

He hadn't. Instead he'd tap-danced around one simple, unavoidable fact. He had a son that he'd given away.

He hadn't told her. He hadn't needed to tell her.

Maybe he wasn't as different as he liked to think he was.

Maybe she wasn't, either.

CHAPTER TWENTY-THREE

Where are you?

IAN HIT SEND on the text. The odds of Lacy answering him were fifty-fifty. The morning after the fight—if you could even call it that—Lacy had suggested that maybe they take a little break. They were done running to two or three separate rodeos a weekend, after all. Maybe, she'd suggested in a weirdly calm voice, it might do him some good to spend time with his family. His *real* family.

He'd asked her if that's what she wanted.

And she'd said yes.

So he'd packed up his things and driven to South Dakota. He'd sat down with his father and told him about Eliot. The same with June and Tony and a couple of other cousins he was close to. They'd all pretty much had the same reaction— shock at first, followed by the hope that Ian would make sure Eliot knew what it meant to be Lakota, make sure he knew he'd always have family out on the grasslands.

Throughout the ten days since he'd left the Straight Arrow, Ian had kept up a steady stream of texts to Lacy. He'd texted her when he'd gotten home. He'd texted her after he told his family about Eliot and told her how they'd reacted. He told her the name of the hotel where he'd booked a room—which was a hard thing to stomach because they were supposed to be sharing a big fancy suite together. Instead, he was rooming with Jack. Again.

Every night he'd text Lacy when he went to bed and tell her how much he missed her and that he hoped she was doing okay. That he wanted to see her in Vegas—just to talk. Those were the texts she tended to reply to. Yes, she was okay. She was glad to hear he was making peace with his family.

But not that she missed him. Not that she wanted him to come back. And there was no mention of getting together.

So he drove to Vegas with June and Travis, checked into his hotel, sent a text to Lacy and buckled down for two days of media interviews. Mark Soleus hadn't been lying—Ian and June had a lot of interviews. Ian kept having to come up with new ways of saying, "No, it doesn't bother me that June's the better bull rider, really," because by God, reporters were going to keep asking it.

Someone had located a YouTube video of Ian

wrestling Rattler to the ground, so he had to explain what the hell he'd thought he was doing a lot, too. And after watching that clip a good ten or fifteen times with reporters at his side, waiting for his reaction, he had to admit—to himself at least—that he had no idea what he'd been thinking. He should have been trampled by Rattler.

When he wasn't answering the same five questions over and over, he tried to keep himself busy. It wasn't that hard—either June or Travis always seemed to be around. They knew about the meeting with Eliot, and they knew Ian had come back to the rez without Lacy. If Ian had to guess, he'd say that they'd decided it was best if he wasn't left alone.

Ian *missed* Lacy. It was a hell of a thing, really. The only thing he'd ever felt that was even remotely comparable to the pain he felt whenever he thought of her was how he felt looking at pictures of Chris and Eliot together—but this wasn't the same. Over the years, he'd trained himself not to think about Eliot all the time. It had been enough to know that his boy was happy and healthy and loved.

But Lacy? After living with her for a summer—working cattle with her, taking his meals with her, sharing her bed—there was no place he could go that didn't make him miss her. Every single thing he did all day long was a painful reminder that he wasn't by his side—and that it was his own damn fault.

Finally, Wednesday arrived. This was it—the big night. The Future All-Stars rodeo started at six. Eliot's parents were going to meet Ian behind the chutes at five twenty. That would give them about twenty minutes to visit before Ian had to focus on his job. Twenty minutes seemed like a safe amount of time. If the meeting didn't go well, then the built-in time limit would keep things from being awkward. But it was long enough that, if it did go well, Ian could pitch the idea of future meetings—like when he hopefully came back to Vegas next year, or like having Eliot come out to the rez and meet the rest of his birth family.

And he still didn't know if Lacy was coming to the meeting. She was here—that much he knew. She'd arrived yesterday with Rattler—but she hadn't agreed to meet Ian for dinner.

He could do this, he thought for the four-hundredth time as he set out the presents he had for the Bergers. A stuffed toy bull of No Man's Land for Eliot. A box of tea for Rayanne and a TCB T-shirt for Chris. Tobacco and paper would have been more traditional but he didn't think Chris would get the significance.

Lord, Ian was nervous. Instead of spending the past two weeks looking forward to this, he'd been stuck in an awful limbo of not knowing

what was going on with Lacy or if he could fix
it—or if he should even try.

He'd wanted to do this with her by his side
Somehow, he'd convinced himself that she would
understand—but at the same time, he'd been sure
he couldn't tell her. It was damned hard for her
to understand something she didn't know about

His phone chimed. I'm here.

Can I see you?

There was a long pause. Why?

It sounded callous, but he could hear the question in Lacy's voice—the same one she'd used
when she'd asked him why he insisted on helping her.

Except the answer then had been the same
thing he'd said to her that night as she stared at
the picture of his son. Because he'd wanted to
help her, wanted to be someone she could depend on.

That wasn't the answer this time. Meeting
Eliot and his family soon, he wrote. Nervous. I—

He took a deep breath.

I need you. He hit Send.

That's what it came down to. For most of their
time together, she'd needed him and he'd needed
to be needed. The sex was great, but it hadn't
been part of the deal at the beginning.

Now he was about to do something that scared the ever-loving hell out of him. He would face what he'd done and meet his son. And he didn't know if he could do it by himself.

He needed her. He hoped like hell she understood.

He sat on the bed and stared at his phone. The little text bubble was thinking. Maybe she was about to tell him off.

Where are you?

Ian exhaled a breath he hadn't realized he was holding. He texted his room number to her.

On my way.

LACY KNOCKED ON the door, fighting down the butterflies that had her stomach doing nervous flips. Was this the right thing to do, meeting him like this? She didn't want him to think this was some sort of act of forgivingness.

A part of her had spent ten days wondering if he really needed her or if he just wanted to bask in the glory of saving the hot mess she was. So when he'd *said* he needed her, she'd left Murph to watch over Rattler down at the arena where they'd been set up for two days now.

Ian opened the door, and she could tell he

hadn't been lying—he was nervous. Strangely this helped calm her butterflies. "Hey, babe," he said, as he'd said all summer long.

In that moment, Lacy realized exactly how much she'd missed him.

But she didn't rush into his arms. Instead, she hung back and said, "You okay?"

"Sure. Great." He laughed in a strangled kind of way as she walked into the room. There, on the bed, was a stuffed toy bull, a T-shirt and a box of tea. "Do you think he'll like the bull?" Ian picked up the animal and held it for her to see. His hands were shaking. "Or is six too old for a stuffed animal? It's No Man's Land. The bull June rode. I thought that'd be cool."

There was something endearing about Ian debating with himself about a plush animal. "I think he'll like it."

"Okay, good. Great." He set the bull back down on the bed and scowled at his hands. "Sorry. Really nervous."

"I'd be worried about you if you weren't." She couldn't even imagine what kind of mess she'd be if she were going to meet her birth mother. The thought was so unsettling she immediately had to *stop* thinking about it.

The alternative was thinking about her and Ian, and that wasn't exactly relaxing, either. "You're meeting them at the arena?"

"Yeah." He blew out a big breath and turned to

face her. "I've done a lot of thinking in the past few days and I wanted to tell you that you were right. I should have trusted you like I expected you to trust me."

She blinked at him. Was he serious? "Yes, you should have. But you didn't."

His mouth curved up into a half smile at her smart mouth, as if he'd expected nothing less. "I didn't. It was—well, it was the coward's way out. I didn't want anyone to know how I'd failed. Because that's how I saw it. I'd failed. Someone else had to raise my kid because I couldn't do it. I couldn't let anyone know that."

He was trying to make her feel sorry for him. She wasn't going to let him know it was working. "You did the best you could. Nothing to be ashamed of."

He took a step toward her. Maybe it was the time they'd spent apart—she'd missed going to sleep in his arms, missed the simple comfort of his touch. Whatever it was, she felt the air between them sharpen with tension. "That goes both ways. You don't have to be ashamed of being adopted, either. We're two sides of the same coin."

"Still trying to save me from myself?" she asked him.

"No—still trying to find the way to make things right between us."

"For the record, that wasn't it."

That got her a full smile, the one that made her want to melt into his arms and kiss him until she didn't remember anything but the way he'd made her feel safe and secure and wanted. She was Lacy and he'd wanted her. Not terribly long ago, that'd been enough.

"I missed you," he said in a low voice.

"Better." Suddenly, her voice was breathy. He'd told her once that he'd never missed anyone before. That he still missed her after she kicked him out was—well, it was something.

His smile this time was more uncertain. "Even if we're done—which is not what I want—I really appreciate you coming with me for this."

What was she supposed to do with *that* statement? Hell, she didn't even know what to call this—whatever this was that had her in his room, talking about toys for children. Were they still together? Or were they friends? She didn't know if they could be just friends. Not anymore.

"You said you needed me. So I came." That, at least, was the simple truth.

He took a step toward her. "Is that what you want? To be done?"

She'd spent days asking herself that question. Days. And it always came down to the same thing.

Yes. No. I don't know.

She wanted him. But she wouldn't stand for

people keeping secrets from her. She couldn't do anything about her parents, but Ian? "I think—"

The door popped open, causing her to jump as Jack walked into the room. He took one look at her and pulled up short. "Oh—hey, Lacy. You're here."

Hell. "Hey, Jack," she said. Behind her, Ian cleared his throat. "Big show tonight, huh?" It was a lousy attempt at small talk, but it was the best she had.

"We've got to get ready…" Jack nodded to the open closet, where their matching red-and-black shirts hung. Then he cast another nervous look around the room. "Everything okay?"

"Yeah. She's going to come with me," Ian said. "Before the show. To meet Eliot."

"That's cool." Jack gave Lacy a tight smile.

Yeah, she didn't need to be here while they changed. "I'll wait for you guys in the lobby, okay?"

"Hang on—here." Ian gathered up the plush bull and the other gifts and shoved them into a bag. "Take this down. I don't want to forget anything." He handed it to her and, in a quiet voice, said, "Can we talk after the show?"

She nodded. "After the show." After he'd met his son and done his job protecting the riders.

God, she hoped she was strong enough for that conversation.

IAN AND JACK had an area behind the chutes where they could set up their stuff. Lacy stood behind Ian's chair, which held the gifts.

Ian was trying not to pace, but that meant he was bouncing on the balls of his feet as he scanned the crowd for familiar faces.

"Boy," Jack said, "you are making me nervous."

"Sorry." Then Ian caught a glimpse of someone he knew—but it wasn't the Bergers. June and her husband, Travis, were making their way behind the chutes. "Are they here yet?" June hugged him and then hugged Lacy, but she didn't ask any questions about Lacy's sudden reappearance.

"No." Ian managed to shake Travis's hand. He checked his phone. Five eighteen. They should be here any minute.

The next thing Ian knew, Lacy slipped her hand into his. "You've got to save your energy for the rides," she said, holding tight to him.

"Sorry," Ian repeated again. Then he saw them.

Chris Berger was taller than Ian would have guessed from the pictures. His balding head stuck out in the crowd—all the more noticeable because he wasn't wearing a cowboy hat. "There—that's him," he said, nodding toward Chris. "Eliot's dad."

Jack stood and June and Travis moved off to

the side. Lacy started to follow them, but Ian refused to let go of her hand. "Stay with me," he said in a low voice. "I can't do this without you."

"I'm right here," she whispered, squeezing his hand even tighter.

Chris saw Ian and waved cautiously. Ian managed to wave back. He tried to smile a welcoming smile, but he didn't make it.

Then the crowd of bull riders parted and there he was.

Eliot.

Oh, God. Ian's chest locked up. No air moved in, no air moved out. He couldn't do anything but stare at his boy. *Tall*, he thought. He knew Eliot was tall—ninetieth percentile for height had to count for something—but Ian hadn't realized what that actually meant. Eliot was already half as tall as Ian and built like a tank.

The boy stared at the bull riders and bulls in total awe, a wide smile on his face. He looked the way he did in all those pictures Rayanne sent—but seeing him in the flesh was still completely different. Ian realized the kid had on a backpack—the Rocket Raccoon one Ian had bought him.

Chris nudged the woman whose hand he was holding—Rayanne. She had bright red hair and wore a long, flowy skirt and was pretty and delicate looking. She, too, was staring at all the cowboys, although she looked overwhelmed by

the crowds and the noise. When she looked in
his direction, Ian somehow found the strength
to wave. She smiled in recognition, which made
Ian feel better. He hadn't known what to expect.
The letters always had a friendly tone but would
this really be a happy meeting?

Rayanne bent down and said something in Eliot's ear, then pointed at Ian.

In the moment it took them to make their way
over to him, Ian panicked. This wasn't right.
Eliot didn't belong here. It'd been better when
he was just a kid in the pictures, a cute smile
and a strong resemblance to Tall Chiefs everywhere. Now he was a real person—one that Ian
had given away.

"Ian!" Eliot shouted. Then, without waiting
for an answer, he broke out in a run.

He was running toward Ian. He was smiling.
Laughing, even.

Oh, God. His son was happy to see him. Ian
fell to one knee, his arms out. If this was all he
ever got, he wanted to hold his boy once.

"Hi, Ian!" Eliot said as he executed an impressive flying tackle. He hit Ian with such force
that, if Ian hadn't been kneeling on the ground,
he might have tipped over.

"Eliot," he managed to get out. Then his voice
choked up and all he could do was hug his kid.

Something in him seemed to break free, and
suddenly he was swimming in all these emo-

tions, these feelings that he couldn't name. This was too much and not enough and the only thing he really knew for sure was that he'd never be the same.

It didn't take long before Eliot squirmed out of the hug. He grinned a huge, toothy grin at Ian, and then spun around, looking at the bull riders and the bulls and all the people. "This is *so* cool! You get to do this all the time?"

"Mostly just on the weekends," Ian said, straightening up. His voice cracked, so he cleared his throat and tried talking again. "I work on ranches when I'm not at the rodeo."

Eliot spun back around and looked up at him in wonder. "You mean—like riding horses and stuff? You're a real cowboy?"

God, it was like looking at himself in a time machine mirror. This was him, twenty years ago. "Sure am, buddy."

"I brought my backpack!" Eliot spun around in another quick circle, showing off the Rocket Raccoon on his back. "It's so cool!"

"Sure am glad to hear that." Ian fought the urge to wrap his arms around the boy again. That might not go over real well. He didn't want to confuse the kid—or upset him. Instead he ruffled the boy's hair.

"Ian," Chris said, shaking Ian's hand. "This is my wife, Rayanne."

"Ma'am," Ian said, nodding his head in her

direction. "I sure do appreciate you coming out tonight." He looked to Lacy. When he reached out his hand to her, she took it and moved forward. "This is Lacy Evans."

"Hi," Lacy said, shaking hands with both Chris and Rayanne. "I'm Ian's girlfriend. It's nice to meet you."

Eliot looked up at her. "Are you my birth mom?"

Ian glanced at Lacy, who'd gone as white as a sheet.

"No, I'm not," she said. "I'm a friend of Ian's."

Eliot looked back at June. "Is she my birth mom?"

"No," Ian said. "That's my cousin, June Spotted Elk. That makes her your cousin, too."

June and Travis came forward and Ian introduced them. After everyone shook hands with everyone else, Ian linked hands with Lacy and said, "Well, this is my family."

Eliot looked disappointed. "But my birth mom's not here?"

Rayanne said, "Eliot, honey," in an exasperated tone. "We talked about that, remember? She isn't going to be here."

"You—" Lacy swallowed. "You know you're adopted?"

"Sure," Eliot said with a shrug. "Mommy and Daddy say Ian's the daddy who made me and they're the mommy and daddy who raise me."

He gave Lacy a funny look, as if parents were okay but girlfriends might have cooties.

Lacy crouched down to Eliot's level. "I'm adopted, too," she told him. "I had two mommies and two daddies like you do."

Eliot's little face relaxed into a grin. "Mommy says that means more people love me—right, Mommy?"

Rayanne stood next to Eliot, a gentle hand on his shoulder. "That's right, sweetie." She looked at Lacy and Ian. "Sorry about that. We've explained about his birth mother before."

"She loved you, too," Ian said. "She wanted to make sure you had the very best parents."

"Do you still know her?" Eliot asked.

"I don't, buddy. But she was a very nice person." Next to him, Lacy held out the bag. "Oh, yeah—hey, I got you a present for tonight's show."

"You did? Awesome!"

Ian pulled out the stuffed bull. "This is No Man's Land—the meanest bull in the world," Ian told him. "And our cousin, June, is the only bull rider to ride him."

Eliot looked at June with superwide eyes. "*Cool*. Are you going to ride tonight?"

"No, I'm going to ride tomorrow night." June's voice had a funny pitch to it, as if maybe this was too much for her. Well, it was too much for Ian, too—and if June got emotional, he had no idea how he would keep it together. "Tonight's Ian's night to be in the arena," June finished. "He's a bullfighter—you'll see. He's pretty cool, too."

"Eliot, honey," Rayanne said, smiling at June. "What do we say?"

"Thank you," he said, hugging the stuffed bull. "Can I call him Manny?"

Everyone laughed. "Totally, buddy," Ian said. "I brought these things for you guys," he said, handing the tea to Rayanne and the shirt to Chris. "The Lakota—that's our people—we give gifts."

"Oh! I brought you a present, too!" Eliot tore off his backpack and pulled out a piece of paper. On it was a larger figure with the name *Ian* over his dark head. Next to Ian was a smaller figure labeled *Eliot*.

The two figures were holding hands. And along the bottom was the word *Buddies*.

The tightness in Ian's chest clamped down again. He was having trouble breathing. "You made this for me?"

"Mommy wrote out the words and I copied them," he said proudly. "I can write my own name and everything!"

"That's great, buddy. I'm going to hang this on my fridge."

That made Eliot grin in an embarrassed kind of way. Then he said, "I'm Lakota, too, right?"

"You sure are. Both your birth mom and I are full-blooded. Maybe…" Ian swallowed hard and spoke to Chris and Rayanne. "Maybe when Eliot's older, you guys can come out to the rez and meet the rest of our family, our tribe. Eliot will always be welcome out there. He can find out what being a Lakota Indian means."

Eliot's little forehead wrinkled up in confusion. "What does it mean?"

How was Ian supposed to sum up his tribe, his culture, in a way a kindergartner would understand it? "It means powwows and drums and horse races and buffalo."

Eliot perked up at the mention of drums and horses. "Can we go now?" he asked his parents.

Chris and Rayanne exchanged a look before Chris said, "Not now, kiddo. You're in school, remember? Maybe when you get older, like Ian said. We want Eliot to know about his culture," he added to Ian.

Behind Ian's back, Jack said, "We've got about five minutes before we need to get ready," in an apologetic voice.

"Can I get a picture with him?" Ian asked Eliot's parents.

"Sure," said Rayanne.

They spent the next five minutes taking different pictures—Eliot and Ian with Rayanne and Chris, with June, with Lacy—and a whole bunch of just Eliot and Ian together.

"Now, you be good for your mom and dad," Ian said, kneeling down to give Eliot another big hug. "You do your chores and your schoolwork. Christmas will be here soon."

"Okay," Eliot said, hugging Ian back. Then he whispered in Ian's ear, "*Star Wars* Lego, okay?"

Ian laughed. This kid. His kid. "Can do. We'll always be buddies, Eliot. You know that, right?"

Eliot looked as serious as a six-year-old possibly could. "Yup. And maybe when I grow up, I'll be a cowboy, too!"

Then it was time for the Berger family to head back to the seats Ian had gotten for them, up close to the arena where Eliot could see all the action. Ian shook hands with Rayanne and Chris, and they made vague plans to meet again if Ian was back in Vegas next year.

Ian watched his son walk away with his parents. Once, Eliot turned around and waved his bull, Manny, at Ian, but then the crowds closed in around him and he was gone.

For Ian, it was like watching a part of his heart walk away.

Lacy was beside him, her arm around his waist. "You okay?"

"I just— I need—" But all those emotions were jumbled together and suddenly he couldn't talk. He couldn't breathe.

"Come on," Lacy said, pulling him away from the noise and the crowds and the concerned faces of his family and friends.

He stumbled blindly after her. He didn't know

where she was taking him but he didn't care. All he knew was that he needed her. He needed her to tell him it was better this way. He needed to tell her he was sorry.

He found himself back underneath the stands in the arena, in a poorly lit hallway that echoed with the sounds of hundreds of people finding their seats. Lacy turned and looked at him, then threw her arms around his neck.

Ian started to sob. He buried his face in her hair and wept for everything he'd given away when he'd signed the papers—his son's first smile, his first word, his first steps. Christmas mornings and birthday parties and bed-times stories, the thousands of small moments of being a father that weren't his because he'd signed the papers and done the right thing.

Lacy held him tight and he clung to her. "I'm here," she whispered again and again as he cried.

He couldn't remember the last time he'd cried. Maybe when his leg had broken during that last game? But even then, it wasn't like this. It wasn't this flood of emotion and confusion and pain that threatened to swamp him entirely. It was self-ish, this crying—because Eliot was obviously a happy, well-adjusted kid. Ian wasn't crying for the boy. He was crying for himself.

And then, almost as quickly as the storm had hit, it passed and he felt better. He stood a little straighter, but he didn't let go of Lacy. "Sorry," he mumbled when he saw she'd been crying with him. "Don't know what came over me there."

She snorted. "Don't make excuses, Ian." She used the sleeve of her shirt to wipe the tears away from his face. "He's a great kid."

"He is, isn't he?" But even saying that out loud made his eyes water again.

Heavy metal music began to blare. It was time for the show to start.

"I don't know if I can do this right now."

Lacy cupped his face in her hands and hauled him down to her level. "You can and you will. You listen to me, Ian Tall Chief. You're going to get your head in the game and you're going to do an amazing job protecting riders from bulls because that's what you do. You're going to show your son that his buddy is cool. You're going to show the promoters you've got what it takes to be right back here next year."

He took a deep breath. "And you? You're the only thing missing from that pep talk."

She gave him a watery grin and the next thing he knew, she was kissing him—hard and long. It was everything he'd missed for the past two weeks. He wanted to bury his hands in her hair and bury himself in her body and know it would all work out.

He didn't get the chance. "Now get out there and show 'em what you've got!" she said when she pulled away. She spun him around and swatted him on the butt before she pushed him toward the arena entrance.

"You would've made a hell of a motivational coach, Lacy."

"Less talk. More rock!"

The announcer was introducing the riders, which meant Ian had run out of time. He hustled to where Black Jack was waiting in time for their intros. As Ian tipped his hat to the crowd, he saw where Eliot and his family were sitting. Eliot waved Manny at him. Even at this distance, Ian could see the huge grin on the boy's face.

"You got your head in the game, Chief?"

"Yeah." He glanced back to where Lacy had taken up a spot on the top of the chutes. She smiled at him, a quick thing. "Yeah, I think I do."

CHAPTER TWENTY-FOUR

WHAT DID SHE WANT?

As Lacy helped with Rattler's bull rope, she asked herself that question over and over.

Rattler had a hell of a good ride, dumping his rider at the 7.2-second mark. Instead of following her bull back to his pen as she normally did, she stayed up on the chutes, kept her eyes on Ian and tried to answer the question.

She wasn't doing a great job at it—too many distractions. Ian had his game on. He executed a couple of nice saves and backed Jack up when he needed to. He didn't wrestle any bulls, though. Probably for the best.

She'd spotted Eliot and his family and kept an eye on them while Ian worked. Eliot seemed totally bowled over by the bull riders. Every time a rider went flying, he'd get this huge look on his face and turn to his mom like he was saying, *Did you see that?*

Maybe it was different for Eliot and Ian. After all, Ian had always sent presents and Rayanne had always sent pictures. Eliot had always known of Ian, his buddy.

If Lacy's parents had told her she had a birth mother when she was six, what could she have done with that information? She thought about how, even though Eliot knew who Ian was, he'd still asked about his birth mother—several times.

Lacy never would've been able to put a name or a face with this concept of "birth mother." There would have been no presents, no buddies. She would have spent the next decade wondering who she was, who her mother was.

Yeah, it had sucked to find that box and discover she was adopted. It had sucked a lot. But she was a grown-up.

How much more would it have hurt if she'd been a little kid?

For the first time, Lacy understood her parents' choice. They hadn't been hiding it from her—as her mom had said in the letter, they hadn't wanted to confuse her.

They had done everything they could to love her.

Because she was their daughter.

Lacy exhaled as a sense of peace settled around her. When she got back home, she might try organizing Dad's office again. She wasn't afraid of that box or the papers it contained anymore.

The rodeo ended with the Preacher taking

first. As the crowd filtered out, Lacy searched for Eliot's family again. When she found them, Eliot's dad had picked up the boy and was carrying him. Eliot had his head on his dad's shoulder, but he was still looking at the arena—at Ian.

And Ian was looking back. Eliot lifted the hand that held Manny the bull and Ian waved. Then the Bergers were gone, swept away in the crowd.

Ian made his way over to where Lacy was perched. He looked as if he'd been run over by a truck but was trying to pretend he hadn't been. "Lacy..."

"You need to get out of here?"

"Yeah."

She sent Murph a text to make sure he was taking care of Rattler, and then took Ian's hand. Without meaning to, she headed back to her room. But that, she realized, was what she wanted—part of it, anyway. She wanted to finish the conversation they'd started earlier, to show Ian the pictures she'd snapped of him and Eliot—to be there for him as he'd been there for her.

They didn't speak on the walk back to her hotel or in the elevator. She could tell he was trying to come to grips with the whole afternoon. Hell, it might take weeks before he'd processed it all. She was still working through her own adoption issues and she'd had months.

"Is this where you're staying?" he asked, his voice low behind her as she opened the door.

Her heart pounded. What was she thinking, bringing him back here after everything that had happened? He probably needed his space to think about his son right now, not to hash through whether they were going to figure out their relationship. "Yeah. I—we—we don't have to be here. We can go somewhere else."

He took a deep breath and put his hands on her waist. Then she was being propelled into the room. "I don't care where we are. I just need someplace quiet—someplace with you."

He dropped his duffel to the ground, but he didn't let go of her waist. And she didn't pull away.

I need you.

That's what he'd texted her earlier. That's what his actions had said when he'd introduced her to his son's family.

He pulled her hat off, and then his arms were around her and he pulled her into a hug and she let him because that was what she wanted, too. Someplace quiet, someplace with him.

He buried his face in her hair and she laid her arms on top of his and held him to her. They stood like that for a while. She wanted to tell him how much she'd missed him, how she wanted him to come back—how she hadn't felt quite like herself without him beside her.

But she didn't. She didn't want to make this moment all about her, and she didn't want to gloss over the reasons she'd asked him to leave in the first place.

So she said nothing and focused on the way his body felt against hers, warm and muscled and safe.

"Babe," he whispered after several moments. "I just...thank you."

"I wanted to be here for you." She spun in his arms and stared up at him. "I wanted you to know that the reason I asked you to leave—it's not that you had a son."

The shame on his face was a hard thing to see. "It's that I didn't tell you."

"It's not even that. I mean, it is—but it's *why* you didn't tell me, don't you see? You thought I couldn't handle it. After all we went through—after all we shared—you thought you still had to protect me from the truth."

She swallowed, hard. Ever since she'd watched him drive away, she'd thought long and hard about what had happened—all of it. From the very first moment she'd seen him, wrestling Rattler to the ground, he'd been trying to keep her safe. "I'm not a bull rider. It's not your job to protect me because I'm *not* your damsel in distress."

"I—I don't know how else to be." He sounded as if she'd punched him—hard. "I made this job my life—it's who I am. I keep people safe."

"It's not who you are," she insisted. "I don't want you to give it up, being a bullfighter. But there's so much more to you than being a fighter—or a football player."

He sat heavily on the bed, his head in his hands. "What do you want? Do you want to be done?"

Once upon a time, he'd told her to be honest with herself and with him. This was her heart on the line. Anything less than total honesty would be a betrayal to them both. "If you and I are ever going to work, I want to be loved—as I am. I may be a mess sometimes, but that doesn't mean I need you to rescue me. I need you to love me. I don't want your job. I want *you*. That's all."

He looked at her, his eyes watering. "Babe, I'm so sorry. It's just that, when we started, you needed protection. And I..." He swallowed. "And I needed to protect you. I needed to prove to myself that I was a good person, a good man. That I wasn't the same stupid kid who gave up his son and abandoned his girlfriends. I thought... I thought I could redeem myself by helping you out."

"Was that all I was to you? A path to redemption?"

Abruptly, he stood and closed the distance between them. He brushed a curl out of her face and cupped her cheek in his palm. She sucked in air but she didn't let herself hold him. Not yet.

Not until she'd heard him out. "No. You were never *just* my redemption, Lacy. From the very first moment I saw you, there was this spark about you—between us. I thought that if I could ignore that spark, ignore the way you made me feel, it'd prove that I was different. That I was a better man than I'd been."

"You held yourself back from me," she said, but there was no missing the breathy whisper her voice had become. "You held the truth back from me."

His gaze searched her eyes, and then he touched his forehead to hers. "Because this is the truth, babe. I love you. I've never loved anyone in my life before, but you? I love *you*."

She exhaled. He'd never said the words before. She'd never thought she needed to hear them—but now?

Then he went and ruined it. "And I don't deserve you. I never did. I'm still the same selfish, stupid guy. I haven't changed. I thought if I could keep you from knowing the truth about me, I'd get a little more time with you."

He dropped his hands away from her and took a step back. The loss of his touch was a physically painful thing.

"So now you know the truth about me. I'm not good for you. You can do better than me."

She gaped at him, but he was serious. And that made her mad. "You're doing it again."

"What?"

"You're deciding what's best for me. Dammit, Ian, knock it off!"

"I'm not—it's—I'm *not* a good person," he sputtered in frustration. "Can't you see that?"

That statement was so completely ridiculous that she burst out laughing. Ian's head popped up and he stared at her in shock. "No, I can't see that. Let me tell you what I do see. I see a man who sends Christmas and birthday presents to a child he didn't ask for and didn't know. I see a man who defended his cousin's right to ride bulls and my right to own them. I see a man with friends he'll go out of his way to help and friends who know they can count on him when they need a hand. I see a man who literally saved my life when others would have gladly stood by and let me get trampled." She went to him and wrapped her arms around his neck. He tilted his head to the side and closed his eyes, as if he could physically deny what she was saying. "And I see a man who is so stuck on some crappy choices he made years ago that he can't see what I see."

"I'm not good enough for you," he said, his voice hoarse.

"You weren't, six years ago," she corrected,

pulling him down to her lips. "But I think you are now."

"Lacy…" But she cut him off with a kiss. She kissed him as if she might never get another chance.

When the kiss ended, Ian's chest was heaving. "I tried so hard," he whispered against her skin. "I tried to be the man who deserves you."

"I don't need you to deserve me. I just need you." She got the feeling she wasn't going to convince him, not with words.

However, words weren't the only way to get through to him. She pushed him back and said, "Strip."

His eyebrows about cleared his forehead. "Lacy?"

She yanked his hat off and threw it on the bed, then started on his shirt's buttons. "I owe you one. You're going to cash it in. Shower."

"You don't have to do this," he said—but he didn't grab her hands and he didn't shove her away.

"I want to, you idiot. That's what you can't see—that I want you as you are." She paused, her hands frozen at the top of his jeans. "Unless you don't want me?"

This time, there was nothing soft or gentle about the way he wrapped his arms around her or the way he crushed his lips down on hers. "I want you so much, babe," he said, threading his hands through her hair and tilting her head back so he could kiss her neck. "God, I want you."

"Good. Shower. *Now*."

His erection was huge as she soaped him up and rinsed him off. He moaned in protest when she knelt before him, grasped his shaft and stroked.

"You've always taken care of me, Ian. It's my turn," she replied, stroking him again. "You got a problem with that?"

"No," he groaned as she ran her tongue around his tip. His fingers tangled with her hair. *"Lacy..."*

She licked over his length a few more times before asking, "Here or the bed?"

"Bed, babe. Please."

She got the towels and dried him, then led him to the bed. There, she rolled on the condom, and then mounted him. When she surrounded him, she shuddered. "I missed this," she whispered as she rode him.

"I missed you so much," he growled, wrapping his arms around her and holding her against him while he thrust into her. "I don't ever want to miss you again."

Then he kissed her and sucked on her breasts until her body bore down on his and he unleashed his climax on hers. Spent, they collapsed together, panting hard.

"Now what?" he said in an awestruck voice.

Wasn't that the ten-thousand-dollar question? When she'd come up to his room earlier, she hadn't intended to wind up back in bed with him. But watching him with Eliot...

She leaned up on his chest and gave him a look. "I wasn't going to kick you out in the hallway naked, you know."

Ian snorted. "I appreciate that, but you know what I mean." He took a deep breath. "What about us?"

She lay back down on his chest and traced the tattoo. "This is Eliot's, isn't it? After you left, I looked it up. The heart is your love, and each side of the triangle is everyone in the adoption—him, you and his parents."

"It is." He covered her hand with his and held it against his tattoo. "I got it about six months after I signed the papers. Rayanne sent her first update with a picture of this fat little baby smiling and...that was when I knew I'd never be one of those fathers who walked on without looking back."

He cupped her chin in his hand and tilted her head up so he could look her in the eyes. "Thank you for being here for me. It was..." He exhaled. "It was a *hell* of a day."

"That it was." She tried to look stern but, given Ian's grin, she didn't think she made it. "Any other secrets? Anything else I should know about?"

"Just that I want to try again. I want to do better by you—*with* you," he quickly corrected before she could jab him with her elbow.

She propped herself up on her arms again. "You want to hear something? I get it now—why my parents didn't tell me about my birth mom. Seeing Eliot with his parents—it made sense. He's their son. I mean, he's your son, but he's their son, too. Twice as many people love him."

"Twice as many people loved you." Ian pushed her hair away from her face. "I love you."

"You're not just saying that because it was a hell of a day, are you?"

He grinned at her prickliness. "No. I've never loved anyone before and I did a poor job showing you how much I loved you," he said. "I guess I thought protecting you was how I showed I loved you. But I can't walk on, Lacy. Not from you." He ran his fingers over her skin. "What do you want?" His voice wavered, but he didn't look away. "Honestly."

"I want to figure out who I am. Like when you said to Eliot's parents, how you wanted him to know the Lakota culture? I want to know what it means to be Puerto Rican. I'm still working on who Lacy Evans is, and that's part of it. I want to have a family. I want to belong to someone." She touched his face, tenderly stroking the curves of his cheek. "I want to belong to you. But that means you have to belong to me, too."

For most of the past year, she'd been an orphan twice over, with only the Straight Arrow and Murph to ground her. But since she'd found Ian, she'd found a place to belong.

His arms tightened around her waist as he leaned down to kiss her. "I already belong to you, babe. I've been yours from almost the first moment I saw you. Let's go to Puerto Rico together," he said. "I want us to work. I want to be your family. I want to marry you and I want to have kids. I want to be a good father and a good husband. I want to be a better man—for you. *With* you."

All the air whooshed out of her lungs and she was suddenly dizzy. "That's—that's pretty good. As apologies go."

Ian's grin got huge. "Will you marry me?"

"Yes."

"Right now? This is Vegas, after all."

Lacy burst out laughing. "Nope. I know I'm this huge tomboy, but I want the big wedding with all our family and friends there. Mitch showed me pictures of June and Travis's wedding…" She shrugged apologetically. "I don't want to rush it. I'm only getting married once. I want to do it right."

Ian nodded thoughtfully. "That's what you want?"

"Yup. Come to the Straight Arrow, Ian. Come home with me."

"I promise I will always come home to you. And," he added with a wicked smile as he rolled into her, "I'll always keep my promises."

"You better," was all she said before he kissed her.

But she didn't need to worry.

He did just that.

EPILOGUE

"THAT'S A LOT of people." Murph said as he peeked through the open gym doors.

Lacy grinned. "It's a big family." In a few short minutes, it would be her family. The thought was exciting. Not quite as exciting as marrying Ian, but still.

Murph turned to look at her. "You look beautiful. Your parents would be *so* proud of you."

She touched his cheek. "Thanks. I wish they were here."

Murph's eyes started to water. Then the music swelled and he held out his arm for her. "Here we go."

They swept into the high school gym and down the wide aisle between the folding chairs. The place was packed, but they hadn't gone with the traditional groom's and bride's sides of the aisles. Mostly because Lacy only had a couple of people on her side, including Murph, who was walking her down the aisle.

It didn't matter. This was her family now, this

sea of loved ones who were here to celebrate the union of Ian Tall Chief and Lacy Evans.

Lacy knew people were smiling at her, but she didn't see anyone except Ian at the front. He wore an honest-to-God tuxedo and she'd never seen him look more handsome. He had the biggest smile on his face as she walked toward him. When she was close enough, he notched an eyebrow at her—and then he winked.

She grinned at him. As she neared the front, Eliot Berger turned around in his chair and waved at her. She gave him a little wave back. They'd talked about asking Eliot to be their ring bearer, but everyone had agreed that putting the kid on display his first time on the rez was a bad idea. Lacy was thrilled the Bergers had made the trip for the wedding in the middle of February. They were used to the heat of Las Vegas. South Dakota was *cold* right now.

Then Murph handed her off to Ian and Jack Johnson handed Ian the rings and June held Lacy's bouquet. "You look beautiful," Ian whispered to her as the Preacher waited for the music to stop.

"You look handsome," she whispered back.

Then they were blessed by the tribe's medicine man, and they recited the vows after the Preacher, and then they were married. Everyone clapped and whistled as they were presented as Mr. and Mrs. Tall Chief, and Lacy had this amazing sense of belonging. She'd made this family her own—Ian and June and Mitch and Paulo and Jack, Eliot and his family—this was where she belonged now.

"You got your bikini ready for Puerto Rico?" Ian asked as they walked down the aisle. Then he leaned over and whispered in her ear, "You're Lacy Tall Chief and I want you."

She knew who she was. She was Lacy Tall Chief. She was his.

And he was hers.

* * * * *

Pick up June's story,
RODEO DREAMS.
Available now,
only from Harlequin Superromance!